Wings & Roots

THE SCIONS: BOOK THREE

GEMMA WEIR

Wings and Roots
The Scions: Book Three
Copyright © 2020 Gemma Weir
Published by Hudson Indie Ink
www.hudsonindieink.com

Cover design by Rebel Ink Co
Interior design by Rebel Ink Co

Wings and Roots/Gemma Weir – 2nd ed.
ISBN-13 - 978-1-913904-00-5

To Becky,

Here's to the books that refuse to be written the way you planned. Brain, this is all your fault.

I need my room Right now more than I need my wings #scions

♡ x oxo

Scion

noun
Sci-on

Definition

- DESCENDANT, CHILD *especially*: a descendant of a wealthy, aristocratic, or influential family
- HEIR sense: *scion* of a railroad empire

EMMY

As I stare at my beautiful friend, I realize that as much as I hate to admit it, I'm incredibly jealous of her. Nova is gorgeous, tall, vivacious, and brave; so fucking brave. For the last six months I've watched as she's battled with her own mind and won.

The thing is; until she fell apart, I'd have called myself a selfless person. I'm always the first to offer to run an errand, do a chore, or volunteer for whatever's needed. But the day I watched my best friend fall to the floor, lost to her own fear and self-loathing, I realized just how selfish I actually am.

Our group—'The Scions' as we recently found out the kids at school call us—is made up of me, Nova, Zeke, Griffin, and now Valentine. We're the children of the Doomsday Sinners MC; the next generation, the scions.

My daddy's the president of a biker club and a total badass who most people are terrified of. My mom's a genius; a self-made millionaire and general all-round Wonder Woman. Then there's me. I look like a watered-down version

1

of my mom. I have her coloring: the fair skin and red hair, but where she's tall and gorgeous, I'm small and freckled.

I'm not looking for sympathy or expecting anyone to feel sorry for me because I come from impressive stock. This is just me being honest. In an extraordinary family, I'm ordinary.

I'm surrounded by people who stand out. Nova's gorgeous; Zeke's the golden boy, a larger-than-life personality who everyone wants to be friends with; and Griffin, the happy-go-lucky charmer, is someone you're just compelled to like.

The circumstances of our births brought us together, and a lifetime of friendship is what's kept us that way. Every single one of my firsts was with them. My first steps were taken at Nova & Zeke's house, my first kiss was with Griffin. They're my constant, an ever-present part of my life. We're family, or as close as you can get without matching DNA.

But growing up as the only normal one in a group of special people is hard. I'm not a social butterfly. I'm not likeable. I'm not easy to befriend. I don't like parties. I don't want to date a hundred boys. I don't like to gossip.

I'm boring.

I'm tolerated.

I'm weird.

Nova, Zeke, and Griffin know who I am. They accept my flaws and mostly that's okay. Over the years they've refused to let me sink into the background and so I'm a Scion, even if I don't want to be.

As I watch Nova pull back her shoulders and visibly steel herself, I try to decide if I could ever be as strong as she is. We're at a party in a field about a mile away from our high school. I don't want to be here and neither does she, but nevertheless here we are, because she's determined to fight her own insecurities.

I'm in the middle of an epically good book and the urge to read, to lose myself to a fictional world is calling me. Glancing around, I search for anyone who will care if I mentally check out of this godawful party, but all I can see is a crowd of kids, and no one is paying me any attention.

None of these people are my friends, and even though that's probably as much my fault as it is theirs, that doesn't change the fact that I don't like anyone here and they don't like me. Brittany, Nova's ex-friend, always took pleasure in reminding me that I didn't deserve to be popular; that the only reason people tolerated me was because of Zeke, Griff, and Nova, and as much as I always disliked the bitch, she's right. My dad's reputation and my friends are the only thing keeping me on the top tier of a social sphere I have zero interest in.

Scanning the crowd, I search for their familiar faces. Zeke's in the middle of a group of football players, his head tipped back laughing while the rest of the guys look on. Nova is sat on Valentine's lap, completely ignoring everyone but him as the group surrounding them try to get the attention of the most popular couple in school. Griffin is wrapped around a girl, her blonde hair all I can see as his lips devour hers.

And I'm alone.

Other outsiders stare longingly in the direction of the beautiful people, hating their places on the outside looking in. But for me, I'm not the outsider. I'm one of the popular ones. I'm part of the inner circle and instead of basking in my posi-tion, I'm jealous. I envy the ones looking in; I want to be them and isn't that just an ironic twist of fate.

The metal tailgate beneath my butt is cold, and I wiggle my weight from side to side trying to find a comfortable spot.

What would this party be like if no one here knew who I was? If I was completely anonymous, a stranger.

A cold laugh escapes me. As if that's even possible. I doubt there's a single person here who doesn't know who I am, or the notoriety that haunts me and my friends. Some people spend their whole lives desperately trying to be seen, but I just want to be forgotten in a world so narrow that I can't be invisible no matter how hard I try.

My gaze moves back to Nova and Valentine and I exhale wearily. If Valentine hadn't come into our lives, I doubt I'd be here right now. When school finished for summer last year, I made the conscious decision to distance myself from my friends. Back then it had all seemed so simple. The future was looming ever closer, and all I had left to do was get through my senior year, get into a good college and get as far away as possible from Archer's Creek. I hadn't cared about anything else.

I didn't think about the friends I was leaving behind. I was selfish enough to only think about myself, what I wanted and how dissolving the bonds I had to my home would make my escape a little easier.

Everything changed the day I watched my best friend fold into herself and lose the battle with her demons. I had no idea how much she was hurting. I was clueless to her struggles. But I promised her that I'd hold her broken pieces together until she figured out a way to make them all fit again, and I couldn't do that from a distance.

"Hey," Valentine says, hoisting himself up onto the tail-gate beside me.

"Where's Nova?"

"Dancing with Zeke," he says distractedly, his eyes fixed on his girlfriend dancing with her brother. He isn't looking at me, but I can still feel the intensity rolling off him in waves. "Why are you sitting by yourself?"

"I don't mind being alone," I answer. He and I aren't close. I've forgiven him for what he put Nova through, mainly because she has, but I haven't forgotten.

"You're not like them," Valentine says in that succinct way of his that has you flinching beneath his hard tone.

"No, I'm not," I admit, and even though I've always known it was true, for some reason it hurts me to admit it.

We fall silent and strangely it's more comfortable than I was expecting. Valentine's an outsider too. I don't know him well enough to know if he's always been this way, or if his history influenced it; but even though we're not talking, it's nice to have someone to be silent with.

I'm not sure how much time has passed when Griffin barrels over to the truck and leaps up into the back, lifting me up and stealing my spot before dropping me back down into his lap. "Eww, Griff," I cry, pushing at his hold on me and climbing out of his lap, "You smell like sex and cheap perfume."

Griff smiles, his eyes a little glazed. "Ahh the sweet smell of being eighteen."

"Gross," I groan, as Valentine chuckles beside us.

"Don't be like that, Em; come cuddle with me," Griff whines, dropping his arm over my shoulders and pulling me into him.

"No, eww, I don't want to smell like that skank you were dry humping."

His sigh is loud and so full of exasperation that I have to bite at my lip to stop myself from laughing. Reluctantly, he lifts his arm releasing me and I edge away from him and closer to Valentine.

"I'm starving. Let's go find something to eat." Nova

announces, as she prances across the field, Zeke following closely behind her. Skipping the last few steps, she moves straight between Valentine's legs and into his waiting arms, wrapping herself around him and pressing her cheek against his chest.

"This party sucks. Let's go back to ours and order a pizza," Zeke suggests.

"I should probably—" I start.

"Nope," Griff interrupts me. "You're coming too, no excuses."

"But."

"Nope," Griff says again, jumping down from Valentine's truck and scooping me over his shoulder before I have a chance to say anything more.

The others laugh loudly and I glare at them from my upside-down position. They simply smile and follow as he strides purposefully to the cab, opening the door and placing me onto the seat, before climbing in after me. Nova slides in after Griffin, pulling the door closed as Valentine and Zeke get into the front seat.

"What happened to your shirt?" Nova asks Griffin, and I see he's removed it, his warm tan skin exposed to the cool night air.

"Emmy said I smelt like skank," Griff says with a chuckle.

"Which skank?" Nova asks, her body swaying a little from side to side.

"It was either Erica or Rebecca. I can never remember," Griff replies with an offhanded swish of his hand.

"Dude, they're nothing alike. Erica has enormous tits and dark hair, Rebecca's blonde and tall." Zeke says, twisting around in his seat.

Griff shrugs. "Might have been Jill then. Who cares? I only made out with her a little bit."

"You're a pig," I hiss, shaking my head.

"No, I'm not," he insists, draping his arm over me and pulling me into his side. "Don't be like that, Em. You know I only want you, so none of these other girls even matter. Say the word and I'll never look in their direction again."

The others laugh and I can't help the chuckle that pulls at the corners of my lips. Griff's such a joker and tease.

Everything in Archer's Creek is close to everything else, so a few minutes later we're out of the truck and climbing down the stairs into the basement den Auntie Liv and Uncle Echo made for us to hang out in.

"Pizza's gonna be here in ten, someone grab some sodas," Zeke calls.

Crossing to the refrigerator, I pull out a bunch of sodas and carry them back across the room, placing them on the coffee table in front of the huge sectional couch. Nova is in Valentine's lap in one corner, so I sit down in the opposite corner, curling my legs beneath me.

Griff sits down beside me, pulling my legs up and laying them back down over the top of his. "Come snuggle with me, shortcake. I'm lonely," he whines.

Rolling my eyes at him, I reach for a can of soda, cracking the ring pull and waiting for the first hiss of air to escape, before lifting it to my lips. Zeke's messing with the TV, loading a game into the Xbox and collecting controllers. I take a second sip before the can is taken from my fingers and Griffin lowers it to the table.

"Emmy," he gripes. "I need my snuggle ration." Then he looks up at me with puppy dog eyes and Nova gigglesnorts.

Spinning my head in her direction, I glare at her, but she

just smiles back at me unrepentantly, her head resting against Valentine's chest.

"You already had snuggles from Jill or whatever her name was," I chide him.

"Nuh huh. You promised me you would always be available for snuggles. I'm calling it in," he says, flashing me a playfully smug look.

"What the fuck is with all the snuggle talk?" Valentine asks, his brow furrowed.

Nova giggles then lifts her head. "When Griffin first moved in with Duke, we were what, seven, eight?"

"My parents had just died," Griffin interrupts. "One day when I was really sad, Emmy told me that snuggles always made her feel better and that all I had to do was ask and she would snuggle with me until I was happy again," he says, looking at me expectantly.

Sighing, I shake my head softly. "But you're not sad."

Griff pouts, dipping his chin until it's almost touching his chest. "You won't be my girl, Em. I'm real sad."

"God, you're such a dick," I hiss, lifting my legs from where they're draped over his and turning into his waiting arms. He pulls me into his chest and rests his chin against the top of my head, wrapping me in the tightest hug.

"Dude, that was pathetic," Zeke says deadpan.

"Got my snuggles though, didn't I?" he says, with a low satisfied chuckle.

EMMY

The next morning, I'm lying on my bed reading the last chapter of a brilliant book, when my door flies open and Griffin marches in.

"Okay, I'm here, the epicness can start," he announces dramatically, throwing his arms out wide as if he's expecting me to start applauding him or something.

I glance at him then pointedly turn my attention back to my book. He won't allow me to ignore him for long, and a smile forms unbidden on my lips as I silently count down in my head.

5

4

3

2

1

The bed lurches as he bounces onto it, jostling me into the air. He uses my distraction to rip my book from my hands and fling it to the other end of the comforter. "Books are boring; let's go do something," he moans dramatically.

Griff and I have always been close, we're best friends. But since Nova's illness retightened the bonds I was deliberately loosening, he seems hellbent on making sure I don't try to distance myself again. "I was reading that," I say glaring at him and pursing my lips.

"I know. It must be my psychic vibe that warned me you needed me to come and save you and here I am."

"Don't you have a girl you can go pester? There must be someone in our class you haven't fucked yet. Maybe you could leave me alone and go track her down?"

He clutches at his heart and mock gasps. "You wound me. I've fucked all the hot ones except you."

I roll my eyes so hard they actually hurt. "I'm not hot and I'm never going to fuck you."

"You're right, you're not hot," he agrees, nodding.

My chest pangs. I know I'm nothing special, but hearing him say it in such a blasé way actually hurts.

"You're fucking stunning, Em. Above and beyond any of the girls at school," he says so effortlessly that I'm thrown by the sincerity in his voice.

My lips part and my mouth falls open.

Seeing my shock, his brow wrinkles. "What? Don't act like you don't know you're hot, Em. All that fucking hot red hair and banging rack."

The crass words help me shake off my surprise at him calling me stunning. He didn't mean it. He's just a good friend, a best friend, and he's being nice. "Why are you here? I thought you and Zeke had football practice."

"Nope. Football is done. We didn't make the playoffs so there are no more practices for seniors. Plus, we have important shit to do today."

"What important shit? Is Nova okay?"

"She's fine, but we have decisions to make."

"What decisions?" I ask, sitting up.

"It's time to open all those college letters you've got stashed beneath your bed."

My eyes glance to the floor. How could he possibly know that I've put off opening my letters? "What?" I say, pretending not to know what he's talking about.

He flattens his lips into a straight line and arches his eyebrows.

"Fine," I sigh, twisting my legs off the side of the bed and reaching beneath it to pull out the large pile of letters.

"Jesus, Em, how many do you have there?"

"Twenty-five," I admit sheepishly.

He shakes his head, reaching out and taking the pile from me as he stands and moves to wait by the door. "Future's calling, shortcake. You can't ignore it, no matter how much you try. Now get ready, the others are waiting."

Resigned, I stand up, pulling down the back of my shorts as I slide my feet into sneakers and palm my cellphone.

Six months ago, I was eager for the future; ready to run off to the other side of the country and start a new life where no one knew anything about bikers, except what they've seen on the TV. I was so excited to create a new college Emmy. One who's unexceptional and who blends in with a crowd.

I had it all worked out: get accepted to Dartmouth and be a ten-hour flight away from this tiny, artificial bubble we live in. Only now I'm not so sure it's what I want anymore. Nova's 'meltdown' as she likes to call it, changed more than just her. It changed me, Zeke, and Griffin too.

In the blink of an eye I went from distancing myself from my childhood friends, to refusing to leave their sides as we frantically clung to the shreds of Nova's sanity. That first week we spent almost every moment together, and it made me realize that I didn't really want to be as alone as I thought.

Back then we needed each other just like we always had. I hadn't realized I'd forgotten that, or maybe I chose to pretend that our bond didn't exist anymore. I'm not happy with my life here, but at least now I realize how lucky I am to have such amazing friends. I don't want to lose that by moving to New Hampshire without them.

Walking behind Griffin, I follow him through the house, pausing as my dad greets him with a manly handshake and Mom fawns over him. My parents obviously didn't even know he was here. We didn't knock, we never have. We just let ourselves into each other's houses because we're family and family don't stand on ceremony. They barge in and help themselves to a candy bar, knowing that they're always welcome.

I have a pretty charmed life. My parents are awesome, my little brother's a pain in my ass, but I love him, and I have the most amazing extended family. My life is great, but I can't help feeling this overwhelming sense of dissatisfaction.

Archer's Creek is small, quaint, and safe, but my dad's position within the community has meant that I was brought up under a magnifying glass. The motorcycle club my dad is the president of isn't a lawless club, they're not 1% or criminals, but regardless of that when thirty guys on huge motorcycles are together in a group, they make an impact.

My dad, my grandpa, and every single one of my uncles are total badasses. They're men's men, with traditional alpha male values that rankle my inner feminist. My parents are completely in love, totally devoted to each other; but to my dad, my mom is his. His woman, his property, his old lady. Mom's no mouse. She could bring him to his knees with a single word, but still, that's not a future I see for myself.

If I was a guy, I'm sure I'd jump at the chance to be a part of the club, to be a brother and gain all the advantages that come with it, but as the daughter of a biker, if I stay in this town, continue living this life, there's no future for me beyond ending up as some macho biker's property.

The need for something new has been pressing down on me for years, and I thought I'd have to leave behind my friends to be able to get it. But maybe that's not true. My eyes glide to the pile of letters Griff's holding, and my heart skips a beat. In those envelopes is the key to my new life, to a future where maybe I don't have to give up my roots to spread my wings.

"So you're finally going to do something with those envelopes, rather than just have them catching dust bunnies?" Mom asks, pulling me from my internal musing.

"Huh?"

"I thought I was going to have to open them for you," she smirks.

"I always planned to open them," I say snippily, defending myself.

Griff scoffs and I elbow him in the side, making him laugh beneath his breath.

"Come on, Judas," I hiss at him, pushing him as hard as I can and hating that his huge rock-hard body barely moves.

"Aww don't be like that, shortcake," he says, pulling me into his side and ruffling my hair affectionately.

"Bye, honey; bye, Griffin," Mom calls as I let Griff guide me out of my house and toward his car parked at the curb.

He opens the door for me, smiling annoyingly as I slide into the passenger seat, then closes it behind me. "Dick," I mutter under my breath as he circles the car and climbs into the driver's seat.

Handing me the pile of envelopes, he looks at them pointedly and arches his brow. "So where did you apply? I can see some pretty fancy names, but there are more than eight schools there."

"All the Ivy Leagues, the top ten private schools, and everywhere Nova applied to," I grudgingly admit.

His eyes widen for a second, before a slow, raspy chuckle escapes his lips.

"What?"

"Should have seen this coming," he says cryptically.

"What?" I ask again.

"Let's go, the others are waiting," he says, turning the key in the ignition and letting the engine flare to life.

The drive to Nova and Zeke's place is quick and only a few minutes later, Griffin opens my door and I climb out, annoyed that he seems smug about something I have no clue about. We walk straight into the house and immediately head for the basement, waving to Uncle Echo and Uncle Sleaze who are watching a baseball game on the huge flat screen TV.

The sound of muted chatter filters into my ears as I push into the room and I'm unsurprised to find Nova, Zeke, and Valentine already in here. What is a surprise are the piles of envelopes on the table in front of them.

"What's going on?"

Valentine looks up at me with an imperious arch of his brow. "Apparently we're opening college letters," he says dryly.

"Why haven't any of you opened them already?"

"Why haven't you?" Griff counters, dropping his own pile of letters onto the table before plopping down onto the squishy couch.

"I—" I say, unsure how honest to be with my answer. "I wasn't ready to make a decision yet."

"When I spotted that first envelope hidden beneath your

bed, I told the others and we agreed to wait and open them all together," Griff says with a shrug.

Tears fill my eyes, but I'm not sure why. Maybe it's that tonight could see us all heading in different directions and I'm just not ready. Pulling in a shaky breath, I lower myself in between Griff and Nova and pull my stack of envelopes toward me, the funeral march playing on repeat inside my head.

This should be exciting. I should be over the moon, but instead I'm sad and filled with trepidation. How can a few short months change everything so dramatically?

"Let's do one each. We can go round the table starting with Griff," Nova says excitedly, shuffling forward to the edge of the couch and pulling her own pile toward her.

I notice that my pile seems to be almost twice the size of everyone else's except for Valentine's whose pile looks tiny in comparison. "Where are the rest of your letters?"

"Mine came in early," he says.

"What, all of them?"

"Yep."

"So did you get in?" I ask.

"Yep."

"To all of them?" I say incredulously, wondering how it's possible that I didn't know Valentine had done early admission applications.

His nod is dismissive.

"So which schools did you get into?"

"None that I plan to attend," he says vaguely, his eyes flicking to Nova and softening perceptibly.

"Come on, we can talk about that later." Nova cries excitedly. "Griff, open your first letter."

One by one we tear open the envelopes, celebrating and commiserating with each person in turn. But the more letters that are opened, the more obvious the similarities in the schools becomes. Despite our closeness, we've never discussed going to the same college. In fact, I think we all just assumed we'd separate after graduation. Thinking about it now, it seems really weird that we never talked about which schools we were applying to. I mean, sure, I knew where Nova was applying and they all knew I planned to attempt the Ivy League route, but we never really came out and told each other what our choices were.

Only maybe we did know, because consciously or subconsciously, we've managed to apply to several of the same schools. "Did y'all know where you were applying?" I ask, suspiciously.

"I knew where Zeke was applying," Nova admits.

"I knew where Nova was applying," Valentine says.

Turning, I look to Griff who just shrugs. "I might have had some idea."

"So did we all deliberately apply to the same schools?"

"I was hoping I'd end up at the same school as at least one of you," Nova says quietly.

Valentine lifts her up and drags her into his lap. "Princess, I applied to every single school you did. There's no way I'm not following you to college."

Her eyes widen and her teeth pull at her bottom lip. "But you got into so many amazing schools."

"Where did you get early decisions from?" Zeke asks.

"Harvard, Brown, Princeton, Yale, and a couple of others," Valentine says offhandedly, like he didn't just casually throw out that he got early admission to four out of the top eight schools in the country.

I open my mouth to speak, but when I see the way he's looking at my best friend it's obvious that all that matters to him is her. That spark of jealousy jabs at my gut again. I don't want Valentine, but for the first time I'm a little envious of the way he so obviously adores her.

Guys aren't exactly on my radar, but I can't ever imagine having someone look at me the way he's looking at her right now, like she hangs the moon, like she's his everything. Most people look at me like they were expecting something more; like I should be more and instead I'm ordinary and for some reason that always seems to surprise them.

"This is awesome," Zeke cries. "Which schools did we all get in to?"

It takes us a moment to organize the piles of thick college brochures, separating the single sheets that denote a rejection. In the end my pile has acceptances for Dartmouth, Yale, Cornell, and ten other schools I applied to.

"So if Valentine is following my sister to school, instead of going to a fancy pants Ivy League school, then the four of us could actually stay together while Emmy runs off to be an overachiever," Zeke says excitedly.

"Emmy's going to Dartmouth, that's the dream, right? I'm so proud of you. I knew you could do it," Nova cries, throwing her arms around my neck and hugging me tightly.

I hug her back, waiting for my own enthusiasm to kick in. Lifting up the glossy brochure for Dartmouth, I slide my thumb across the shiny card. This is it, the dream I've wanted for years, here in the palm of my hand ready to be grasped. Only now I'm not so sure I want it anymore.

It's one thousand, nine hundred and three miles from my house to the front entrance of Dartmouth college, a nine-hour flight, a thirty-one-hour drive. Going there would be like moving to another world and that's what I want, or at least what I thought I wanted, what I used to want.

Now that it's here waiting, it doesn't seem quite so bright and shiny as I expected. The thought of being at a new school, alone, while the others start their futures together feels wrong. I thought that a new start in a place where no one knows me would be the most important thing in the world, but if I change who I am, will I forget the person I am at my core?

Normal.

Special.

Invisible.

Seen.

Does any of that matter if I have no anchors?

My heart starts to pound and a herd of elephants burst to life in the pit of my stomach. I don't want to be left behind, I don't want to be alone, I don't want to forget who I am.

"I'm not going to Dartmouth," I announce.

EMMY

Everyone speaks at once and I grimace as Nova, Zeke, and Griffin fire questions at me all at the same time.

Despite the noise, it's Valentine's pointed silence that pulls my attention. His lips tip into a small smile, his eyes softening with understanding. He offers me a single nod and I know that he gets it. He understands and that lingering doubt I had about him evaporates because he understands.

"Emmy, you're going to Dartmouth," Griffin snaps, his tone domineering and stern.

"No, I'm not."

"Yes, you are," Zeke cries.

"No, I'm not. I changed my mind."

Three voices all start to talk over each other until Valentine whistles. The shrill noise silences everyone, and all eyes turn to look at him. "Let her tell you why," he says slowly, his gaze moving to me as he dips his chin, encouraging me to explain.

Exhaling loudly, I stand up and walk around the coffee table. "I don't want to go to Dartmouth anymore."

"But why? That's your dream, Em. It's what you've been aiming for. Why now when it's right there and all you have to do is reach out and take it would you change your mind?" Nova asks, her voice pleading for me to explain.

Reaching up, I tuck my hair behind my ears. "Dartmouth was the furthest away."

Zeke's brow furrows and he leans forward, resting his elbows on his knees.

"I wanted to go there because it was the furthest place from here. I picked it because I wanted to get away, to start over in a place where no one knew me or who my family are."

"So what's changed?" Griff demands, anger sparking in his eyes, his fingers clenched into tight fists at his sides.

"I have," I say simply. "You guys love this life, this town, the club, and so do I, but I'm not sure I want it to be my future. I thought that running as far away as possible was the only way I could see what life was like when I wasn't a Scion. I backed away from you guys. I chose to distance myself so when it came to the time to leave it would be easier. Then Valentine moved here, and everything with Nova happened and I couldn't be distant anymore."

"This is bullshit, Em," Griff growls.

"What's bullshit? That I want a different life; that I want to be normal and not be the odd one out anymore? I agree it's bullshit. But it's how I felt. It's still how I feel, sort of. But being with you guys, being the Scions and owning it, has made me realize that I'm not ready to start my new life yet. I'm not ready to give you all up. I want roots and wings, Griff, and you guys are my roots. Fuck Dartmouth. It's not where I want to be if you're all together somewhere else."

"I understand," Valentine says, his voice a low rasp. "I ran, thought I'd be better on my own, but I was fucking kidding myself. Nova, this town, you guys, Brandy and Sleaze, you're home to me now. I get it Emmy, fuck Dartmouth."

A shuddering breath escapes me and I nod at him, a silent bond forming between us, an understanding that only outsiders like us will get.

"Fuck Dartmouth," Nova cries, shocking me. "I want us to go to college together. I always have. I even thought about trying to get into an Ivy League, but I'm not smart enough. So fuck Dartmouth. Let's find the best college we can and go there together."

A smile spreads across my lips and I grin at her. This girl is my sister, my best friend, and I need her just as much as she needs me, if not more.

"Fine, fuck Dartmouth," Zeke says, throwing his hands into the air and reaching for the pile of acceptance letters in front of him. "Let's figure out which schools we all got into."

My eyes drift to Griffin. His lips are still pressed together in a firm line and I can almost see the tension that's rippling across his body. "Griff," I say quietly, biting at my lip apprehensively.

"Dartmouth's your chance, Em."

I shake my head. "No, it would be a mistake. This is what I want; it's why I've put off opening those letters. I need my anchors so I don't forget who I am. I love you guys and I'm not ready to give that up. Please try to understand."

As I watch him, his shoulders relax a little and the fists at his sides unclench. "I do understand. Fuck, we've all done the exact same thing, applying to the same schools because we don't want to be alone either." Pushing up from the couch, he reaches me in two strides, pulling me into his chest and squeezing me. "Fuck Dartmouth," he whispers against the top of my head.

"Okay, let's do this," Zeke calls.

I reluctantly push away from Griff's warm embrace and move back to my place on the couch, pulling my own pile of brochures toward me.

"Texas State, Auburn, Arizona State, Wilson Hill, Addington Hall, University of Kentucky, and Hayhurst College," Nova reads from the notepad in front of her. "Does anyone have any preferences?"

"Texas State is a little too close to home," I say, hating to admit it, but really hoping they agree.

She doesn't say anything, just draws a line through Texas State, then looks up. "Anyone else want to veto any of them?"

I glance at the others and find them shaking their heads.

"Wilson Hill, Addington Hall, and Hayhurst are the best academically," Valentine offers.

"They're all smaller, private schools too, so less people, probably better food," Zeke says, flicking through the brochure for Wilson Hill.

"Okay, so location," Nova says, her voice upbeat. "Where is Wilson Hill?"

"Duluth, Minnesota," Zeke says, turning the glossy booklet in his hands around to show us.

"And what about Addington Hall and Hayhurst?"

"Addington Hall is in Iowa, and Hayhurst is Alabama," Valentine says.

"Are we ruling out Auburn, Arizona State, and the University of Kentucky?" I ask.

"You and Valentine both got accepted to more than one Ivy League school. You guys should go to the best school possible. Addington, Hayhurst, and Wilson Hill are the best of the ones we all got into." Griff says solemnly.

It's obvious that despite his earlier words, he's not

completely onboard with the idea of me not going to Dartmouth, but I don't call him out on it. Hopefully once we pick a school, the reality of all of us being together for the next four years will change his mind. Regardless of his opinion, this is the right decision, I can feel it.

"Let's go visit those three then. We can road trip or fly in if it's too far to drive. We've all put off campus tours, so it makes sense to do them now," Zeke says, lazily flopping back onto the couch, his arms stretched over his head.

We debate the merits of the three schools for the next hour or so, then as a group head out of the basement, emerging into the kitchen only to find music playing and the smell of BBQ permeating through the house.

"Looks like Mom activated the Sinners telephone tree," I say sardonically. "I'm gonna guess that all of our families are here."

"Looks like it," Zeke says, stepping forward and heading toward the backyard. "I'm starving."

I follow him, shielding my eyes from the bright sunlight as I step outside and immediately spot my mom sat on the patio with Brandi and Auntie Liv.

"They're here," Phoenix shouts and everyone's attention turns our way.

"So," Auntie Liv asks, standing up from her seat and wringing her hands together nervously. "Where did you all get accepted to?"

My gaze hits the ground. I don't want to talk about my reasons for wanting to run away from Archer's Creek. Although my reasons are all valid, I'm fairly sure I'd end up upsetting all of our families who love it here. When Zeke steps forward, I sigh with relief.

"There are a lot of shiny booklets for colleges downstairs. We haven't made any final decisions yet, but we've narrowed it down to three schools: Hayhurst College, Addington Hall, and Wilson Hill," he says.

"What about the rest of you?" Auntie Brandi asks.

"The same for all of us," Valentine says, stepping up next to Zeke.

"You've all picked the same schools?" Duke asks, his tone light and amused. Griffin's brother is the youngest of all the parents and has the least parent-like tone.

Sucking in a lungful of air, I lift my head and lock eyes with my mom. "Yeah, we've decided to pick a school so that the five of us can stay together."

I expect to see her disappointment and brace myself for it, but instead her smile is wide and happy. "Those are three great schools, kids. I'm so proud of all of you."

Tears pool in my eyes, but I refuse to let them fall, blinking them away and leaning into Zeke for support. His arm snakes around my waist and he squeezes me quickly, sensing my relief.

"We're going to take a trip out to the three schools and have a look around, then we'll pick our favorite." Nova announces, bouncing across the patio to where her dad is flipping burgers on the grill.

With the big announcement done, we all disperse, grabbing plates and drinks. I settle on a lounger overlooking the beautiful sky-blue pool. It looks so tempting I consider going to grab the spare swimwear I keep in Nova's closet for when I come around.

Griff drops down onto the end of my lounger, his plate overflowing with potato salad, chicken, and a huge burger with cheese melting down the side. For a long moment we sit side by side, neither of us saying anything.

His appearance isn't a surprise. His agreement about my change of college plans was too easy, and I've been expecting the speech I'm sure he's about to make ever since.

"You were so desperate to get away from us, you were going to pick the school farthest away." Griff growls, his eyes narrowing, as anger slips into his tone.

"I wasn't desperate to get away from you, just to get away." I admit. "Going to Dartmouth and being in New Hampshire, somewhere so different than here just felt like it would be a completely new life."

"What the fuck is so wrong with this life, Emmy? Explain why you think what we have is so fucking bad?"

I can hear the anger building inside of him and I sigh trying to decide how I can explain how I feel to him. "Nothing and everything. This," I say, gesturing around the backyard at all of our family. "Is all I've ever known. I've only ever lived in this town. I've only experienced the Sinner way of life."

I expect Griffin to say something, but he doesn't.

"Don't you want something more?" I ask.

"I think we always want more," he says quietly, his eyes softening as he looks at me, with a wistfulness that I don't really understand reflected back at me. "But it can all be taken away in the blink of an eye, and this life feels pretty good to me."

Groaning, I lift my hand up to cover my eyes. "It is a good life, but maybe something different could be better than good. What if it could be great?" Sighing, I blink slowly, letting my eyes lock with his, hoping he can see what I so desperately need him to understand. "I don't know what I want anymore. I don't want to stay here, but I don't want to run away either."

Griff pulls my hand from my face. "Come here," he says, urging me to curl into his side.

I move, placing my head on his chest as he curls an arm around my back and brushes my hair away from my face with his other hand.

"We'll figure it out, I promise," he whispers against the top of my head. "Roots and wings. I've got you, shortcake. Always have, always will."

GRIFFIN

Inhaling deeply, I rest my cheek against the top of her head. I just promised her that everything would be okay and I have no idea if that's true or not. We've been losing her for years and then all of a sudden she came back to us and it was just like it was when we were kids. Emmy was one of us, all the way in, a Scion.

I think we all knew that our time together was limited, but Nova, Zeke and I were just so fucking happy to have the fourth member of our group back that we all just pretended it would last forever.

A big part of me wants to cling to this bomb she just dropped on us and be excited that she wants to forgo her ambitious future for one that includes the five of us going away to college together. For a moment I was over the fucking moon when she stood in front of all of us and said that she didn't want to go to Dartmouth, but how good a friend are we if we just let her give up a dream she's had for years?

Her arms are wrapped tightly against my waist and

memories of us doing this a thousand times before all flash into my mind. Emmy's home to me, the closest I've had since the last time my mom hugged me and I don't want to give her up.

My gaze wanders around the garden to the people who are here, chatting, eating and being a family even though they're not related by blood. How can she think there's something out there that's better than this?

Unlike Emmy, I've seen a little more of the world, lived somewhere other than here, but that only makes me even more certain that what this town has, what the Sinners have, is unique. I was born a Sinner. My dad was the president of our hometown chapter and I spent the first seven years of my life living as part of the club, but it was nothing like this.

My dad was cold, detached and ruthless, and my mom, me, and Duke were his property. Our future was cemented into place the day we were born. We would follow in his footsteps regardless of if that was what we wanted or not. I loved him because he was my dad, but now that I've seen what it's like to be supported and loved from this group of people, I'm not blind to his faults.

Emmy has every opportunity. She has a loving family, she has great friends, a great home town and an entire club full of people who would fall over themselves to make sure she's safe, loved and protected. This place is a bubble, but she wants to live in a world without the Sinners.

Everything inside of me wants to protect her from discovering that the world outside of our lives isn't all it's cracked up to be. My instincts tell me to protect her, to shelter her and cosset her from anything that could hurt her, but I can't do that if she's thousands of miles away.

I should release her, but instead I grip her a little tighter. My inner fucking caveman is screaming that if I can keep her close, maybe I can stop her from drifting from us again, but even while I'm touching her it still feels like I'm losing her.

I'm not ready to consider her actually turning down her place at an Ivy League school to follow the rest of us to one of the three schools we've narrowed it down to. Because as much as I want it to be true, I don't ever want to be the ropes that are holding her back.

What's that cliché saying…? If you love it set it free. My gut says fuck that; if you love it keep it close, but what do I know? I'm an eighteen-year-old kid.

Sighing, I reluctantly let her go and she looks up at me with glassy eyes. "It'll be okay, Griff," she whispers.

I nod, not believing it, but wanting it be true. Hoping that we can keep her in our lives without clipping those wings she so desperately wants to spread.

EMMY

In the next few weeks we fly out to both Wilson Hill and Addington Hall to do campus tours and look around. Wilson Hill is in the middle of a city in Minnesota and even though I've always loved the idea of living in a bustling metropolitan city, after a couple of days I was almost glad to get back to the sleepy pace of life at home. Thankfully, the others felt the same way and we all agreed to cross Wilson Hill from our shortlist.

Our visit to Addington Hall was more of a success. The campus seems to have fallen straight out of a Harry Potter movie, with gothic turrets and towers that made my inner bookworm start squealing with glee. The one big downfall for the school was that the location made Archer's Creek look positively hectic. The town of Addington was the closest bit of civilization to the school's campus and even that was still nearly ten miles away and consisted of one long street with a bar, two diners and a handful of shops. So we were still on the fence about if the school, with its fantastic facilities and outstanding academic results, was worth living in the middle of nowhere.

It's been three weeks since our last trip out of state and our upcoming trip to Hayhurst seems to be taking forever to arrive. Nova has been gushing excitedly about how after our trip to Alabama our futures will be sorted soon and how awesome it will be when we're all together at school.

But the closer we get to making a decision, the more apprehensive I get. I'm not changing my mind about staying with my friends for school; there's just something about picking a future and committing to it that scares me half to death. What if I make the wrong choice and the road I pick leads me straight back here?

We're starting our road trip to Alabama in the morning. When we announced that we wanted to drive the thirteen-hour journey to visit Hayhurst, my daddy just about lost his mind, and though I know he's just an overprotective Daddy with his precious daughter's interests at heart, it was another reason why I wanted some independence away from home.

One Week Before

"Hell, no," Dad says, looming over me, his chest heaving with angry indignation.

With my hands on my hips I tilt my head back and just look at him, my eyebrow arched in an imitation of the way I've seen my mom look at him when he's exasperating her.

"No, absolutely fucking not. There is no way I'm allowing you to drive for thirteen fucking hours with some punk kids."

"Daddy, you really shouldn't use that language," I scold, barely keeping a smile from my lips.

"Emmy," he growls in warning.

"You're being dramatic. The punk kids I want to visit our

potential university campus with are your nephews and nieces, and I'm not asking your permission, I'm telling you what I'm doing."

"Little girl, don't you sass me. I'll ground your ass til you turn twenty-five and I've got an entire club full of your uncles that'll back me up."

"Daddy," I sigh.

"I'm not happy about this," he growls, his lips pursed into an aggravated scowl.

"I'm eighteen. I'm going with family and it's only Alabama for one weekend."

"If you want to go see that school, your mom and I will take you."

"Dad," I whine, rolling my eyes. "I'm not a little girl anymore. I'll be going away to school soon, so you need to start trusting me."

"I do trust you."

Scoffing, I give him a pointed glare. "If you trusted me, you wouldn't be refusing to let me go. We're going to look at the school. It's hardly going to be a rager with drugs and beer and boys."

"I don't understand why you can't just go to Texas State. Then you could live at home."

"Cam," Mom scolds, crossing the room and sitting down in Dad's lap.

"What?" He says innocently.

"She's not a baby anymore."

"She's my baby. She always will be and I don't want her to go to a school fourteen hours away."

"Daddy, I got into schools all over the country. I could be much further away than Alabama. Hayhurst is only a short flight. If I'd decided to go to Dartmouth instead it would have

been over eight hours on a plane, and nearly thirty hours to drive."

My dad huffs disdainfully, but I ignore him and cross my arms across my chest. "I want to go to school with the others, and you didn't have any issues with us going to visit the other schools. I know you're not happy about us driving, but I'm sorry, this weekend I'm going on a road trip to Hayhurst College. I don't need your permission, I'm an adult. If you force my hand, I'll go without your approval, but I don't want to do that. I want you to see that I'm a sensible, mature woman and that a road trip with my friends, your nieces and nephews, isn't something dangerous. I'm not stupid or reckless and you need to trust that I'm capable of looking after myself."

His sigh is gruff and pained. "I know how capable and mature you are, baby girl. I'm just not ready to lose you yet."

I watch as Mom wraps her arms around his neck and whispers something I can't hear against his ear. "Fine, you can go, but you need to be careful, and I'll be telling those boys that if they ever want to be a part of my club, they better keep you safe," Dad growls, holding Mom tightly to him.

Rushing over to him, I throw my arms around his neck and both he and Mom hug me. When I pull back, I press a kiss to his cheek. "Love you, Daddy."

"Love you too, baby girl," he replies and I swear I hear a crack of emotion in his voice.

Present Day

My dad is completely unprepared for me to go away to college, even though he's always known it was going to happen. Maybe it's that he knows once I move away it's unlikely I'll ever live here in Archer's Creek again. He can sense the dissatisfaction in me, much more so than anyone else.

I may look like my mom, but my personality is alarmingly similar to my dad's. He feels so much more than he lets on and he and I are exceptionally in tune for a father and daughter. My dad raised me to be his baby girl, but he also prepared me for life as well. He, more than most knows I'm capable of looking after myself, because he taught me.

A pang of loss hits me in the middle of my chest and I roll to my side. Until now I hadn't really thought about how much I'd miss my mom and dad; hell, even Phoenix too. Resting my palm beneath my cheek, my other hand holds my Kindle tightly as I try to distract myself with another world.

It doesn't take long for me to dissolve into the story, to allow the words to become the tide and pull me under, drowning me in a vivid story about love and loss and choice. I see familiarities in each scene, each character, feeling their struggle as though it were my own. To some a book is merely lines on a page, but to me, it's an escape. It's somewhere I don't have to be me. It's a chance to leave this narrow world of mine and experience more, so much more, and all without ever leaving my room.

In real life I'm not brave or bold. I don't take risks or put myself out there for adventures, or love or experiences. But between the pages of a book, I can be whoever I want to be and that freedom is the most liberating thing I've ever experienced in my eighteen short years of life.

Just as I'm busy wallowing in pathetic self-pity, my Kindle screen turns black as my battery dies. My cell beeps, signaling a text message and I roll to my stomach to reach for it, glancing back to my Kindle, just in case by some miracle it's now fully charged, but it's still dead. Awkwardly, I pull my cell from my pocket and bring the screen to life, clicking into the text message app.

Griffin
Stop reading.

Prying my other arm up from beneath me, I quickly type out a reply and hit send.

Emmy
I'm not reading

The three dots barely flash before a message pings up.

Griffin
Bullshit.

Emmy
I swear I'm not reading.

Griffin
The battery dead on your Kindle?

Emmy
Yes :(

The fact he knows me so well makes me smile. Rolling back onto my back, I twist my head and stare at the setting sun through my bedroom window. With my storybook escape beyond my reach for the moment, my mind drifts to tomorrow, our trip, and the choices I'm going to be expected to make after we get back from this weekend.

This is why books are better than real life. In my books, the world is full of magical beings and unknown latent powers. Every boy is beautiful and every love story has a happy ever after. Friends last forever and betrayal is left to villains. What college to choose isn't exactly important when the fate of the world is in your hands.

Sometimes I wish my life was more like the plot of one of my books, but I suppose to someone else, the life I lead could be fictional. My family are bikers, my dad the president. There are literally thousands of romance novels dedicated to MC's and the people who are a part of them. Only I'm not a character in a book and my life isn't a story.

My family is great, my friends are great, this town is idyllic. But I yearn for something else. I want to live in one of my books. I want my soulmate to rescue me from a bad guy and for it to be love at first sight; for them to take me on adventures. I want an epic love story, full of new experiences.

Sighing wearily, I watch the sun sink lower and wonder if one day I'll slip so far into my imagination that I won't be able to get out. Would it really be so bad?

My door swings open and Griffin strides into my room. His eyes search for me, and when he finds me on the floor he chuckles, shaking his head, his eyes glimmering with amusement. When we were kids we used to spend so much time together, just the two of us. We'd joked that as Nova and Zeke had each other, Griffin and I had to have each other's backs.

At eight years old, that made complete sense, and so he would beg his brother to drop him off at my house and then we'd play together, do our homework, and tell each other secrets. There was a time when he and I knew everything about each other. Things started to change around the age of twelve or thirteen. Puberty hit and the boy/girl divide got wider. All of a sudden it was easier to tell my secrets to Nova and so his secrets stopped being mine too. When Griff and

Zeke found girls, the divide got even wider. He never stopped being my family, one of my best friends, but our friendship changed.

When Nova's illness brought me back to our group, it mended something between Griffin and I too. I can't be sure when our relationship became more like it was when we were younger, but over the last several months he's become an even bigger part of my life: my comfort, my protector, my safety net.

More than anything, our rediscovered closeness has only confirmed that I'm not prepared to lose the most important people in my life. I need my best friends, I need him.

"What you doing, shortcake?" He asks, his one brow arched in question.

"Cooking pasta," I deadpan.

"Sweet, I could go for some spaghetti," Griff replies brightly, as he lowers himself to the floor and lies next to me. "We plotting world domination?"

"Something like that," I murmur, my head tilted toward his now; my gaze half on him, half on the sunset painting the sky outside.

"You okay?" He asks, his eyes crinkled at the corners in concern.

"Yeah, just thinking."

"That's dangerous stuff. Probably better you stop doing that shit. Go with the flow instead, face things as it happens."

Rolling my eyes, I offer him a small smile that I know doesn't make it to my eyes.

"You worried about this weekend?"

"A little," I admit.

"The drive or the school?"

I inhale, wondering how honest I should be. Griff tries to understand, but he doesn't really get it. He likes it here. He loves our town, our lives, and I think deep down he just doesn't understand why I wouldn't pick this place as my future.

"Come on, Em. Just tell me," he urges, rolling fully to his side and resting his palm beneath his cheek.

"Once we've seen Hayhurst, we have to make a decision. I'm worried that I'll make the wrong choice," I admit, laying it all bare for him.

His eyes widen slightly and then wilt into a sadness that makes my chest hurt.

"I'm not changing my mind about us all going together," I say quickly. "I'm just not sure what my future looks like and because I can't see it, I have no idea if whatever school we pick will be the right one. Does that make any sense?" I ask.

His head slowly moves up and down in a small nod. "Yeah, I think I get it. But you don't have to pick a future this weekend; we're just picking a college. Where you go to school doesn't have to define you. It's just the first step on the path. We're still kids. We don't have to be adults for years, so try to enjoy it. Make choices without thinking of the consequences. Be reckless, be brave, and have some fun. That's what being a kid is all about."

"But…" I try to interrupt him.

"No buts. Stop thinking so hard, shortcake, and just see what happens. Do what feels right, what makes your heart beat faster and your soul sing. Life can be over in the blink of an eye. Make the time you have the best possible."

When his lips stop moving, I roll toward him and wrap my arm around him, hugging him tightly. Sometimes I forget that Griff's parents aren't here, that they were ripped away from him when he was far too young to lose them. It's only in moments like this, when he reminds me that things can be gone in a split second, that I see the pain that's always there beneath the surface with him.

He acts like he doesn't have a care in the world. Laughs the loudest, parties the hardest, and lives to the fullest, but he also feels deeply. It might have been ten years since his parents' deaths, but he's still sad, still grieving.

I have everything in the world and yet I'm so desperate for something new that I'm agonizing over if picking the wrong college could ruin my chances of getting away from this town. I'm so selfish.

"You're right," I say into his neck.

"Of course I am," he snickers.

"This weekend is going to be great and whichever school we pick will be great, because we'll all be there together and at the end of the day that's what's important."

Griff pulls back and rests his forehead against mine. "We're Sinners, Em, and Sinners take care of their own. Staying together is right. We need each other. You were right and I get it now. I still think you should go to Dartmouth, but I'm so fucking glad that you're not. My world wouldn't be whole without you in it."

"Mine wouldn't be whole without you either," I say quietly.

Chapter 6

GRIFFIN

I can't do it. I can't be the type of guy who sacrifices his happiness to give someone a chance at their own. Emmy is my best friend. She's too fucking important to me, to let her leave and go to a school across the country.

Maybe a different kind of man could do it, but apparently I'm too fucking selfish for that. It's time for plan B. I love this girl. She's in every single one of my happy memories, and Nova, Zeke, Valentine, and I need to do whatever it takes to keep her in our lives.

We've visited two out of three of our shortlisted schools. Wilson Hill was too busy, Addington, too remote. Fingers crossed Hayhurst is perfect, it needs to be.

We're the Scions, our futures are intertwined. Emmy untied a few of those knots, but between the rest of us we can tangle them back up again. We're family and family is everything.

I can see her glancing at her dead Kindle next to her on the floor, but I have no intention of letting her charge it and then losing her to the pages of a story again today. Fiction is great, but real life will always be better, even if it's not as simple and it doesn't come with a guaranteed happy ever after.

She needs to spend a little more time living, instead of watching other people live through words. I chuckle to myself as I think about all the ways I can stop her from reading and keep her in the here and now.

I'm gonna drive her crazy, but she'll thank me for it in the end.

EMMY

The next morning, we all pile into Valentine's truck, loading our bags into the back. Looking out of the window I smile at the row of adults who are stood together at the curb to see us off, like we're actually leaving for college, not just visiting for the weekend.

"Do you have the address for the hotel?" Auntie Brandi calls.

"Yep," Valentine replies.

"And you have enough gas and your credit cards?" Auntie Liv asks.

"No, Mom, we decided to only put in enough gas to get us to those cornfields where all the serial killers hang out." Zeke deadpans.

Auntie Liv's eyes narrow and she purses her lips.

"We have a full tank of gas, and five credit cards as well as some cash," Nova tells her mom.

"Griff, don't get anyone pregnant," Duke offers with an amused smirk.

Griffin salutes him, laughing, while Auntie Brandi,

Auntie Liv, and my mom all turn and glare at Duke as he holds his hands up in surrender.

"Valentine," Brandi calls, taking a step up to the driver's window.

"Yeah."

"Don't forget your way home," she says quietly.

"I won't," he says. Then he glances to Nova, before turning back to Brandi. "Plus, we're gonna need to sign those adoption papers when I get back."

I watch as Auntie Brandi's mouth falls open and tears fill her eyes. She leans fully in through the window and pulls a slightly stunned Valentine in for a hug. He awkwardly pats her back until she releases him, her lips trembling. "You still need to work on that hug."

"When we get home on Monday," Valentine agrees with a small smile.

"Okay, drive safe, love you," she says, cupping his cheek before looking at the rest of us. "Take care of each other."

"We will, Auntie Brandi," I say, as the others all agree.

She takes a step back, straight into Uncle Sleaze's arms, then Valentine starts the truck's engine and all of the adults move forward to surround her as they wave us off.

"Road trip, baby!" Zeke cries the moment we turn the corner and our parents are out of sight.

"Road trip," we all chorus back and I throw my hands in the air and laugh with excitement.

By the time we reach Alabama that night we're all exhausted. "Oh my god, longest drive ever," Nova cries as we climb out of the back seat of the truck.

Stretching my arms into the air, I tilt my head from side to side, trying to crack my stiff neck back into place. "Whose stupid idea was it to drive? It's less than a two-hour flight; we could have been here hours ago."

"Duh, it's not a road trip unless you drive," Zeke says, ruffling my hair as he moves past me to grab our stuff from the back of the truck.

Our parents insisted on booking us into a suite at the hotel we're staying in this weekend. It's extravagant, but they excused the expense saying something about us being safer if we were all together. Honestly, I'm not complaining because the thought of a soft hotel bed is looking pretty good right now. Griff grabs my bag from the bed of the truck, while Valentine grabs Nova's and we all head for the hotel's front entrance.

It doesn't take us long to check-in and fifteen minutes later I'm dropping my bag to the floor of a beautiful bedroom, off a large sitting area and kitchen. Falling backward onto the bed, I groan with pleasure as I hit the marsh-mallowy hotel comforter and sink into the soft, white cotton.

The suite has three bedrooms and I know Auntie Liv and Uncle Echo assumed that Nova and I would be sharing a room, but really that was never going to happen. Something else I'm not complaining about as I make the most of the huge King bed and starfish, spreading my arms and legs wide, giggling to myself as I do it.

"I'm starving. Room service or out to eat?" Zeke calls from the sitting room.

Forcing myself off the bed, I kick off my shoes and pad barefoot out into the sitting room. "Room service. I'm hungry and I want to finish my book, because someone." I glare at Griffin. "Wouldn't let me read in the truck."

Griff smirks at me completely unashamedly from his position on the couch. "I'm good with room service."

"I vote room service too," Valentine says, when he and Nova emerge from their room.

"Room service it is," Zeke says, reaching for the menu and reading it. "Anyone know what they want?"

The menu's passed around and we each pick, relaying our order to Zeke who calls it through to the reception desk. "Food's going to be twenty minutes, so we have some time to talk about what the plan is for tomorrow. There are no official campus tours this weekend, so should we just head over there and have a wander about?" Zeke asks, taking charge in the way he so often does.

"Sounds good to me. At least this way we can get a feel for the place, then we can find a party to hit tomorrow night so we can see what the nightlife is like." Griffin says, getting up and crossing the room to the fridge in the suite's kitchenette.

My gaze drifts to Nova and I notice that her eyes are crinkling a little at the edges, her teeth worrying at her lower lip. "We don't have to go to a party," I say, knowing that she hates them almost as much as I do.

"What? You're not gonna just sit—" Griffin starts to say, looking at me before glancing at Nova. "Oh shit, Nova, I wasn't thinking. Don't worry about the party thing, we can just play it by ear and see what's going on once we're done looking round."

Nova's smile is small and a little sad. "We can find a party, Griff. I'm getting much better with them."

"Don't even worry about it, sis," he says. "We can find trouble some other way."

We chat about what we want to do and see while we're here until a knock on the door ends the conversation. Zeke jumps up and opens it, and I watch as a hotel employee pushes a cart into the room, resplendent with several plates of food. He quickly unloads it onto the table, accepts the tip Valentine offers him and closes the door as he leaves.

I descend on the burger I ordered like a wild animal, stuffing fries into my mouth and groaning when the hot, salty goodness hits my tongue. By the time my plate is empty, my belly is full, and after a long day stuck in a car with four other people, I'm desperate for some peace and quiet.

I head back to my room, strip out of my clothes and step underneath the hot shower to wash away a long day's traveling. I luxuriate under the water for longer than I normally would, letting the heat soothe the knots in my shoulders, then dry off and put on a cotton tank and shorts before climbing beneath the bedsheets.

The exhale that falls from my lips is both relief and satisfaction. My door's closed, it's quiet, and it's unlikely any of the others will disturb me. Inhaling slowly, I take a moment to enjoy the calm silence of my room. Even the most social person in the world would need a little bit of solitude after a fourteen-hour truck ride with my excited friends, and I'm most definitely not the most social person. Griff seems to take a perverse pleasure in stopping me from reading. In fact, more and more in the last six months he's been determined to keep my attention off whatever book I'm devouring. He distracts me the moment I pick up my Kindle at school, regularly texts me to obnoxiously tell me to stop reading when I'm at home, and has even gone so far as to take my Kindle off me at family BBQ's and parties.

But he's not here now and the unsettled butterflies that are jumping around in my stomach can easily be calmed with the distraction of another world, another life to experience. Grabbing my Kindle from where I placed it on the nightstand, I open the new book that only released a couple of days ago and start to read.

For the first time in ages the story I'm reading is a contemporary romance, rather than the paranormal or high fantasy I usually pick, but it still doesn't take me long to become completely consumed with the story. Set in college, the heroine meets the hero at a campus tour and sparks fly. The story is sweet, the hero a cute nerdy type and within a few chapters I'm engrossed in the world and watching the story play out from the heroine's eyes.

When my door opens, I'm aware of someone standing in the doorway, but I don't put my Kindle down long enough to acknowledge whoever it is. A moment later my mattress depresses and I glance down to find Griff climbing onto my bed next to me. He pokes my arm with his finger, but I swat him away.

"Em."

I ignore him.

"Em."

"I'm reading," I hiss, not lifting my eyes from my screen.

"Em, Em, Em, Emmy, Emmy, Emmy," he whines.

I can't help it. I giggle, closing my eyes for a second and shaking my head. "What do you want?"

"I'm bored, entertain me."

"Entertain yourself, I'm reading."

"That's boring," he says with a groan.

"Not for me," I reply, focusing back on my eReader. "Go harass Zeke."

"Can't, he's asleep, and Nova and Valentine are in their room probably fucking, so you're it."

"I'm reading," I say again.

Griffin sighs loudly and flip flops around on my bed, before eventually settling on his back, his head next to mine on my pillow. He grabs the remote from the bedside table and switches the TV on, turning the volume down low. The screen flickers as he flips through the channels until he finally settles on something, dropping the remote to the comforter.

47

Surprisingly comfortable, I lie in bed and read while he watches the TV. I must fall asleep, because when I open my eyes there's sunlight filtering through the gaps in the drapes. Griffin's warm body is next to me. At some point he must have undressed, because his chest is bare and he's only wearing sweatpants. He's still on top of the covers, his dirty blond hair disheveled and his face relaxed in sleep.

Rubbing at my eyes with my hands, I wiggle up the bed until my shoulders are leaning back against the wall. My movement must disturb Griff, because his eyes slowly blink open and he twists his head up to look at me. As his eyes focus, his brow furrows with confusion. "What?" He croaks, his voice rough with sleep.

"We must have fallen asleep," I say.

A faint red blush fills his cheeks and he looks away for a moment, before sitting up, and adjusting his sweatpants. "Sorry," he says. "I meant to go back to my room."

"Err, it's okay," I mutter, a little embarrassed by his obvious embarrassment.

The bed jostles as he clambers up and off, scurrying to the other side of the room. "I'll see you in a bit," he mumbles as he opens the door and leaves.

Well that was weird. Maybe he had morning wood and didn't want me to see? I have a brother, I know all about the weird and disgusting things teenage boys do. Shrugging, I snuggle back under the comforter and grab my Kindle.

Two hours later, I pull my black sweater over my head, slide my feet into my fur lined Dr. Marten boots, then push open my bedroom door and head into the sitting area. It's nowhere near as cold in Alabama as it was in Minnesota and Iowa, so although I'm still in boots and a sweater, I'm not freezing to death in a blizzard.

The sitting room is empty, but the smell of freshly brewed

coffee fills the room, so someone must be awake. As if on cue, Nova's door opens and she steps out wearing a blue check shirt that I know belongs to Valentine; black skinny jeans; and short, black suede UGG boots. Her hair is braided back into two tight braids against her head and she looks as effortlessly stunning as always.

"Morning," she says through a yawn.

"Morning."

"You want coffee?"

"Always," I say, scoffing and following her as she pads to the kitchenette and retrieves two cups from the cabinet. She makes us both a coffee and slides one cup to me, before bringing the other to her lips and sipping.

Her sigh is audible. "God, I swear I don't know how I functioned before I became a caffeine addict."

"Are the others up yet?

She nods as she lifts the cup to her lips again. "Zeke's dressed; he went for a run at some ungodly hour this morning. Valentine's just in the shower, and I'm not sure about Griff, but I heard someone moving around a couple of hours ago, so maybe he went to hit the hotel gym or something."

For a moment I consider telling her that he fell asleep in my room last night, then I decide not to. I don't really know why. It's not like she would care, we've all shared rooms in the past. But for some reason this feels like one of mine and Griffin's secrets, something that's just between the two of us, like the secrets we had as kids.

The door to his room swings open and Griff emerges, dressed in fitted jeans with rips across the knees and a gray, long-sleeved Henley that's stretched across his ridiculously huge arms. "I'm fucking starved, what are we doing for breakfast?" he demands, his tone more brusque than I'm used to.

"There's a buffet downstairs. Zeke went down to see if we have to make a reservation," Nova tells him without lifting her eyes from the coffee in her hands.

The suite door opens and Zeke strides in looking fresh-faced and awake. "Morning. The buffet looks delicious, let's go eat," he says, resting his arm against the doorjamb.

"Valentine, dude, breakfast," Griff hollers in the direction of their room as he hops around pulling on sneakers.

"Yeah, I'm coming," Valentine says, emerging from the room, his head down, his eyes barely open. He's dressed in his usual black jeans; white t-shirt; and scuffed, black leather boots.

"What the fuck's up with you?" Zeke says with a laugh.

"He's not a morning person," Nova says brightly, jumping up from the couch and bouncing over to her boyfriend. "Come on, sweetie. There's coffee and bacon downstairs."

Valentine nods, grabbing a hoodie from the back of the couch and letting Nova lead him out of the room.

The breakfast is amazing and I fill my plate with waffles and drown them with maple syrup, washing it down with a latte and freshly squeezed orange juice. With my stomach full, I lean back on my seat and watch as the others eat. Nova is leaning against Valentine and his eyes are on her, smiling down at her as she sips her coffee.

Another pang of want hits me. I want what they have. I want someone who looks at me the way Valentine looks at Nova. I want all of that, and until this moment I hadn't realized just how much. Guys have never really been on my radar. I've had crushes and the occasional date in middle school, but since the start of high school when the reign of the Scions began, I've shied away from guys. The doubt over their reasons for paying me attention has always stopped me from engaging, but in college all of that will change.

No matter which school we pick, no one there will know who I am or who my family is, and that thought is blissful. Any friendships I make will be genuine, any boys who ask me out will be asking me out, not asking Emmy Devereaux, daughter of the Doomsday Sinners MC's president out.

Excitement ripples through me and I feel a smile spread across my lips. "I have a good feeling about this place."

"Yeah?" Griff asks, looking up from his plate and grinning at me. "Why's that?"

"I don't really know; I just feel like this might be the one."

Twenty minutes later, we walk outside, stepping onto the sidewalk in front of the hotel.

"It looks like a nice day; shall we walk over to campus?" Nova asks, practically jumping up and down on the spot with barely restrained excitement.

I nod and she rushes forward and links her arm with mine. Our hotel is in the center of the small town of Hayhurst and as we walk, I eagerly take in every detail of the town.

"Okay, so on our pro list for Hayhurst was the small-town location," Nova reads, pulling the list we made the other night from her purse.

"It's pretty. I like it better than being in a big city like Wilson Hill was," I admit, eyeing the cute stores and coffee shops, full of what I guess are probably students judging by their age and appearance. Hayhurst is not that much bigger than Archer's Creek, but unlike the town we live in, it feels more metropolitan, or perhaps it's just that we don't know anyone here and they don't know us that makes it feel like a much bigger world than the one we inhabit now.

My excitement from earlier builds as we meander through the quiet, tree-lined streets. Rows of brownstones line one side, while restaurants and bars fill the other. It's a Friday, and even this early in the morning, the whole town feels alive and eager for the day ahead. The feeling is addictive and with each step I take I feel more invigorated, as if the place is seeping into me and settling into my core.

Hayhurst is definitely not a big city like Minnesota, nor a remote hideaway like Addington, but it's new and somehow it already sort of feels like home. People talk about you having the opportunity to reinvent yourself at college and as my feet move me forward, I really feel like it's true. Here I could simply become a face in a crowd.

When Nova's illness was first diagnosed, she admitted that she felt desperate to blend into the background and I understand that need completely; only in Archer's Creek that's never been an option. Hayhurst has a freshman class of around a thousand students. If we were to come here, I could be no more special than anyone else. I could just be normal.

When we reach the college campus my step falters as I take in the impressive iron archway with the words *Hayhurst College* shaped into the curving metal above us, marking the entrance. Butterflies burst to life in my stomach and a glimpse of my future flashes before my eyes. I scan the green lawns and manicured cream gravel paths that weave their way across the grounds and up to the impressive pale gray stone of the college's buildings. Mature trees, bare of leaves, are dotted here and there, with wrought iron benches placed every so often. Even before spring kicks in and makes it green and lush again, the place looks idyllic.

Stepping beneath the archway, I feel like I'm passing through to another world, and maybe in a symbolic way I am. A gasp slips from between my lips as I take in the almost castle-like structure ahead of us, with narrow curved windows and turrets that seem to burst from the roof. It's stunning, an architectural masterpiece that blends effortlessly with its surroundings, content in its place and ready to stand tall for the next hundred years.

A sense of rightness settles over me. All of my worries over making the right decision about school dissolve and right here in this moment, with my feet barely inside the campus, I fall in love with the place.

Nova's fingers entwine with mine and I squeeze her hand lightly. She squeezes me back, then with a giggle she pulls me forward. "Come on, let's go and have a look around."

Following behind, I let her tow me along the path, but I don't really need to look any further. This is it; this is the school I want to go to, now I just need to hope that the others feel the same way. One by one Nova lists the pros and cons we thought of, but we easily dismiss each shortcoming, all of us equally impressed with the thought of what our lives would be like if we went here.

My feet barely seem to touch the floor as we explore, and being here makes me feel hopeful, like this is exactly where I'm supposed to be, with exactly who I'm supposed to be with.

By lunchtime, my feet ache, but I haven't stopped smiling. I think we've explored every inch of the place and even sat in on a modern English literature class. No one looked at us with more than passing curiosity and it was blissful.

I slide into the red leather booth at the student bar we found not far from the campus and watch as the others follow suit.

"I love this place," Zeke declares once everyone is sitting down.

"Me too," I say, enthusiastically, looking between the others, trying to gauge their reactions. I've no idea what I'll do if they don't all want to go here. It's only been a morning and I already have my heart set on moving here in the fall.

I catch Griffin's eyes and his dance with excitement as his lips spread into a wide grin. "Me three."

We all turn to Nova and Valentine expectantly. His gaze is firmly fixed on her, the look in his eyes saying that he doesn't care which school he goes to, as long as it's the same one as her.

"I love it," Nova says, her lips spreading into a wide grin.

"Oh my god," I cry. "Are we doing this? Are we all going to go to Hayhurst?"

"Are you guys sure?" Nova says, worrying at her bottom lip with her teeth.

"I am," I say quickly. "I want us all to stay together, at least for the next few years. I'm not ready to lose you guys yet."

"Neither am I," Griffin says. "You're all my family. I don't have that much left anymore so I'm keeping you. And I'm not talking distant, 'postcards on the holidays' family, I mean 'walk into each other's houses, know each other's business' family, the nosy as fuck kind that drive you crazy but that you couldn't go a day without talking to."

Zeke's bark of laughter echoes through the bar. "Hell yeah," he says, holding his hand up to Griff for a high five.

Nova looks over her shoulder to Valentine who's beside her. He nods at her and she smiles at him before turning her head back to me. "I love you guys. Let's do it. Let's all go to Hayhurst."

"Yes," Griff hisses, dropping his arm over my shoulder and pulling me close. "To Hayhurst," he says, lifting his glass into the air.

"To Hayhurst," I say, mimicking Griff's action and lifting my glass up. The others quickly follow suit and we clink our glasses together.

The waitress arrives a moment later and we all give her

our orders. When she leaves, Griff speaks, garnering all of our attention. "Where are we going to live? I didn't see any co-ed dorms and the girl's dorms are on the opposite side of the campus to the guys. I don't like the idea of you girls being so far away from us."

I open my mouth to argue with him, to tell him off for suggesting that Nova and I aren't capable of looking after ourselves, but Valentine speaks first. "Maybe we could get a place off-campus," he suggests. "I could look at buying a house for us."

"Firstly, Nova and I will be absolutely fine in the dorms, and secondly, I'm fairly sure my dad's head will explode if I tell him I want to live with three guys," I admit on a laugh.

"Nah, Prez would rather you live with us and have us keeping you safe, than live on your own or in dorms," Zeke says, waving me off.

I turn my incredulous eyes on Nova. "Are you hearing this? Do you think your dad will seriously let you live with Valentine?"

Nova shrugs. "He'll probably say no at first and he definitely won't like it, but once he has a chance to think about it, like Zeke said, I think he'd rather we all live together than alone."

"But will we really get the full college experience if we don't live in dorms? What about all the parties and mixers and camaraderie of dorm life? If we move into a house off-campus we'll miss out on all of that," I say, watching as the others all turn to look at one another.

"I've lived in plenty of group homes and dorms at school. It's not all it's cracked up to be. Communal living with strangers is ugly; people are noisy and dirty and you have to share a bathroom with strangers. Plus, it would be cool for us to live together," Valentine says quietly.

Valentine is the newest member of our group. He doesn't share the history the rest of us do and honestly, if he didn't love Nova as much as he does, I'm not sure any of us would still be speaking to him after the shit he pulled when he first moved to town. But now, watching as his hopeful eyes scan our group, then soften when they land on Nova, I exhale a sigh. He's here for her, prepared to follow her to whatever school she picks, but he wants us along for the ride too.

"We don't have to decide right away," I say.

Nova smiles at me, before looking back at Valentine, a happy grin gracing her lips as she lifts her face up to him for a kiss. He obliges, leaning down and pressing his lips against hers. It's not a heated kiss, not a prelude to more. It's a loving, adoring, infatuated kiss and I wonder what it would be like to share that with a guy.

After our food arrives, we excitedly chat about the campus, what the university offers and the classes we could take. Every word is full of excited hope and it energizes me. What a difference a day makes. Wednesday night in my room I was worried about the future, about making the wrong choice, but right now I've never been more certain that Hayhurst is the right decision.

With my certainty comes a confidence I've never really felt before. We leave the restaurant as a group, but each step I take feels full of possibility. This town will be our home, this school our future and I'm ready.

GRIFFIN

Fuck, we actually picked a college. Hayhurst seems like a great school, but more than that Emmy loves it and even if I hated the place that would be enough to convince me this was the best place for us all to attend.

I swear she spent the entire day smiling so widely I bet her jaw was hurting, but I love seeing her so happy. I want her to be happy. It's really happening, we're all going to be together for at least the next four years. We're not losing her, I'm not losing her, and I feel like I can breathe for the first time in months.

Until last summer I didn't realize how dependent on my friends I am, but fuck, Emmy distancing herself and Nova having her meltdown has made me realize that I'm not me without them.

It's codependent and messed up, but who I am is so intrinsically linked with them that without them I have no idea what I'd do. Some people might think that would make me want to give myself a chance to explore who I am on my own, but I really don't care.

Growing up, I learned that family can be the people you choose, just as easily as the ones you share blood with. Emmy, Zeke, Nova, and now Valentine are my family by choice and I can't think of a single reason why I'd want to be alone when I can be with them.

I watch Emmy's face as she talks about living in the dorms and for a split-second I feel guilty that she won't get that experience if we all live together off-campus. None of us would stop her if that's what she really wants, but I hope we can change her mind. We're her roots, a little taste of home in this big new world and selfishly I want to keep a part of her with us while she starts her new life.

Chapter 9

EMMY

College Move-In day.

"Are you sure you have everything you need?" Mom asks me, her lower lip trembling with emotion.

"Yes, Mom. We have more stuff than an Ikea store. You guys got us everything we need and just as much stuff that we'll never ever use," I say on a laugh.

"Don't be a smart-ass," Mom mock scolds, as she pulls me in for yet another hug. "I'm going to miss you."

"I'm going to miss you too, but we'll be home for Thanksgiving and you can all come down for parents' weekend to make sure we're still alive."

Mom hugs me tighter, eventually releasing me and turning me into Dad's waiting arms.

"Be safe, baby girl. The boys will look after you, I'll kill them if they don't, but I need you to be smart too. No parties, no boys, no drinking."

I laugh against his chest. "Okay, Daddy, because I spend so much time drinking at parties with boys."

"You're still my baby girl. I don't like you growing up this quick."

That had become obvious with the amount of time it took him to debate between whether I should live in dorms or with the boys. Living with the boys won, after he'd told them all in no uncertain terms what would happen if they didn't protect me. I loved him dearly but sometimes he could be soooo embarrassing.

"I'll always be your baby girl," I say, stifling the tears that are threatening to fall.

"Always," Dad says, his voice gruff and full of emotion.

Eventually he releases me, pulling my mom into his chest and rubbing her back as she cries silently. I look around me and see Auntie Liv sobbing while she clings to both Nova and Zeke, Duke slapping Griffin on the back in a tight 'bro' hug, and Auntie Brandi openly sobbing.

"I only just got you. It's not fair that you're leaving us so soon," she cries, her fingers gripping Valentine's shirt tightly.

"I'm only going to college, Brandi, not leaving forever." Valentine says.

"Promise you'll come home for Thanksgiving," she pleads.

"I promise," Valentine says earnestly, his cheeks a little pink.

Unable to resist, I watch as Uncle Sleaze steps forward and pulls Valentine into a tight hug. Pulling back, he lifts his hands and places them on either side of Valentine's face. "Love you, kid, see you soon."

Valentine nods. "You'll come for parents' weekend?" He asks quietly.

"Of course. We wouldn't miss it for the world."

Valentine's gaze falls to the floor, then he mutters. "Love you guys."

Both of his adoptive parents surge forward and engulf him in a tight group hug and I look away, already having intruded on their private moment for too long. When I focus my attention back on my own parents, the reality that they're about to leave, to get on a plane and go home without me finally dawns.

Rushing forward, I wrap my arms around their waists and hug them both tightly. "I love you," I say into my dad's chest, my voice breaking as tears fill my eyes.

After several more rounds of goodbyes, our parents load into the huge SUV they rented and drive away.

In the end our parents hadn't let Valentine buy a place, but instead purchased the house we just moved into between them.

Our new home is a five-minute walk from campus. It's a craftsman style house with a wide front porch that circles the entire place. It's far too nice really for a group of college students to live in.

The house is a five bed, two bath, with a family room, large kitchen, and a basement. Uncle Echo insisted that Nova's bedroom be as far away as possible from Valentine's, but I think we all know that they'll be sharing a bed every night from now on.

Our families decked the house out with everything we could possibly need, including all brand-new furniture and even an entire basement full of gym equipment for the guys to use. It feels a bit surreal to be living in such a nice place when we should be living the proper student life in a crummy apartment with thrift store furniture, but at least we're together.

I would have liked to experience dorm life; this house and all this stuff feels a little bit too much like home. But even as I think that I feel ungrateful. We only just moved in and I'm already unsure how I'll juggle my past with the new life I'm hoping to make here, because I'm not sure I'll be able to bring any new friends I make back to the house. How would I explain away this luxury without telling them about my family?

"College, baby," Zeke shrieks, scooping me up off the floor and twirling me around.

Pushing all of my doubts and fresh fears down I smile and shout "College, baby," as Nova, Valentine, and Griffin shout too. Then as a group we troop back into the house, *our* house, and shut the door behind us.

Hours later when the sun has dropped and crisp fall air coats the evening, I sigh exhaustedly. The last couple of days have been overwhelming. From packing up all of my stuff, to loading the U-Haul's and making the long journey from Texas to Alabama; to saying goodbye to my mom and dad and knowing I won't see them for at least a month, I feel completely drained.

The need to curl up beneath my comforter and lose myself in words is almost overwhelming, but I fight it and my solitary nature and force myself to stay with my friends. This is the new me, the one who can laugh and joke and be social. This is college me: brave, bold Emmy. I don't have to live in books because this is a brand-new world to explore, and maybe if I give it a chance it could be just as exciting, just as invigorating as a story is.

I spend the rest of the night quietly watching my friends laugh and joke and smile. It's moments like this when I'm reminded how different I am to them. I wouldn't consider myself a loner, but I'm also not the type of person who needs constant company or to be entertained. Sometimes I'm just content to sit and watch the world go by.

I love the idea of living with them all for school, so much more than being in a tiny dorm with a stranger, but I'm also terrified of never having a moments peace. Zeke and Griff love to be around others. I'm not sure they even know how to be on their own. It's not a bad thing, it's just not something I fully understand.

When Nova was diagnosed with anxiety earlier this year, she fought to regain control of her own mind, and force herself out of her comfort zone. Sometimes I'm in awe of her strength. But I'm not like her. I don't find parties stressful; I just don't see the purpose.

I want a new life, new experiences, but I'm not sure I'm brave enough to push my own boundaries. Maybe I just want to be a voyeur on a new life, to watch without actually having to participate?

The idea of meeting new people without the preconceptions that come with being a Scion is titillating. But really, what's more likely to happen is that I'll watch others make those connections while I sit with my noise-cancelling headphones on, surrounded by the music flowing into my ears!

Internally I scold myself. No. This is my future. A fresh start with lifelong bonds. The new and old blending together in a brand-new future that I can't wait to start. I have to force myself to be the person I so desperately crave to be. No one can do that for me. No one else can make me reach for those dreams I've put on a pedestal and longed for. I have to do it for myself.

From now on this house will be my safe harbor and my friends my anchors. They're my binding to this version of myself, while I experiment with a new me. Inhaling deeply, I take another moment to look at the family surrounding me and for a tiny second, I wonder why I would ever want anything more than this.

Growing up is so confusing. I'm content and restless. Happy, but wistful. I'm a swirling maelstrom of contradictions.

Suddenly I'm drowning and adrift beneath a wave of apprehension, doubt and fear. I reach over and grab Griffin's hand and his attention turns to me. There's a knowing look in his eyes, as if he sees right through me, to the very core of me, and he can tell without me saying a thing that I need a tether.

"I need my snuggle time, you've been slacking recently," he says with a laugh that doesn't reach his eyes. Then he pulls me into his arms and holds me tightly, calming me, binding me. In this moment, he's my anchor, my axis and I allow my body to crush against his, needing him more than I have in years.

The next morning, I wake up early, the unfamiliar bed and room disturbing my sleep. The morning light filters through my drapes and I pull in a deep breath and let it out slowly, the sound of my exhale loud in the silent house.

The straight out of the packet sheets rustle beneath me and I snuggle further under my comforter, enjoying the way the crisply starched sheets feel against my skin. My new bed is incredibly comfortable, my room calm and relaxing, but even though it's filled with lovely things it isn't home and a pang of longing for my childhood bedroom hits me.

I shake my head, banishing the maudlin thoughts away and instead focusing on the fact that I just spent my first night in my new home. The one I live in without my parents, the one I share with my best friends. A small squeal of excitement bursts from me and I kick my heels against the mattress.

Reaching for my cellphone, I check the time. It's not even

7am and we don't have anywhere to be until the freshman orientation fair this afternoon. I could, should, get up and go explore our new town, or I could be lazy and stay in bed, something I've never been allowed to do at home.

Smiling widely, I fluff the pillow beneath my head, reach for my Kindle and decide to stay put, warm and cosy in my new bed and read. Like every other time I find an amazing book, I lose all concept of time. I imagine myself in a land full of Fae and mythical creatures, my heart racing as the hero dives through a shower of arrow fire to rescue the woman he loves, his destined soulmate, his one and only.

When my bedroom door flies open, I know my solitude is done and I'm only slightly annoyed by the interruption. "Griffin, have you forgotten how to knock? I could have been naked."

"At least that would have been interesting. Jesus, Em, turn your Kindle off and get up, the freshman fair starts in an hour," he says, bouncing down next to me on my bed.

My eyes widen and I check the time on my cell. It's after noon. I've been reading for nearly five hours.

Griff reaches over and plucks my Kindle from my hand and turns it off, lifting it out of my reach when I try to grab it off him. "Nope, you've read enough today," he says, arching his eyebrow at me and daring me to argue with him.

"Griff," I warn. "Give it back."

"Nope," he says again, popping the letter p and smirking at me.

"I can still read on my cell you know?" I say tauntingly.

A sadness masks his expression and he sighs, dropping my Kindle to the comforter. "You know I love you, right, shortcake? But you need some time out of your own head. These last few months, you've been more with us than you have in years. You've been my little shortcake again, like you were when we were kids. I know you've checked back in because of everything that went down with Nova, but I don't want you to disappear back into your books again. We missed you, Em. I missed you. I know you don't think you really fit in with us, but that's just some fucking bullshit you've told yourself to make you feel better about leaving us. You wanted this, you wanted us all to be together again, it was your choice. So if you're in, be in. I'm not saying you have to be with us twenty-four-seven, we all need time to ourselves. Just please, please, I'm begging you, don't lose yourself between the pages of a book again."

His voice cracks a little as he begs me, literally begs me, to get out of my own head and be present.

Swallowing thickly, I feel my bottom lip tremble. "I'm sorry," I whisper, so quietly that I can barely hear myself.

"Don't cry," Griff says, pulling me across the bed until I'm half splayed on top of him, my face pressed against his chest. "I'm sorry. I shouldn't have said anything, ignore me," he says, his lips pressed to the top of my head, his fingers stroking down the length of my hair.

"No, you're right. I do get lost in my mind," I say slowly, knowing that it's true but finding it difficult to actually say the words. This is the first time any of my friends has ever told me how they feel about my need for solitude. I always thought they understood and didn't care, but maybe they do and I've just been too far gone to notice. Have I been hurting them all this time? I assumed that they hadn't cared when I'd distanced myself, but was I wrong?

None of them ever tried to pull me back in. Or did they and I just didn't realize that's what they were doing? Nova always insisted on including me, asking me to every party, always picking me up for school and making sure I sat with her at lunch.

Zeke went above and beyond to make it up to me after I overheard him saying I was boring last year. In fact, now I think about it, he was almost frantic to make sure we were okay, apologizing again and again, turning up at my house with my favorite candy and the blueberry sweet tea from the next town over.

As I think about it, I realize that they've been frantically holding me to the group, while I selfishly kept cutting each new bind they made. I'm an asshole.

"I shouldn't have said anything. Only this is a big new adventure for us. We could barely hold you in a tiny town. I'm fucking terrified of losing you in this big, wide world. I can't let you go, Emmy, so maybe it would be okay if every now and then I pull that string that keeps you tied to me, to us, and reel you back in, so you don't get too far away, or so lost in those other worlds you love so much that the binds break and you drift off completely."

Tears pool in my eyes at his words and I nod against his chest, biting my bottom lip to keep it from trembling. "Okay."

"I fucking love you, Em."

"Love you too, Griff."

GRIFFIN

I sound like a fucking pussy!

I'm begging her, literally begging her to stay with us, and I swear to God my balls just got a little smaller from how pathetic I sound. But we're here now, we're in our new house, in our new town and the adventure starts today. This is our new life, we're all on the precipice of change and while Emmy is running toward the edge, I'm clinging to her and begging her not to jump.

We all saw the way Valentine's eyes got haunted when he talked about living with strangers, so Zeke, Valentine, and I agreed that we would live off-campus even if the girls didn't want to. Zeke and I might have told Prez this and it wasn't long after that when he decided it would be safer for us all to be together.

Was what I did manipulative? Yep it totally was. Do I feel any regret for making sure the girls ended up living with us? I don't regret a fucking thing.

I don't want a new life, I don't want new friends or a new family, I have all those things. What I want is to experience college with the most important people in my life. I want to become an adult, screw up, get drunk, celebrate my victories and commiserate my failures surrounded by people I know will be in my life forever.

I'm ready to take the next step toward my future, but why can't that be with my family by my side?

That's the balance Emmy doesn't understand yet, she really thought the only way to experience and grow as a person was if she was alone, until she truly considered what being alone meant. She's always thought of herself as this introvert outsider, but that's not true, she chooses to keep herself isolated because she truly believes that she's only one of us because of who her parents are.

The reality is that Emmy is a magnet, she draws people to her and without her I'm not sure the Scions would be as close as we are, at least not the way we are now. We all cling to her, we always have. She's the glue that binds us and she has no fucking clue.

I love Nova like a sister and Zeke a brother, but I *need* Emmy and I refuse to lose her.

EMMY

I stay wrapped in Griffin's arms for a few minutes longer, then peel myself from him, wiping the tears from my cheeks. "I should get ready," I say, avoiding looking at him and busying myself in my closet, pulling out clothes for the day.

Alabama in August is hot as hades, so after washing my face and brushing my teeth, I pull on a simple green sundress and flipflops, quickly braiding my hair into a loose braid that falls over one shoulder and applying some mascara and lipgloss.

I take one last look in the mirror, then leave my room with my cell in my hand, walking into the living room and finding all of my friends waiting.

"There are muffins on the counter and sweet tea in the refrigerator," Nova says. "That dress is cute. Is it new? Can I borrow it?"

I roll my eyes. "As if you need to ask. Not that it would make a difference if I said no. You help yourself to everything in my closet anyway," I throw over my shoulder, as I head into the kitchen grabbing a blueberry muffin. Taking the plastic cup of sweet tea from the refrigerator, I pull the paper cover off the top of the straw and drop it in the trashcan as I pass. "Y'all ready?" I ask.

"We've been ready for the last hour, Em," Zeke says, his fingers tapping on the doorjamb agitatedly.

I part my lips to apologize, when Valentine stands. "Let's go then. We walking or taking the truck?"

"Walking," Zeke answers. "No point searching for a space in the lot when it's only a five-minute walk."

Valentine looks to each of us and when no one disagrees we make our way out of the front door and down onto the street. I eat my muffin and sip my tea as we walk while Nova chatters animatedly about everything from how well she slept, to how liberating it is to be living on our own.

When we reach the campus, I'm surprised to find the beautifully manicured lawns in front of the school's main buildings filled with booths, tents, and a sea of excited freshman just like us. A tingle of excitement runs beneath my skin, making my limbs itch to rush into the fray and explore. Hayhurst is new. This isn't Archer's Creek where we've been everywhere a hundred times and everything is overly familiar and boring. Every day from now on is a brand-new experience, something none of us have ever done before and now that we're here, only a few steps away, I can't wait to get started.

Turning my head, I glance at the others and find them all with the same expression of excited awe that I'm feeling. Griff spots me looking at him and his smile widens. "Ready?" He asks as he reaches out a hand to me.

I nod, and reach for him, entwining our fingers together. He yanks me toward him and I shriek out a laugh as I'm propelled forward, his fingers releasing mine, so he can drop his arm across my shoulders.

Together we step beneath the huge metal archway at the entrance to the grounds and onto the campus for the very first time as enrolled students.

The booths are buzzing with people. Kids—some in groups, some with their parents—meander from stall to stall, laughing and smiling and enjoying themselves. No one is looking at us, no one cares, and with that knowledge is the freedom I've been desperately craving for so long.

This is my opportunity to step out of the shadow of my legacy; it's all of our chances. At Hayhurst we're just freshman, five new faces with no history and nothing but the opportunity to be whoever we choose to be.

I don't have to be the daughter of a biker, or the nerdy friend of the popular kids. Here I can just be Emmy. No one knows anything about me, and any friends I make will be friends through common interests or circumstance. They won't know that my dad is terrifying or that my family is wealthy. Here I don't have to question people's motives, because there's nothing to gain from knowing me.

That realization has me standing a little straighter, rolling my shoulders back and walking with an ease and confidence I'm not sure I've ever felt back home. Nova dealt with the pressure of our heritage by pretending to be something she wasn't, but although my mask has never been as extreme as hers, I've still been wearing one. I didn't conform like she did. Instead I decided to be invisible.

It's unavoidable to be seen, but you can choose not to see. Being a Scion means that flying under the radar has never been an option, but over the last few years I've figured out how to ignore everything that's going on around me. I figured out how not to notice. To be blissful in my ignorance and I love it.

My eyes roam the crowd and a thousand possibilities

burst to life. From here on out, my life can go in two ways. I can be truly invisible, withdraw in the anonymity that comes from everyone being a stranger, or I can create the version of myself I always wanted to be. My world just got a lot wider.

"Hell yes, free condoms." Zeke shouts, darting off in the direction of a stall.

Excitedly, I scan the booths, trying to decide where to start. "Shall we meet back here in a bit, then we can go over to orientation together and get our ID's and schedules?"

"You gonna be okay on your own?" Griff asks, his brow furrowed in concern.

I roll my eyes. "I'll be fine. I know my dad probably threatened you to watch me at all times, but you know I'm more than capable of looking after myself."

The wrinkle in his forehead relaxes slightly. "I know you are. It's just a new place and we all still need to get our bearings."

"Go have fun, I'll see you guys back here," I say, kissing Griff on the cheek, before turning and strolling off toward the stalls. At least fifty booths are spread across the lawn, housing everything from fraternities and sororities, to Young Republicans, with a Wiccan society booth next door. The smile that's etched across my face is huge and genuine and I can't help the small laugh that escapes my lips when I spot a booth for motorcycle enthusiasts. If only they knew who my family was.

Without looking back, I step into the melee and enjoy wandering from booth to booth. Within minutes my hands are full of more condoms than I will ever be able to use, and I have the information for four sororities who insisted I should rush. It didn't seem to matter to the girls manning the booths that I told them I wasn't interested in joining. They were adamant, and in the end it was easier to just take the baggies full of information about the various sisterhoods and what they could offer me, than argue with them.

Who knew at a small private college like Hayhurst that there could be enough interest in so many random societies? As I stroll toward a stall advertising free book tokens, the guy behind the table catches my eye and smiles. He's cute, in a preppy, hipster way, with black-framed glasses, a button-up shirt, a bow tie, and khaki shorts.

"Hey," he says when I reach the table.

"Hey."

"Would you like a free book token? You can use it at the campus bookstore to either get a free novel or as a credit toward a textbook."

"Oh, er sure thanks," I say, reaching out to take the token he's offering.

"I'm Kent.

"Emmy."

"So you're a freshman?" He says, then cringes. "Sorry, obviously you're a freshman. This is the freshman fair."

I laugh lightly, but nod. "Yeah, I'm a freshman."

"Cool, how do you like it so far?" He asks, stepping out from behind his table and leaning against the edge instead.

"Well we only moved in yesterday, but so far so good."

"Are you in Calhoone or McKenzie?" He asks, listing the names of the girl's dorms.

"Neither, we're in a house off-campus,"

"Nice," he coos approvingly. "I tried to find an off-campus for this year, but everywhere I found that was even half decent was already full, so I'm stuck in dorms again."

I'm not entirely sure how to respond. Do I commiserate on him having to live in the dorms? Are dorms bad here? Do I apologize for having a nice place to live in? I really need to figure out how to talk to people I haven't known my whole life.

"So, are you going to the Fresh Meat party at Kappa Tau tonight?" Kent asks, angling his body a little closer toward me. "Frat parties aren't normally my thing, but the KT's always have the biggest event during Move-In week."

"I'm not sure," I say, fidgeting with the bags of stuff gripped tightly between my fingers.

"Hey, Em." A voice calls from behind me and I spin around to find a smiling Griffin and Zeke striding toward me.

"Hey," I say as they reach me. Griff looks from me to the guy in front of me, then drops his arm over my shoulder and turns his hard gaze on Kent.

"Guys, this is Kent," I say, gesturing toward where Kent has now retreated behind his table. "He was just telling me about a party at the Kappa Delta house tonight."

"Kappa Tau," Kent corrects. "They have the Fresh Meat party this time every year. You guys should go, it's a great way to meet new people."

"A party sounds like fun," Griff says, curling his arm around my neck and pulling me in a little closer. "I'm Griffin by the way and this is Zeke," he says, pointing to Zeke who has positioned himself on my other side.

"Nice to meet you both. Would you like a book token?" Kent says a little stiffly, visibly swallowing as he takes in my huge friends.

"Sure," says Zeke, reaching out and taking the proffered token. "Thanks."

"You ready to go find the others?" Griff asks, turning me toward him and away from Kent.

"Yeah, sure," I say. "Nice to meet you, Kent," I say turning back to face him.

"Yeah, you too," Kent says, his lips pressed into a hard line.

I let Griffin lead me away from the stall, and I offer Kent a small wave before someone else steps up to his table blocking me from his view. He was cute. Not in a 'Wow! How hot is that guy?' kind of a way, but in a nerdy, hipster way.

"So, are we going to hit up that frat party tonight?" Griff asks.

"Nova hates parties," Zeke says.

"Yeah, true," Griff agrees thoughtfully.

"We can see what she thinks though. I know she wants to try to push herself to deal with crowds, so maybe we can go for a bit. If she stresses, we can just leave," Zeke suggests.

I nod, crossing my fingers at my sides and hoping that Nova doesn't want to test her boundaries tonight. Frat parties are not my thing. *Maybe they are now* my inner voice taunts, and it's true, I've never been to a frat party, they could be my thing. College Emmy might love frat parties full of drunk horny guys and drunk sex-starved girls. Nope, nope, I'm fairly sure college Emmy won't enjoy them either.

When we walk past a coffee cart, I nudge Griffin. "I need caffeine, you want anything?"

"I'll get it, you stay with Zeke," Griff says, unhooking his arm from around my neck and waiting for Zeke to come to my side before stepping up to the cart and ordering us all drinks.

"What's in the bags?" Zeke asks, snatching them from my fingers with a laugh.

Pursing my lips, I prop my hands on my hips and arch my eyebrows at him.

He ignores my very obvious annoyance and starts rooting through the bags, chuckling to himself at what he finds. A moment later, he lowers the bags to his sides and smirks. "So you're planning on joining a sorority and having a very well-protected gang bang?"

I try so hard to keep my stern, annoyed expression, but I fail and burst into laughter. "A gang bang?" I splutter, between laughs.

His laughter is low and addictive and I find myself laughing even more. "Fuck, Em. I knew college might change you, but we've only been here for a day," he says, doubling over at his own joke.

"What the fuck's up with you pair?" Griff asks, his smile bemused, a drinks holder with three cups in his hand.

"The new Emmy is a little racier than I expected," Zeke says between laughter.

Shoving Zeke, I shake my head, giggles still escaping from my lips as I step toward Griffin and the delicious smelling coffee. "Which is mine?" I ask.

"Caramel latte for you," Griff says, lifting one of the cups and handing it to me. "Americano, extra hot for the laughing asshole and a filter coffee with hazelnut creamer for me."

Lifting my cup to my lips I take a sip and sigh happily.

"Valentine says he and Nova are back where we came in." Griff says.

"Cool, let's go find them," Griff says, taking the drinks holder back to the cart, then striding back to us, his cup gripped tightly in his hand.

It takes us ten minutes to fight our way back through the busy stalls filled with students and when we finally spot Nova and Valentine, I'm glad that I had the guys to shelter me from the hordes of people who have appeared since we first got here.

"Hey, guys," I call as soon as we get close.

"Hey," Nova says. "I wondered how long it would take

you to get to us. It's gotten so busy." She says, looking a little apprehensively at the crowds.

"We've had to fight our way back down here. Thank God the guys are so huge and everyone moves out of their way," I say with a smirk.

Nova chuckles. "What's in the bags?" She asks.

"Emmys thinking about joining a sorority," Zeke says derisively.

Something about the arrogant tone in his voice makes me instantly defensive. "Maybe I am," I snap, glaring at him.

Nova scowls at her brother, grabbing my arm and linking hers though mine. "Let's head over to the administration building and get our schedules and student ID's. I'm so freaking excited."

I wait for Zeke to make another obnoxious comment, but when he wisely keeps his mouth shut, I let Nova pull me away.

An hour later we step back out into the afternoon sunlight with our brand-new laminated student ID's and brown envelopes holding our schedules. Holding the small plastic rectangle between my fingers, I stare down at it, surprised by how significant such an insignificant item is. This card says we're officially students and it somehow makes this whole thing suddenly seem so real. "We need to celebrate," I say, biting at my bottom lip as I rub my thumb back and forth across the word student.

"Yes!" Nova shrieks. "We can try out our fake ID's finally."

"We actually heard about a frat party," Griff says sheepishly, his expression tense.

"Oh," Nova says, her eyes widening a little. "We should go," she says slowly, as if she's trying to convince herself to say the words.

"Princess?" Valentine says, asking if she's okay. Checking if she really wants to do this, or if she wants him to punch Griff in the face for suggesting it, with just that one word.

"No, we should go," she says more decisively. "This is college. We should be going to frat parties and having fun, trying new things. If it gets too much I can leave, just like I did back home."

"Where is it?" Valentine asks.

"Kappa something or other," I offer.

"Kappa Tau," Griff says, shaking his head, an indulgent smile tipping at the corner of his lips.

"I was close," I mutter, ignoring him and looking appraisingly at Nova. Her smile is a little brittle, but she seems okay, not panicked at least as far as I can see. But then she hid her anxiety from me for over a year, so maybe I wouldn't be able to see even if she was falling apart. "Are you sure?" I ask her, staring at her intently, hoping to be able to read her, to see something.

"Yes," she says. "Yeah, I'm sure. Let's go home, grab some food because I'm starving, then go to our first frat party as official Hayhurst students."

When she smiles again, it's a little less practiced and a little more real and it dawns on me that I'm going to my first ever college party, and the first party I've been even slightly excited to attend since I was nine years old.

Staring at my reflection in my mirror in my room, I frown. I don't dislike the way I look. I'm not that girl who hates the person looking back at them, but tonight I'm scrutinizing my reflection a little more than normal.

Nova offered to help me find something to wear. She even suggested I wear something from her closet. But for my first foray into the world of college life, I want to be in control of people's perception of me.

79

I've no doubt if I'd have let Nova play dress up with me I'd look flawless. I always do whenever she does my makeup and dresses me. But tonight, I need the armor of looking like myself and that won't come if Nova's in charge of my outfit.

Glancing at myself again, I rip the white lacy tank top over my head and pull my jeans off, dropping them onto my bed. I step up to my closet and start to flick through the hangers when my eyes fall on the peach colored skirt my mom insisted I buy a few months back. I pause, eyeing it and debating if I'm feeling brave enough to wear it.

My fingers reach out without my consent and brush back and forth over the soft fabric. On a whim I pull the skirt off the hanger and step into it, smoothing it down before I spin and look at myself in the mirror. The peach color complements my fair skin. The skirt hits mid-thigh, not too short, but the perfect length to make my short legs look longer than they actually are.

Turning to the side, I check out my butt and bite my lip at how much I like the way it fits. Spinning around, I step back into the closet and root through my tops, searching for something that will work. A top I don't recognize jumps out and I pull the hanger from the rail, pursing my lips trying to figure out if this is actually mine, or if something of Nova's has gotten put in my closet by mistake.

"Hey, Em." Nova calls, pushing my door open and walking straight into my room. She blinks when she finds me in only my bra and skirt. "Cute skirt," she comments, jumping onto my bed and flopping back into my pillows.

"Is this top yours?" I ask lifting it up to show her.

"No, but it's cute. I'll have it if you don't want it," she says on a laugh.

"It's in my closet, but I swear I've never seen it before."

Rolling off the bed she moves to my side, examining the top, her brow furrowed. "It still has the tags on."

Pushing the top into her hands, I move back to my closet and carefully examine the clothes, finding more things that I don't recognize towards the back, the tags still in place. My mom hung all of my clothes in my closet and I barely even looked in there when I pulled my dress out this morning. Exhaling shortly, I stomp back to my bed and grab my cell from where it's charging on the nightstand. Clicking into the screen, I dial my mom's number, listening to it ring twice before she answers.

"Hi, sweetie," she says brightly.

"Did you buy me a bunch of new clothes and just put them in my closet without saying anything?" I demand.

Her chuckle is throaty and amused. "It took you this long to notice?"

"Mom," I hiss.

"Oh, Emmy, stop moaning. Most teenage girls would love that their mom stocks their closets with beautiful new clothes and you complain. Show Nova, at least she'll appreciate it. Tell her there are a few things in her closet too, and the boys as well."

"Mom," I hiss even louder. "You bought all of us new clothes and just hung them up? Seriously that's way past the realm of normal."

"Pah," she spits on a laugh. "Who the hell wants to be normal? Anyway, your brother is with Dill and Leo and your dad and I were in the middle of something, so unless you need anything else, I'm going to go."

"Ewww, Mom that's disgusting, I don't want to know about you and Dad."

"Okay then, baby. I'll speak to you soon, love you," she

says, then ends the call, leaving me a little skeeved out and exasperated.

"Your mom bought you new stuff I take it?" Nova asks.

"Yep, apparently there's stuff in your closet and the boys' too. She went on a shopping spree for us all."

Nova laughs then scurries from the room, running into the bedroom her parents think she's using every night and squealing with joy when she finds the new clothes my mom put there for her.

Shaking my head, I move back to the mirror and bring the top up in front of me. It's definitely not something I'd buy for myself, but I can't deny how pretty it is. The black fabric is super soft, and when I slip it over my head, it fits like a glove. It's cropped, exposing three inches of skin between the shirt and my skirt. The neckline is Bardot, exposing my shoulders, and the sleeves fit tight to my elbow, then flare to my wrists.

Somehow, I feel sexy, but covered up; it's perfect. I slide my feet into nude chunky sandals and pull some product through my hair before teasing it into long loose curls the way my mom showed me how to do. Makeup isn't really my thing, but I add a couple of coats of mascara then cover my lips in the red-tinted gloss my mom badgered me into trying. I love it, but I'll never admit that to her.

Adding a spritz of perfume, I slide my purse over my shoulder and head downstairs, ready, if not prepared, for my first college party.

"What the fuck?!" Griff shouts when I push through the door and into the living room. "No! Hell. Fucking. No."

"What?"

"You are not going out like that. Absolutely fucking not," he says, jumping up from the couch and stomping toward me.

"What? I like this outfit." I say, glancing down at my skirt and top and wondering what could be wrong.

"Like. Are you fucking kidding me? Your dad would ground you for the rest of your fucking life if he saw you dressed like *that*." Griff says, his brows drawn together in an angry line.

Resting my hands on my hips, I tip my head to the side. "And what exactly am I dressed like?" I ask, my voice clipped.

"Like you're looking to get fucked," Griffin rasps, stepping toward me, forcing me to retreat.

"What the hell are you talking about?" I hiss, taking another step back when his chest touches mine.

"You look like walking fucking sin, Em. Is this the new you? Tiny little skirt so you can see how tight your ass is. Tiny little shirt so every fucker at the party can see your perky tits and your eager nipples," Griff growls, moving forward as I move back, pursuing me, chasing me until my back hits the wall and his chest touches mine.

"Griffin," I warn. But it doesn't sound like a warning. My voice is husky and there's something unfamiliar teasing at my tone.

"You're too fucking beautiful like this, shortcake." He inhales slowly, his eyes locking with mine. "You looking to find someone to help you ruin all that innocent Emmy?"

Griff's voice is low. So low I can barely hear him, but somehow, I feel every word he says. His fingers touch my shoulder, sliding up to wrap around the side of my neck and my skin pebbles beneath his touch.

This isn't right. This is my friend, my best friend, practically my family, and yet his touch, his chest pressed so close to mine, doesn't feel wrong.

"Time to party," Zeke calls from the stairs.

In the blink of an eye, Griff's gone, clear across the other side of the room, his face a mask. I stare, unsure if any of that happened or if I just imagined it.

"Emmy, where the fuck you been hiding all that? You look hot," Zeke says, scooping me off the floor and leaning me back over his arm in an exaggerated dip.

"Zeke," I cry, giggling.

"Come on, hottie. Time to get our party on," He says, lifting me back up and twirling me in his arms until my back is pressed against his chest, his arm looped around my waist.

Nova walks through the door and into the room, Valentine on her heels and I almost gasp at how perfect they look together. Nova's willowy body is covered in skintight, cropped leather pants that fit her like a second skin and a simple white cami tucked in, with a long necklace hanging between her breasts. Tall, black pumps are on her feet and her hair is hanging loose and straight around her shoulders.

Valentine barely seems to have made an effort in his black ripped jeans, scuffed boots, and ratty looking band tee, but somehow together they look like they just fell off a runway. For the first time I take in Zeke and Griffin, who are in similar, slim, ripped jeans. Zeke's in a t-shirt that says 'You're Welcome' on the front and Griffin's in a black button down, the sleeves rolled to the elbow.

They all look gorgeous, the beautiful people, and for a moment I feel truly unexceptional and out of place. I really don't play in the same league as my friends.

Holy shit, am I their DUFF?

I brush the thought away as soon as it pops into my head. Everyone is someone's designated ugly fat friend, even when they're not actually fat and ugly. I only feel plain because they're all so gorgeous.

Note to self, make a normal looking friend.

"Em, you need to lend me that outfit. It's so cute and you look gorgeous in it," Nova gushes, rushing over to me and running her fingers through the end of my curls. "Babe, you look so hot."

"You look beautiful, Emmy," Valentine, says, smiling at me.

"Thanks," I say shyly, not appreciating all of the attention. "Shall we go?"

"Group selfie first," Nova cries, producing a selfie stick from her purse and waving her hand for us all to crowd around her.

We smile for the picture, then leave the house to make the short walk to where the frat houses are located. It's not exactly frat row as the houses are spread over three streets, but the area is clearly frat and sorority heaven if all of the plaques on the houses and the huge insignias landscaped into the front yards are anything to go by.

"We're not in Kansas anymore, Toto," I mutter beneath my breath, as the Kappa Tau house comes into view. The party is raging, people spilled out onto the lawn as lights and music pour from the huge white rendered house. A massive banner reading "Fresh Meat" hangs across half the front of the house, as if people wouldn't be able to guess where the party's at without it.

"Hell yes," Zeke cries happily, striding forward to the guy guarding the front door.

"What are the magic words?" The guy asks in a bored voice.

Zeke furrows his brow, then looks to us, before turning back to the guy. "Fresh meat?" He says with a shrug.

Suddenly the guys expression changes from bored to ecstatic as he throws his head back and bellows, "Fresh meat," into the night air.

A chorus of fresh meat calls back and he steps back from the doorway allowing us entry into the party.

Zeke glances back to us and steps forward, only to have another guy bar the way. He holds out a red plastic cup to Zeke. "Cover charge is ten bucks each. You only get one cup; lose it and you have to pay again in full to get another. Kegs out in the garden, pump it yourself, don't take drinks from anyone. Welcome to Kappa Tau."

Zeke slides his hand into his pocket and pulls out a small roll of notes. He slides five tens off and hands them to the guy.

The guy looks from Zeke to the rest of us, then pulls two tens off the pile and hands them back. "Hot girls don't pay."

Zeke arches a brow, then shrugs, taking the notes back and shoving them back into his pocket. He takes the red cup from the guy and steps forward and into the house. I step forward next, lifting my hand to take the cup from frat guy, but he hands me a square sealed in plastic first.

"Take this. It's a SipChip. There's a plastic attachment so you can stick it to your cellphone. If you open one and put some of your drink on it; it will tell you if anyone slipped anything into it. There are three in the pack, but you can buy more from student services. Kappa Tau doesn't tolerate that kind of bullshit at our parties, but no matter how much we try to keep the kind of assholes who spike girls' drinks out of our house, it happens. Have fun, but don't leave your drink unattended and be careful."

"Thank you," I say, really meaning it. This wasn't what I was expecting from a frat house, or from a guy who would join a frat, but so far I'm pleasantly surprised.

"I'm Van, by the way," the guy says, with a smile that could melt panties at a hundred yards.

"Emmy," I say, biting my bottom lip as I smile shyly back at him.

"Maybe I can find you later for a dance?" He asks.

"Maybe," I answer, just as Griffin drops his arm over my shoulder and pulls me into him possessively.

"Wanna move it along here, shortcake? The rest of us are all waiting on you," Griff says, his tone short and annoyed.

"Oh, sorry, sure." Lifting my hand, I offer Van a quick wave, then step forward and into the house.

The others all take their red cups, and Van offers Nova a SipChip, but he doesn't speak to any of the others and when I risk a glance back at him, his eyes are narrowed and his lips pursed into a straight line.

The house almost seems bigger on the inside than it did from the outside and I let Griffin lead me down the short hallway and through a doorway into the main party. We suddenly hit a wall of people. The music seems to swell and the smell of sweat, lust, and sex permeates the air.

This is hell, I think to myself as we shuffle forward into the mass of writhing bodies. Sometimes being short sucks. All I can see are the people in front of us, so I melt into Griff's hold, letting him guide me wherever Zeke is leading us.

It feels like an eternity later that the crowd thins and we emerge into a large backyard, a firepit off to the left and several kegs lined up to the right.

"I think beer's your only option tonight, ladies," Zeke says with a gleeful laugh as he makes a beeline for the kegs. He waits for the handful of girls ahead of him to finish pumping their own cups, before he steps forward and starts to fill his, handing it back to us and then taking one of the empty ones to start the process all over again.

Looking to Nova, I see her eyes are wide and she's

leaning against Valentine like he's the only thing keeping her upright. "Are you okay? Do you want to go?" I ask her.

She shakes her head, lifting her cup to her lips and sipping. Her chest visibly rises and falls as she sucks in a deep inhale. "I'm okay. I just need a minute, there are a lot of people."

The guys chat back and forth as I watch Nova. She gradually relaxes, standing more upright and less dependent on Valentine. When her cup is empty, she moves to the keg and pumps herself another cup, skipping back to us, a genuine smile gracing her lips.

"Okay, I'm ready to dance now. Em, come on there's a dance floor inside," she says, her voice strong and confident.

"You want to go back inside?" I ask, glancing horrified at the mass of people still squashed inside the house.

"Yep, and you're coming with me."

Ignoring my protests, she grabs my arm and pulls me toward the door we exited out of earlier. She drags me behind her as she pushes her way through the throngs of people until we hit the makeshift dance floor, which is really just the living room, with the furniture pushed to the side.

Girls fill the space, some laughing and dancing with their friends, others putting on a show for the guys that circle the small area. I simultaneously feel both under and over-dressed. My eyes fall on a girl who is only wearing a bikini top and bootie shorts, grinding against another girl who is in a dress so short and tight I can see everything she has to offer.

Considering my dad is an honest to goodness biker, and I'm not naïve enough to be oblivious to the 'club girls' who hang out at the clubhouse to entertain the single members, I'm surprised to find myself a little scandalized with the way these girls are dressed and behaving.

It's not the pseudo lesbian show they're putting on, per se, but for some reason I wasn't expecting them to be so obvious. The thought makes me feel young and inexperienced. Maybe if I'd attended more high school parties, I'd be more prepared.

Nova pulls me onto the dance floor, throwing her arms into the air and swaying her hips to the music. I take another look around me, then lift my cup to my lips and take a long pull before I throw my hands up, close my eyes and start to dance.

The music invades my senses and I lose myself to the rhythm. I might not be a fan of parties, but I've always loved to dance. The song changes, but I don't stop moving, smiling and laughing with Nova as she twirls around me.

When I feel someone step up behind me, I expect to turn around and find Zeke or Griff, but instead I find Van, the guy from earlier. He smiles at me as he steps closer, his back meeting my chest, his arms moving around me, holding me loosely.

I freeze for a moment, looking forward and meeting Nova's excited eyes. "Oh my god," she mouths, nodding and urging me to dance. So I do. I don't grind back against Van, but I dance with my body pressed against his, his arm wrapped around my waist, his thumb rubbing circles against the bare skin of my stomach.

For the length of a song, all I can think about is the cute guy dancing with me until he's ripped away and three huge, angry looking Scions take his place, surrounding me and forcing me from the happy little bubble I was basking in.

"What the hell?" I cry, when Van's arm is literally ripped from mine and cold air replaces the warmth of his body.

"What the fuck, Emmy? Who the hell is this guy? And why are you letting him grind all up against you?" Griff cries, his tone laced with indignant anger.

Anger swirls through me and I spin around to glare at him. "Fuck you, Griff. He wasn't grinding on me, we were dancing, and what the hell does that have to do with you anyway?"

Griff's eyes widen before they narrow perceptively, his brows furrowing, his lips falling into an angry straight line. "What does it have to do with me?" He seethes.

"Yes, what does it have to do with you? I wasn't doing anything wrong. I wasn't doing anything inappropriate. I was dancing. PG13 dancing with a guy. So, I'll ask again, what the hell does it have to do with you?"

Griff steps toward me menacingly, but he doesn't frighten me. I've known him my entire life. He would never, ever hurt me, no matter how angry or ridiculous he's being.

"Hey, dude, calm down. I didn't know she was your girl, chill," Van says, stepping in between Griff and me, his hands raised up in a conciliatory gesture.

Griff growls, honest to goodness growls at Van and I swear I see steam burst from his ears. "She's not my girl, but I will beat the ever loving shit out of you if I see you touching her again."

I open my mouth to argue, but before I can, Zeke wraps his arms around me and lifts me up, swinging me to the side away from an angry, posturing Griff and a confused looking Van.

"Griff," Zeke says, the single word a warning.

Griff's attention spins our way, his eyes calming slightly when he sees me in Zeke's arms. "What?" He cries. "If anyone should be—"

"Enough," Zeke snaps, silencing whatever Griff was about to say. "Parties over, let's go."

Griff physically seethes, his shoulders rising and falling with each angry breath he takes. I half expect him to turn back to Van, but instead he nods his head, purses his lips, then turns and heads for the front door.

Nova and an assessing Valentine follow behind him, leaving just me, Zeke, and a thoroughly bewildered looking Van behind.

Van looks at me, his brow furrowed. I shrug at him, not sure how, or what I could possibly say that would explain the madness that just happened. Before I get a chance to say anything, Zeke gently pushes me behind him, leans in and speaks into Van's ear.

Van listens, pulling back from Zeke, his brow arched slightly. Then he nods, his eyes not looking at me as he turns and walks away.

Zeke looks to me, a triumphant smile on his lips, as he curls his arm over my shoulders and guides me through the crowd who instinctively part, moving out of our way as we head for the exit.

As we emerge from the Kappa Tau house, I spot the others huddled together on the sidewalk, Nova talking animatedly with her hands to Griff, who looks tense and angry, his attention barely on her. As we cross the street, Nova's hands drop to her sides and she smiles at me as we approach.

I ignore her, shrugging off Zeke's arm as I march straight over to Griff. Without pausing, I step up to him, curl my fingers into a fist and punch him in the face. His head barely even snaps back with the force of my punch, but I don't wait for his reaction. I just walk away, wiggling my fingers surreptitiously at the pain in my hand.

I don't look back. I don't wait to see if they follow behind me. I know they will, but right now I'm just too angry to care. How dare Griff behave that way? Like I'm his old lady or his property. It doesn't take a genius to know this is my dad's doing. He will have threatened the guys, tasked them to keep me safe, to keep me away from boys, and used their prospect status as incentive to get what he wants.

Right now, I don't care. All I know is that one of my best friends just embarrassed the hell out of me at my very first college party and I doubt for a single moment that what I wanted or what I was feeling even crossed his mind.

Nova is the first to catch up to me, her heels clipping along the sidewalk as she keeps pace. She doesn't say a word, just takes my hand and walks beside me. Right now, her silent solidarity is exactly what I need and I squeeze her fingers tightly, to thank her for being my friend, for being here for me and doing the perfect thing right this moment.

It doesn't take long to walk home and I sullenly ignore all three guys as I wait for Zeke to open the front door. Brushing past him, I stomp up to my room, slamming my door before I strip out of my clothes, the beautiful outfit marred by Griff's dickish behavior.

Wrapping myself in my robe, I stomp into the bathroom, turning the shower to scolding hot, before I step inside and try to wash away all of the embarrassment of the night. Twenty minutes later, the shower has started to cool and I don't feel a moments remorse at using all the hot water as I dry myself off and wrap my robe around my slightly damp skin.

I'd hoped that a shower would cool some of my anger, but I'm still as furious as I was when I walked into the house. When I push back into my bedroom, I find Griff laying on my bed. "Get out of my room," I hiss, angrily pulling a pair of shorts and a tank from my drawers.

"Emmy," Griff says, his voice coaxing, but I don't want to be coaxed, or soothed.

"I need to get dressed," I hiss. "Unless you want to see me naked, I suggest you leave."

Griff pauses for a moment, then slowly climbs off my bed and leaves, closing my door behind him.

Dropping my robe to the floor, I pull on my pj's, brush my hair out and twist it into a messy braid before I climb into bed, so angry that I know, unless I calm down, I won't sleep tonight.

When my door cautiously pushes open fifteen minutes later, I tense, not wanting to deal with my caveman best friend or his stupid excuses. Griff pokes his head around the door, his eyes shut. "You decent?" he asks.

"Yeah," I say, resigned to having to talk to him and listen to him try to justify his behavior.

"Can I come in?"

"Will you go away if I say no?"

"Probably not," he admits, his lips curling into a wry smile.

"Fine," I say, sighing loudly.

He slowly moves into my room, silently shutting the door behind him. As he pads toward my bed, I realize that he's gotten changed too and is only wearing thin athletic shorts and a muscle shirt that drops so low beneath his arms, that his pecs and abs are visible.

He climbs onto my bed, making the mattress dip beneath his weight, then lies down on his side, looking at me. "Emmy," he says.

"I don't want to hear it, Griff. You were was a dick tonight. I'm not a child and I'm not your old lady. There's no other situation where the way you behaved tonight would be acceptable. I wasn't doing anything wrong and neither was Van. We were dancing, that's it, not even suggestively dancing, just PG13, middle school dancing. You were so far out of line. I'm mortified. More embarrassed than I've ever been in my entire life and you caused it."

"There was nothing middle school about the way he was touching you, Em, or the way he was looking at you," Griff growls.

"If you're going to start again, you can get out. I've had just about enough macho biker bullshit tonight. You guys pull this shit and you wonder why I was planning to run as far away as possible from this caveman, chauvinistic asshattery."

"Shortcake," Griff says and I can feel the warning in his voice, but I've had enough.

"No, Griff, fuck this. You guys run around screwing anything with a pussy and no one says a word. I dance with a guy, once, fully dressed, and all hell breaks loose. Well no. I refuse to put up with this double standard. If you guys keep it up, I'll transfer. I'll leave and I won't tell any of you where I'm going. Nova is fucking Valentine in the same house we're all living in and you don't say a thing, even though you know Uncle Echo wants her to sleep in a separate room to him. But with me you all become my fucking prison wardens. I am not a fucking idiot. I'm not a child and I refuse to let any of you treat me like that. Just go, Griff, I'm too angry to deal with this now."

Ignoring his eyes that implore me to listen, I roll away until my back is to him. Frustrated tears pool in my eyes, but I blink them away, not letting them fall. Instead I close my eyes and try to pretend this entire night didn't happen.

For a long moment he stays still, not speaking, but not getting up and leaving either. He sighs and the sound is pained, but I refuse to make him feel better right now. What I'm feeling is justified. He had no right to behave the way he did tonight, and I refuse to put up with it. If I let him get away with acting like I'm his property now, during our first few days here as adults, he'll never stop.

A warm arm snakes around my waist, his huge body curling around me. "I'm sorry."

Exhaling loudly, I clench my fingers into fists, my body tense in his embrace. "Don't be sorry, just don't fucking do it. This is why I wanted to get away from the world we were raised in. A world where I become property. I'm not an object, no one owns me."

"You'll never be property, Emmy. That's not how it is, although I get how it might seem that way. The Sinners, they revere their women, just like your dad worships your mom. He doesn't own her; it's the total opposite. He belongs to her. She owns his bossy, terrifying ass and he's not ashamed to admit it."

Allowing my body to relax a little, my back melts into the curve of his body and his arm tightens around me, holding me a little closer. "I wasn't treating you like property tonight, shortcake. I was treating you like family. Maybe I went a little too far, but I was acting with the best intentions."

Snatching my body out of his embrace, I sit up and glare at him. "I don't care what your reasons were. If I'd gone and ripped you away from a girl you were dancing with, you would have laughed and told me to go away, but when it's me, you beat your fucking chest like a caveman and intimidate everyone around us. Family doesn't have this kind of double standard. Please just go. I'm too angry to listen to your bullshit attempts at defending yourself. You were wrong, Griff, and I don't want to be around you until you understand that."

"Em," Griff cajoles.

"No," I snap, lifting my hand, signaling for him to stop.

His mouth turns down at the sides and his eyes flash with sadness.

Crossing my arms across my chest I harden my resolve. If I show even an ounce of weakness, he'll jump on it and I'll end up forgiving him, even though he was completely out of order.

"Em."

"No, please just go."

Griff sits up, pausing for a moment before he stands. He takes a single step toward me and for a moment I think he's going to come to me, but then he sighs, visibly sagging, his shoulders slumping as he turns and leaves.

When he quietly closes the door behind him, I crumple back down onto my bed, all of my bravado evaporating. Embarrassment, hurt, anger and sadness consume me, and hot, confused tears fill my eyes.

Covering my mouth with my hand, I stifle the sob that threatens to escape, burying my face into my pillow and letting all of my emotion wrack through my body. For the first time since we spoke about going to college together, I regret my decision. Is this what the next four years are going to be like? Griff or one of the other guys taking turns to control everything I do?

The thought makes another sob burst free. Inhaling shakily, I brush the tears from my cheeks and try to harden myself. Tears are the way children behave and I'm an adult dammit.

Rolling onto my back, I stare wide-eyed at the ceiling, taking deep breaths. Tomorrow I'll tell them that this isn't how things are going to work. They'll either agree and we'll get past this, or they won't and I'll have to figure out what to do next.

GRIFFIN

Shit. I fucked up so fucking badly.

I've never seen her with a guy before. She's never been interested and back home if a guy approached her she would either tell them to fuck off or I'd warn them away. I don't know how to deal with this, I can't.

Emmy isn't the girl who dresses up like a walking wet dream and grinds up against random dudes at parties, that just isn't her. Or at least it wasn't in high school. Fuck, she keeps telling us that she wants a chance to be someone new, but I don't think I ever really thought she meant it. Is this the new Emmy? Am I going to have to watch her meet douchebag guys and hook up without doing anything?

Fuck that. I can't, I'm not that guy, I'm not that strong. I acted without thought today; all I knew was that I needed to get that asshole away from her. My vision went red and I just moved.

It's the world's biggest double standard that I'm pissed at her for doing something I did most weekends back home. We'd go to a party and I'd hook up with a random girl, whoever caught my eye, but tonight watching her do the same made me crazy.

Now she's mad at me. I don't ever remember a time where she kicked me out of her room.

My skin is crawling with the need to go back to her, to make her forgive me, to make her understand that I don't care which version of her she is, I'll never be okay with seeing her with random guys. I force myself to keep moving, to keep walking away from her, because everything's too raw tonight and nothing I say now, when my hands are still shaking and my heart is still pounding, is going to make this any better.

EMMY

I barely sleep and when I drag myself from my room the next morning, my eyes are gritty and red. Padding barefoot downstairs, I step into the kitchen and find Griff sat on a stool at the breakfast bar, his eyes downcast and sad.

When he sees me, he lowers his spoon to his cereal bowl and watches as I enter the room. "Emmy," he says, his voice rough and gravelly.

"Griff, I love you, but think really carefully about what you want to say right now."

He pauses, visibly swallows, then dips his head in a single nod. I wait, expecting him to speak, and when he doesn't, I sigh, shaking my head and scoffing lightly beneath my breath as I stalk into the kitchen. Grabbing a cup from the cabinet, I cross to the coffee pot and pour myself a large cup, adding creamer and sugar and stirring before moving to head back up to my bedroom.

His hand on my arm stops me. "I'm sorry," he whispers.

"What are you sorry for?"

"Right now, I'm basically sorry for existing. Last night, I saw that guy all over you and I just lost it."

"I'm not yours, Griff, and even if I was, I wasn't doing anything wrong."

"I know," he admits quickly. "I know you weren't. I guess I'm just so used to assuming you don't want guys near you. That's always been your MO. If a guy was hanging on you at home, you'd either threaten him or one of us would, so I just did what we've always done."

Huffing out a breath, I roll my eyes. "And it never occurred to you that I might want to dance with him?"

Griff shrugs. "It didn't. You've never shown any interest before. The only guys you've ever let touch you have been us."

I feel my eyes widen as I realize that he's right. I've never been interested in guys. But that doesn't mean he gets to behave like he did last night. "You could have just pulled me aside and asked if I was okay."

He shrugs again and this time an 'aw shucks' smile tips at the corners of his lips. "That probably would have been smarter."

"I was mortified, Griff. Our first college party and you behaved like a caveman. This is a small school. Gossip probably spreads faster here than back home and you just made me look like an idiot."

"I'm sorry," he says, his voice pleading.

"I'm not a child. I'm not your girl, your old lady, or your property. I won't tolerate you behaving like a Sinner here. This isn't Archer's Creek and you aren't a brother. If you want to try that shit, then in terms of hierarchy I rank higher. I'm the president's daughter and you're just the brother of a member. I know my dad probably told you to play guard dog, but no, just no. We're either friends and family, or you're my bodyguard. You can't be both, so pick a side."

When I finish speaking, my chest is hitching up and down, hot emotion filling my eyes and threatening to spill. Griff's face is pale, his eyes wide and I realize I've never spoken to him like this before. I've never needed to.

"I'm not going to stop keeping you safe, Em. That's what family does. What I did last night had nothing to do with the club, or your dad, or me playing bodyguard. That was me doing what I thought I needed to do to keep my best friend safe. I admit that I handled things in the wrong way, I won't go DEFCON 5 again without checking with you, but you can sure as shit believe I'll step in if I think I need to."

My bottom lip quivers and I bite it to keep it still. Griff's intense gaze is firmly fixed on me and I swallow, stalling as I decide what to say. Griff and I have been friends all our lives and I get that he was just being his normal protective self, but I don't know how to make him realize that I have to figure my own shit out and that although I appreciate him, I don't need his help.

"Em," he says, breaking our silent standoff.

Exhaling, my shoulders sag. I feel like no matter what I say right now, I can't win, so instead I decide to just say nothing at all. Twisting my lips into a wry half-smile, I nod once, not acknowledging his point, but not arguing against it either. Then I grip my cup of coffee a little tighter and walk away.

———

My alarm buzzes and I reach across and immediately turn it off. I'm awake and have been for hours. My argument with Griff has plagued my thoughts for the last three days and the result is about three hours of sleep a night and an awful lot of tossing and turning as I play out our conversations over and over in my head.

I haven't actively avoided him or the others, but instead I've drowned myself in my books and used them as an excuse for going MIA for hours on end. My friends have noticed, but they haven't said anything.

Today is the first day of classes, the real introduction to college life and I'm excited and terrified in equal parts. I have no idea what I want to major in yet, but I've got a full course load of required classes and a mix of electives that will hopefully give a better insight into what I might want to specialize in. Rolling out of bed, I stretch up onto my tiptoes and lift my arms above my head. Scooping my hair off my neck I wander to the bathroom and turn on the shower, before stripping and stepping under the life affirming hot water. Just like I knew it would, the heat relaxes my muscles and by the time I've washed my hair and lathered my skin in vanilla scented body-wash, I feel refreshed and excited for the day ahead.

Once I'm dry, I wrap myself in a towel and pad back to my room to blow out my hair and pick my 'first day of school' outfit. As I'm applying my makeup my cell beeps with a text message.

Mom

Have a fantastic first day, sweetheart.
I know you'll be amazing xo.

As I read my mom's words, a smile spreads across my lips. I'm in college. This is it: my first day, my fresh start, and I can't wait. I finish my makeup, step up to my closet and open the door, staring inside like the perfect outfit will jump out and shout 'wear me'.

After scanning my clothes for several long moments, I settle on a cute acid-wash denim skirt with buttons down the front, a deep red fitted t-shirt, and my tan sandals that twist around my ankles and buckle at the back. Turning from side to side I consider my reflection. I feel cute, the skirt's not too short, and the sandals are comfortable enough to wear all day without giving me blisters.

I take a quick mirror selfie and text it to my mom. Her reply is immediate.

Mom

You look beautiful.

When my cell rings a second later, I already know it's her. "Hey, Mom."

"Are you excited?" She asks, her familiar comforting voice the balm I need to settle some of my nerves

"A little. I'm nervous too though."

"You're going to do so great, baby. I'm so proud of you. Did your dad call you yet?"

"No, not yet," I tell her.

Her laugh is infectious. "He's been up since five pacing. He misses you."

"I miss him too," I say, a little sadly.

"What's the matter? What's happened?" Mom asks quickly, her voice rising an octave with her panic.

"Nothing, I'm just... Griff and I had a bit of a fall out."

"Oh, sweetie, what happened?"

Sighing, I consider telling her it was nothing, but before I can brush it off, words are falling from my mouth in a rush. "We went to a party at a frat house. Nova and I were dancing, then this cute guy came and danced with me. He was barely touching me. His name was Van and then Griff completely lost his shit. He ripped the guy away from me, went all stupid caveman and we all ended up leaving. I was so angry and just, gah, so embarrassed."

When I finally stop speaking, I exhale and realize I feel a little better just from telling her.

"Oh, honey," Mom says, her voice soft and sympathetic. "Have you told him you're upset with him?"

"Oh, he knows. The party was a few days ago and I've barely spoken to him since. He says he's sorry, but I think he's only sorry I'm angry with him, not sorry because he embarrassed me and totally overreacted."

"Sweetie, I'm not justifying his behavior, but he's a Sinner. Your dad, your uncles, they're all the same and if any of them saw you dancing with a guy, even if it was completely harmless, they'd all react the exact same way. Maybe cut him a little slack while he figures out the rules now you guys are in college."

I exhale. A part of me knows that's she's right, but somehow that doesn't make me any less annoyed. "You might be right," I grudgingly admit.

"College is when you take those first steps to being an adult, and part of growing up is learning to forgive people when they make a mistake. Not every person, or every mistake. But I think if you really think about it, Griffin was only trying to protect you; something that's so ingrained in him I doubt he could stop doing it even if he tried. By the sound of it he handled the situation in the wrong way, but if you've barely spoken to him for days, I imagine he's learned his lesson. Today is an exciting, nerve-wracking day for all of you, don't start it on a sour note. Make peace with Griffin. He's one of your best friends and if I know him like I think I do, he'll be hurting if you're upset with him."

Sighing, I silently curse my mom. "God, I hate it when

you're right," I say snippily, but with no real heat behind my words.

Mom's laugh echoes through the line. "I'm always right, honey."

"I miss you."

"I miss you more," she says, her voice softening. "Call your dad, then go hug Griffin and have the most amazing first day ever."

"Okay, Mom, love you."

"Love you too."

I end the call and immediately call my dad. We spend a few minutes talking about what classes I have today, then he tells me he loves me and misses me. Grabbing my backpack, I make my way downstairs, and step into the kitchen. Both Zeke and Griffin stop and turn to look at me. A part of me wants to walk into my friend's arms and tell him it's all okay. Hell, all of me wants to do that, so I do.

Dropping my backpack to the floor at my feet, I walk across the kitchen and throw myself at him. Griff opens his arms and tenses like he's half-expecting me to punch him in the gut, even as he pulls me to him and holds me so tightly, I can barely breathe.

"I'm so fucking sorry, Em. I'm so sorry," he coos into the top of my head.

"I know, I know, it's okay," I say, my face pressed up against his chest.

I'm not sure how long we stand there for, but when I eventually push away from his hold, Griff's eyes are red-rimmed and repentant. "Please don't stop talking to us, Em. I was an idiot, not the others, just me. I'm gonna piss you off again, you know I will, but just yell at me, or hit me again. I'd rather you take it all out on me, but the silence, I can't take the silence. Please Em, please."

I nod, emotion clogging my throat and making it impossible to speak. Griff grabs me and pulls me in for another bone-crushing hug.

"Oh, thank God," Nova's voice says and I can't help but hear the relief in her tone.

Pulling back, I look up and find her stood in the doorway, her hands clutching at her cheeks.

"You guys made up. Yay, now we can actually enjoy our first day," she cries rushing over to throw her arms around both me and Griff at the same time. "Get in here, bro, group hug," she calls.

I hear Zeke's low chuckle before his arms wrap around my back and the four of us do a weird group hug with me squished in the center.

Half an hour later we leave the house as a group, the five of us all excited to start our first full day at our new school. "What class do we all have first?" I ask, hiking my backpack a little higher onto my shoulder.

"Biology," Zeke says, an excited gleam in his eyes.

"Philosophy," Nova says with a grimace. "It seemed like a cool pick, but now I'm not so sure."

"Advanced statistics," Valentine says quietly.

"How are you taking an advanced class?" I ask.

"I started taking a few college classes while I was at the boarding school. I finished them online this summer," he says with a nonchalant shrug.

I don't know why it surprises me so much when Valentine lets it slip how much of a genius he is, but somehow it always does.

"Geek," Griff coughs.

A small grin tips at the corner of Valentine's lips. "Genius," he says mockingly.

"What class do you have, Griff?" I ask.

"Computer Science. What about you?"

"British Classics. I'm so excited," I gush, skipping a little.

"Nerd," Griff coughs again.

"Yep and proud," I say, spinning around to bob my tongue out at him.

When we reach the college entrance, I pause, taking a moment to look up at the huge iron gates that loom above us. Inhaling a reaffirming breath, I step through, a smile breaking across my lips as I take in the sea of students just like us that are milling along the paths.

"This is it," I whisper.

"Yep," Griff says, dropping his arm across my shoulders. "Let's go learn some shit."

When we reach the central courtyard, we split, all of us heading in the directions of our first class. "See you guys at lunch," I call, as I wave goodbye and stride purposefully in the direction of my first college class.

My British Classics classroom, is almost full by the time I finally get there and I make a bee-line for the first empty seat I spot, sliding into it and pulling my laptop from my backpack to place it on the desk in front of me.

The girl sitting next to me, smiles. "Hi," she says, her voice squeaking slightly.

"Hi," I reply, lifting the lid of my laptop and bringing the screen to life.

Her chair makes an awful screeching noise as she pushes it back and pulls a notebook from her bag, then frantically searches for something, piling stuff onto her desk. "Err, is there any chance you have a pen I could borrow? I forgot to switch out my laptop battery and put it on charge last night, even though I left myself a note, so I'm going to have to take actual notes today," she says, hysterical panic lacing her tone.

"Err yeah," I say, pulling a pen from my backpack and handing it to her.

"You are a life saver. I'm Avery by the way."

"Emmy," I say smiling at her quickly before focusing my attention back on my laptop.

This girl seems nice, if a little disorganized. I'm so used to only being friends with the other Scions, I haven't made a new friend in years; until Valentine that is. Glancing at the girl at my side, I realize she could potentially be a new friend. I mean she might not be, but I could at least try, right? Do my best to remember that the kids I'm meeting here are nothing like the ones from back home. They don't know who I am, or who my family are, and any friendships I form are just that, simple offers of friendship with no agenda.

I've spent so long wanting to be different, to live a different life, but now I'm faced with a chance to get everything I want, I'm stalling, second guessing myself. It's time to put my money where my mouth is and step out of my familiar bubble with my familiar friends. Maybe this is the push I need, to actually take hold of my new life with both hands, so I turn to Avery and say. "Are you looking forward to this class? I think the reading list is my favorite of all my classes."

Avery smiles widely, her shoulders rising as her excitement practically bubbles from her. "I know. Bronte is great, but I can't wait til we get to Jane Austen. I've read all of her books at least a hundred times, but I'm looking forward to reading them again and maybe getting a new perspective on them."

Before I have a chance to respond, the classroom door flies open and an eccentric looking man strides in, wearing what looks like pajama pants, with sandals, and a button down and tie. "Good morning, class. My name is Professor

Allen and together we will be exploring the intricacies of the British Classics, such as Hardy, Austen, and Bronte."

The room falls silent as the strange looking man talks with such passion about words and stories and books. I'm enthralled and riveted and the next hour is quite possibly the fastest and most interesting one of my life so far. By the time Professor Allen finishes speaking, I no longer care that he looks like he got dressed in the dark. The way he talks about literature is inspiring and I genuinely want to be as cool as him when I grow up.

"That was…" Avery pauses as if she's trying to find a word that would adequately describe what we both just experienced.

"Exhilarating?" I offer.

"Yes," she cries animatedly. "I thought I'd enjoy this course, but now I think this is going to be my favorite class this semester."

"Mine too," I agree, smiling gleefully.

"What class do you have next?" She asks.

"Err, let me check." Pulling my schedule from my bag, I scan the timetable for the day. "Art History. You?" I ask as we walk side by side down the stairs of the lecture theater and into the corridor.

"My major is French so I have advanced translation and French business practices, which is basically just a fancy name for how to run a business in French," she says with a laugh, as we push out of the building and into the bright morning sunshine.

"You've picked a major already? It's only day one," I gasp, my mouth falling open.

Avery laughs lightly, "My parents own a vineyard. We spend a lot of time in France, so my education is all based on me joining our family business. What building is your class in?"

"Clangham Hall," I tell her, glancing down at the map I've clipped to my schedule in case I get lost.

"Oh, that's the next building to where my class is, so I can walk that way with you, if that's okay?"

"Of course," I say with a smile, pulling my backpack onto both shoulders. "So where are you from originally?"

"California. I miss the beach already," she says, a misty look flashing across her face. "What about you?"

"Texas."

"Are you homesick yet?" She asks.

"I wasn't til I spoke to my parents this morning. I miss them, but I have all my friends here with me."

"What dorm are you in?"

I pause, wondering if I should admit that I don't live on campus. It's not that weird to rent a place rather than live in the dorms, right? I second guess myself again. I want to be just a normal student, but I don't even know what normal looks like. "Err, I'm not." I admit, wincing slightly. "We got a house just a few blocks from campus," I say.

"We?" she asks curiously.

"Me and my four best friends. We all came to Hayhurst together."

"Wow! I want to say that must be awesome, but five girls in a house honestly sounds like hell," she says, her eyes crinkling at the sides a little.

I laugh. "Yeah five girls would probably be a nightmare, but I live with one other girl and three guys."

Avery's jaw drops so far, I swear I can see her tonsils.

"Emmy," someone calls from behind me and I turn to find a smiling Zeke jogging toward me.

"Hey," I say, when he reaches us.

"Hey," he replies, dropping his arm over my shoulder and smiling rakishly at Avery. "Introduce me to your friend."

Rolling my eyes, I stab my elbow into his stomach playfully and he laughs. "Zeke, this is Avery, we have British Classics together." I look to Avery. "Avery, this is Zeke, one of my best friends, my housemate, and general pain in the butt."

Avery's smile brightens and she bites her lip as she holds out her hand to Zeke. He takes it and flashes her a panty-melting grin. "Pleasure to meet you, darlin'," he says, letting his accent thicken as he speaks.

Avery blushes and I elbow Zeke again. "Behave," I hiss at him.

"Me, I'm always an angel," he drawls, hamming it up again.

Laughing at his antics, I roll my eyes. "What class do you have?"

"Finance," he says, his lip curling slightly in displeasure. "How was your first class?"

"It was amazing. The professor is bizarre, but I already know it's going to be a fascinating course." I tell him, my excitement from the last hour seeping back in.

"Awesome. Right I gotta go, my class is over there," he says, pointing to one of the large buildings behind us. "I'll see you at lunch."

"Okay," I say. "See you later."

He pulls me closer to him and drops a kiss to the top of my head. "Love you."

"Love you too," I whisper.

Then he waves to Avery and darts off towards his class.

"Are you guys…?" Avery asks, her eyes glancing between me and Zeke's retreating back.

"What?"

"Are you like a thing?"

My eyes widen and I stifle a giggle. "God, no. I've known him my entire life. He's like my brother."

A small grin forms on her lips. "That man is hot with a capital H."

It looks like Zeke has a new member of his fan club. When we reach the path that splits off between our two buildings, we exchange numbers and I wave goodbye.

The next week passes in a blur of classes and homework and I love it. College life is amazing and even living with the others isn't proving as exhausting as I thought it would. I love my friends, but I need more down time than them and surprisingly, none of them moan when I retreat to my room and lose myself in another world or two.

We don't go to any more frat parties, but the others drag me to a couple of the student bars and we get a chance to use our fake ID's, much to Nova's delight.

Avery and I have been chatting through text and today I'm meeting up with her and her roommate for drinks. I thought about inviting Nova to come along, but selfishly I don't want to share my new friend with her. Everyone loves Nova and I'm sure Avery would be no exception, so I'm keeping her to myself until we know each other a little better.

We've arranged to meet outside the library so we can all walk to the bar together and nerves are humming through my veins as I walk across campus. I'm not sure I've ever actually made a real girlfriend. Nova and I have known each other since we were born so that doesn't count and the girls from our elementary and high schools were all her friends who tolerated me.

It's strange to meet people who genuinely knows nothing about me. Back home, the kids all assumed they knew us, because they knew of our families, of the club, but only the Scions have ever known the real me.

Avery spots me and starts to wave, a bright smile taking over her lips. "Emmy, hey," she calls, rushing over to me and pulling me in for a hug.

I hug her back, even though I'm not sure we're at the tactile stage yet. "Hey," I say as I pull away.

"Come meet Veronica," she says with a giggle, hooking her arm through mine and walking me back to where a petite girl with rich ebony skin is standing. Her hair is so long it flows down her back almost touching her butt and she's so gorgeous I almost feel intimidated.

"Emmy this is my roommate Veronica," she says reaching out to place her hand on Veronica's arm.

"Hi, Emmy, nice to meet you," Veronica says, a smile lighting up her face as she does an awkward wave.

"Let's go get our drink on," Avery says, tucking her spare arm through Veronica's and pulling us both in the direction of the bar.

It's early so we walk straight into the bar and easily find a table. "Shall we share a pitcher?" Avery asks as she searches through her purse for something.

"Sure," I say and Veronica nods in agreement.

"Cool, I'll go order at the bar. I'll get some snacks too, I'm starving." Avery says once she's found her wallet and immediately skips away from the table, her blonde ponytail swinging as she walks.

Veronica and I fall into a strained silence and I knot my fingers together in my lap wishing I was better at this. "So, err, are you a freshman too?" I ask.

"No, I'm a sophomore, but I only transferred to Hayhurst this year, so I'm still a newbie."

"What school did you transfer from?" I ask.

Her smile slips slightly and her eyes crinkle a little at the sides. "NYU."

"Wow from New York to Hayhurst, this place must feel like the wilderness."

She laughs and the haunted look I thought I'd seen in her eyes disappears. "This is actually a lot like the town I grew up in, so I don't mind the slower pace of life. New York was a bit too hectic for me."

"I considered going to Wilson Hill, but it's in Duluth and it was the city location that put me off too. I guess you don't realize how much of a small-town girl you are until it comes down to it." As the words leave my mouth, I realize how true it is. I might want to find myself, but one weekend in a big city and I was craving small-town living again.

"That's so true," Veronica says. "But it was actually my boyfriend that lured me to Hayhurst."

"Is he a student? Or does he live in Alabama?" I ask.

"He's a senior; he's actually my ex-boyfriend now though," she says ruefully.

"Eeek, you moved schools to be with him, then you broke up? That's terrible timing," I say with a wince.

Veronica barks out an unexpected laugh. "Definitely. He hooked up with a girl the day after I moved into the dorms. He's always been so sweet to me; I had no idea he was such a dog. But it is what it is, I'm here now so I need to make the best of it."

"Drinks," Avery singsongs as she appears at our table with a pitcher full of amber colored beer in one hand and a stack of three glasses in the other hand.

After she sits down, she pours us each a glass of beer then lifts hers into the air. "To new friends," she says cheerily.

I tap my glass against hers, and smile. This is it, this is what I wanted, to be the new Emmy, to make new friends and experience life away from home, away from the shadow of the club and away from the Scions. So why do I wish Nova was here to share this with me?

———

The library has become my solace. Not that I really need somewhere to hide, but I still enjoy the peaceful silence and homely smell all libraries have: old books and dust.

"Hey."

"Oh, hey," I say shyly to the cute guy who appears in front of me, his hands buried in his pockets, his backpack hanging off one shoulder.

"Look, I know this is a huge cliché and it's probably going to sound like the worst pick-up line ever. But do you remember me? I noticed you sitting over here the other day and by the time I plucked up the courage to come and speak to you, you'd left. I promised myself that If I saw you again, I'd introduce myself and see if you remembered. So hi, I'm Kent."

I feel the heat rise in my cheeks and I glance away, embarrassed and a little confused. Pushing my glasses up my nose, I scan the area of the library I'm sitting in, but other than a couple of people sat studying at the other tables there's no one else up here.

"I'm sorry, I've made you uncomfortable. Shit. As I'm guessing you can probably tell, I don't do this sort of thing very often and apparently, I'm really bad at it. I'm gonna go and hide under a rock for a month or two," he says, pushing his hands deeper into his pockets and swiveling on the spot.

"I'm Emmy."

His movement stalls and he twists back to face me again. Straight white teeth appear beneath his growing smile and a faint pink blush coats his cheeks. He gestures to the seat opposite me. "Can I join you?"

I pause for a moment. "Tell me why I should remember you first."

His cheeks get even redder. "Ah, err, we met at the freshman fair. I was giving out book tokens," he says, cringing slightly.

I nod slowly, narrowing my eyes as I stare at him. He does seem a little familiar. "Yes," I cry pointing at him, "you were wearing a bowtie." I don't tell him that the only reason I remember his bowtie is because I'd never seen anyone apart from a clown at the circus wear one. "I actually think I lost the token though which is shocking considering I'm a total bookworm," I confess, smiling shyly.

He hurriedly pulls out the chair, wincing when the legs squeal as they drag along the floor. Sliding off his backpack, he lowers himself into the seat and I take a moment to allow my eyes to look him over. His frame is slim and lean, but not too skinny. His skin is a little pale considering Alabama is hot as hell, and his hair is neatly styled and a dark auburn color. Beige khakis cover his slim legs and I can see a glimpse of a tan leather belt at his waist. His white button down is perfectly pressed, the top button undone, and he's sporting a pink tie, knotted loosely at his neck. He's cute in a preppy, Young Republican kind of way.

We fall into an awkward, stilted silence and I stare at him, expecting him to speak.

"What class are you studying for?" He asks, after what feels like forever.

"Creative Writing."

"Oh, I was hoping you were going to say something math related, then I could have offered to help. Words aren't exactly my forte," Kent says, blushing adorably.

"That's okay, they're my thing. Words, I mean." The moment the words are out of my mouth I realize how stupid I sound, and my gaze falls to my laptop and the books in front of me.

"I like numbers." Kent declares, a little too enthusiastically.

Lifting my hands onto the edge of the table, I fidget, unsure what else to say. The boys at my high school rarely spoke to me. Sometimes I'd catch them looking, but they never spoke, and I'm not sure if that's because they were terrified of my family, or because I was standing next to my stunningly beautiful best friend.

"I'm sorry," Kent says again.

"What for?"

"Because I really want to be smooth and confident and that's obviously not going well, when all I can think to say is, 'I like numbers'," Kent says, cringing.

"I think I might have started it when I declared that 'words were my thing'," I giggle.

Kent flashes me that sweet smile again and I find myself smiling back at him, unable to resist responding to his animated expression.

Lifting his hand from beneath the table, he thrusts it forward toward me. "Hi, I'm Kent. I think you're stunning, and I'd really like to take you out sometime."

I giggle again. Wow, I wouldn't have said a guy could ever turn me into a giggler. Biting down on my bottom lip with my teeth, I reach out and take his hand, smiling when he wraps his fingers around mine. "Hi, Kent. I'm Emmy and I'd like that."

"Are you busy Wednesday night?"

I shake my head. "I don't think so."

"Can I take you to dinner?"

I nod. "Sure." We exchange numbers and then Kent grabs his bag and leaves, a huge smile gracing his lips.

Later that night, I turn my key in the lock on our front door and push the door open, nearly falling straight through when the door is pulled from my grip. I stumble forward, bracing myself to hit the floor when Griff grabs me, stopping my forward movement and pushing me back upright.

"Whoa, shortcake, you okay?"

"Jesus, Griff, you ripped the door out of my hands," I hiss.

"Sorry," he says smirking, not looking even remotely sorry.

I shake my head at him as I pull myself from his hold and step into the house, waiting for him to move so I can step past. Instead of moving, he pulls my backpack from my shoulder and places it on the table to the right of the door, then he bends down and throws me over his shoulder so quickly I barely even know what's happening until I'm hanging upside down and staring at his jean clad ass.

"Griffin," I shriek. "Put me down, you asshole."

His chuckle is low and throaty, but instead of lowering me to the ground, he turns, closes the door then carries me into the living room. "Look what I found. It's our missing room-mate," he announces.

"Hey, Em," Zeke says, slapping my ass as he moves by us and drops down next to his sister on the couch.

"What the fuck, guys. How have I been missing? I've been here every night this week."

"No, you've hidden in your room every night this week. Tonight's family night and we're going out. No excuses, no get out clauses," he says, as he flips me back upright and sinks down onto the couch, pulling me into his lap.

I slap at his arms until he releases me, then I glare at him as I cross to the other side of the couch next to Nova.

His laugh is loud and unrepentant. "This is the new status quo, shortcake. You hide for a week, then I'll throw you over my shoulder and kidnap you."

Flinging a throw cushion at him, it hits him square in the face, but his smile just gets bigger as he shoves the cushion behind his head and leans back in his seat, wiggling his eyebrows at me tauntingly.

"Where are we going?" I ask Nova, while flicking Griff the bird.

"We thought we'd go back to The Fishbowl, that place we went to last week. The food's good and the beer's cheap."

I nod, "Okay. I need to go get changed. What time did you want to go?"

"It's happy hour til eight."

"Give me twenty minutes, I'll be quick." I tell her.

She nods and I stand up, heading for the door. I glare at Griff, bobbing my tongue at him as I pass. He just laughs, his smile so wide I swear it must meet his eyes. It takes me thirty minutes to get ready and when I make it back downstairs, I see that the others have all changed too.

The Fishbowl isn't a dressy place, so we're all in jeans, the guys in t-shirts. Nova's in a cropped football jersey, and I'm in a plain black tank. The first one I'd found in my closet had a Sinners logo on the back, and for a moment I'd considered wearing it. Normally I'd worry about people recognizing the insignia, but no one here would have a clue. I still pushed the hanger back into my closet and picked the plain one though. This is my fresh start and I can't be the new me, while dressed in clothes literally branded with my past. I ignore the feeling of guilt tinged with homesickness and try to focus on enjoying myself.

"Family night," Zeke shouts, strutting ahead of us, snapping his fingers like a hyped-up valley girl.

I try so hard not to laugh, but a giggle escapes my lips anyway. It reminds me of my giggles from earlier in the library with Kent. He's nothing like my friends, being preppy, and a bit of a geek. He doesn't fit in with us, and I think maybe that's what I like about him. As we leave the house and walk down the sidewalk, I consider telling the others that I have a date on Wednesday, but something stops me. I don't know if it's because I think the guys will go into alpha body-guard mode, like they did at the Fresh Meat party, or if maybe I just want something that's for me; but either way I don't say anything and instead I listen to the familiar banter of people I've known my whole life.

The Fishbowl is busy when we get there, but we manage to snag a big round booth just as the people using it are leaving. The guys gesture for Nova and me to slide in first and once we're settled they join us, shielding us on both sides like we need to be protected. I fight the urge to roll my eyes, until I catch Nova's gaze, then we both simultaneously sigh, exasperated with the guys' overprotective antics.

A harried looking waitress appears to take our drinks orders. "I'm gonna need to see ID's," she says so matter of factly that I've no doubt she asks every table.

We all dutifully pull out our fake ID's and hand them over to her. She studies them each in turn, eyeing us before she hands them back and smiles. "What can I get you?"

"Can we have a couple of pitchers of beer and five glasses, please Fiona?" Zeke says, looking at her name tag and addressing her by name, like he does every time we go to a bar or restaurant.

"Sure thing. Just to let you know table service ends after

happy hour; then you'll have to go on over to the bar to order. I'll be right back with your drinks."

"We need to order some food when she gets back. I'm starving," Griff says, nudging my knee with his.

"I want chili fries again, they were so good," I say, my mouth watering just at the thought.

"Me too," Valentine agrees. "And hot wings."

The waitress returns a few moments later, and we order food as Valentine pours beer into each of our glasses. "To the Scions and our first few weeks at college," he says, raising his glass into the air in a toast.

"The Scions," I say, lifting my glass and tapping it against his as the others all follow suit.

I scan the people sat around me and get a warm fuzzy feeling as I take in the faces of my friends. These people are my roots and in this moment I'm reminded of how lucky I am to have them; how lonely I'd have been if I'd decided to take up my place at Dartmouth instead of following my heart to Hayhurst.

Conversation about our first few weeks, our classes, and the new people we've met flows effortlessly, not even pausing when our food is delivered. When Griff reaches over and scoops the garnish off the top of my fries I don't blink, and neither does he when I steal one of his fried pickles. Even Valentine, the newest member of our group, seems to push and pull in the dance of shared food and confidences like he's been doing it his entire life.

Being here is easy, and tension that I didn't even realize I was holding falls from my shoulders. Leaning over, I press my lips against Griff's cheek. "Thank you," I whisper.

He catches my chin as I move to turn away from him, his finger and thumb holding me gently, but firmly in place. "I'll always take your kisses, Em, but do you wanna tell me what you're thanking me for?" He asks, his voice a low drawl.

"For this, for family night. For pulling me back from my own head, just like you promised me you'd do."

His lips twitch at the corners and he blinks slowly, leaning in until his forehead is almost touching mine, our faces so close I can feel his warm breath on my skin. "You're welcome, shortcake," he whispers, his lips pressing against the corner of my mouth.

EMMY

The next two days pass in the blink of an eye and before I know it, it's Wednesday, the night of my date with Kent. When the doorbell rings, I dart from my room, rushing down the stairs in an attempt to get to the door before any of the others do. Jumping off the last step, I turn toward the front door only to find Zeke stood in the open doorway, one arm curled around the wooden door, the other braced against the jamb, blocking the entrance into the house.

Despite both Zeke and Griffin deciding not to pursue football after high school, they've continued to work out like athletes, lifting weights and doing cardio on the gym equipment we have in the basement. Right now, he's fresh from a shower, wearing nothing but a pair of loose-fitting sweatpants, his hair still wet, the tattoos he got done this summer bold and black against his tan skin.

"Who the fuck are you?" Zeke demands gruffly, sounding scarily like his dad.

"Err, I'm Kent. I'm here to pick up Emmy." Kent's voice is quiet and unsure and I cringe at how intimidated he sounds.

Perhaps I should have warned my date about my living arrangements, or maybe told the others about my date, but honestly, I wasn't ready for my two worlds to collide yet. After our cute, but somewhat awkward meeting in the library when he asked me out, Kent has texted me a few times, but we've mainly exchanged small talk about our days, classes, and homework.

I've almost told Nova about him a hundred times in the last couple of days, but every time I've opened my mouth to tell her, the words wouldn't come. My friends won't understand Kent and I seriously doubt he'll understand them. Kent's nice, our texts have been nice, and I'm sure our date will be nice too. It will all be very, very nice and damn it, I want to see what that's like.

Nova is the only one of my friends who's ever really been in a relationship. Zeke hops from one girl to the next, always running a mile as soon as they want labels and commitment. I know Griff fucks about, I've seen him with more girls than I can count, but never for more than a night; and me, well I've never bothered with guys. What's the point when all the guys at school are either terrified of my family or want to be part of the club and are hoping I'll help them get there.

Kent is basically my first ever date, the first guy who's wanted me for me, or at least his first impression of me. We don't know each other, we don't have any history, or any real preconceptions, and who can blame me for wanting to keep that to myself and not share it with anyone else.

As I watch Zeke's back tense, and his body language become hostile, I realize that the other reason I kept my date with Kent secret is because I knew they would react like this. Months ago, when Valentine manipulated Nova into acting like they were dating, neither Zeke nor Griffin batted an eyelid at them making out in the parking lot. But if a guy comes within fifty feet of me, they both turn into Sinners prospects, charged with protecting the prez's kid, just like they did at the frat party.

I love them for it almost as much as their ridiculous over-protectiveness drives me crazy.

Kent isn't like the guys I grew up around. I'm not talking about the boys I went to school with. I mean the Sinners, their kids, the other Scions. I grew up in a world filled with men's men. Every male role model I have is a biker, a brother. I'm not saying they're all the same person, because they're not, but my dad and all of my uncles are the same type of man. Strong, independent, but with a viciously loyal streak. Resilient, tough, that's how I'd describe all the men in my life. Those familiar character traits are what drew them all to the Sinners. It's what led them to the loyalty and brotherhood the Sinners stand for.

The closest thing I've ever known to a math geek is Puck and though he might be a tech genius, he's still huge, intimidating, and dangerous. Guys like Kent—skinny guys who dress nicely and style their hair with more than water—have just never been a part of my world.

He's nothing like the life I left behind when I moved to Alabama to go to school. He's different and interesting and he has no idea that I'm a Sinners Scion, and even if he did, he probably wouldn't have any idea who the Sinners are.

"What the fuck do you want with Emmy?" Zeke growls, his stance becoming more assertive as he steps forward.

"He's here to pick me up for our date," I say, placing a hand on Zeke's side and pushing him out of the way.

"He's what?" Griff growls, emerging from the kitchen, a half-eaten banana in one hand and a scowl etched across his face.

"Emmy?" Kent mumbles from the porch, his eyes flitting nervously between my two huge pseudo brothers.

"Ignore them," I tell him. "Zeke, Griff, this is my friend Kent. Kent, these two meatheads are my roommates and two of my best friends."

"You live with two guys?" Kent says slowly, eying the posturing men behind me.

"She lives with three guys," Valentine says, walking up behind Kent, a greasy rag in his hands.

"Oh my god," I sigh. "Guys stop it." Pushing past Zeke, I step out onto the front porch and reach for Kent's arm. "Kent, let's go."

"Err," he says again, his eyes darting between all three guys in turn, his complexion turning a little green beneath their hostile scrutiny.

"Wait," Valentine hisses, crossing his arms across his chest and widening his stance as both Zeke and Griff step onto the front porch and surround us.

Griff steps forward and pulls me back, wrapping an arm around my waist and dragging me back into his body. "When did you two meet and where are you going?" He demands.

Kent looks at me, and swallows nervously before turning his attention back to Griff. "We met in the library."

Pushing futilely at Griffin's arm that's locked around my waist, I smile at Kent. "I'm so sorry about this, they're being Neanderthals," I say, apologetically. "Griffin Elijah Bennett, let me go," I seethe, twisting my head to glare up at him.

His grip tightens for a brief moment then loosens enough for me to push his arm away and spin around to face him.

"I'm not happy about this *Emmy Grace Devereaux*." Griff snarls right back, his eyes narrow in anger. "You've never even mentioned this guy's name and you want us to let you disappear with him."

Crossing my arms across my chest, I hiss angrily. "Firstly, you're not *letting* me do anything, because you're not my dad, or my keeper, and secondly I don't have to tell you about every new person I meet, or chose to go out with, because again, you're not my dad or my keeper. Now I'm going to leave before you do or say something to piss me off even more than you guys behaving this way already has." Glaring at Griff, I turn to both Zeke and Valentine in turn, narrowing my eyes in warning.

"I'll see you all later," I say, grabbing Kent's arm and pulling him away from my annoying, overprotective friends.

"I'm so sorry about them. They're so embarrassing." I say, walking slightly ahead of him, toward the shiny unfamiliar Mercedes that's parked at the curb. "Is this your car?" I ask, looking at the almost brand-new model.

"Yes, it was a graduation present from my parents," Kent says quietly, reaching into the pocket of his crisply pressed blue khakis and pulling out a key. The car beeps and I climb into the passenger seat as he strides around to the driver's door and clambers in.

I pretend I don't hear his slightly shaky inhale of breath as he closes the driver's door behind him and starts the engine. Internally cursing, I look out of the window, my eyes landing on Zeke, Griffin, and Valentine; the three of them looking huge and intimidating with matching scowls on their faces as they watch the car pull away from the house.

Kent doesn't speak again as he drives us to the restaurant a few blocks away, and the silence becomes almost palpable as we enter the steak house and follow the overly bright server to a table in the back. I wish I was a little more experienced with guys, at least then I'd know if this date is beyond redemption, or if this strained silence will fade once we order.

"What can I get you both to drink?" The Suzie Sunshine server asks.

"I'll have a beer please," Kent says.

"Sweet tea, if you have it please," I say.

She hands us a menu each, her perma-smile still firmly fixed in place. "I'll be right back with your drinks," she says, as she turns and practically skips away.

"So, you live with three guys?" Kent says slowly.

"And a girl."

"Three guys and a girl?"

"Yep. Nova who you didn't meet is Zeke's sister, and her and Valentine are a couple."

"And Zeke and the other guy are?"

"Family. I actually come from a really big family, lots of aunts and uncles that aren't actually related to me," I say, cringing at how bizarre that sounds. "I've known Nova, Zeke, and Griffin my entire life. Valentine is my aunt and uncle's adoptive son."

Kent nods slowly, obviously trying to join together the tenuous links between me and my pseudo siblings. "And you're all at school at Hayhurst together?"

I nod. "Yeah, we decided that we wanted to go to the same school and it just made sense for us to live together, rather than end up living with strangers if we moved into the dorms."

"Wow, you all must be really close," Kent says, his eyes widening slightly as he leans back in his chair.

"We are. Like I said, they're my family."

Kent nods again, a little easier this time and a small smile graces his lips. "They seem a little overprotective," he says mockingly.

I can't help the laugh that slips from my lips. "Yeah, my

dad worries and I'm fairly sure he made the guys promise to look after me."

Kent's expression softens and his shoulders visibly relax. "My parents worry about me too. I guess that comes from being an only child."

"Do you have cousins that you're close to?"

"Nope, I'm the only grandchild on both sides. I have an aunt, but she never had any kids. It's just me," Kent says with a shrug.

"Wow, you must have been lonely growing up." The idea of not having a big family is unthinkable. They might drive me mad at times and I might choose to spend time away from them to relax, but I can't imagine my life without them.

Kent shrugs again. "I guess so, but I've never known any different. Plus, I had friends so it wasn't too bad."

I nod, just as the server returns with our drinks. She takes our food order then leaves. Unsure what to say, Kent and I fall into a weird silence. This is the first real date I've ever been on and I'm not sure what we should be talking about. I mean do I make small talk? If he asks about my parents, do I admit that my dad is the head of a biker club and my mom is a genius who makes money for a living?

From the very little I know about him, Kent and I don't really have that much in common. He's a sophomore, he's already declared his major as math with a statistics focus, and he lives in the dorms with a roommate called Devon. I'm a freshman who loves books but has absolutely no idea what I want to major in or do for the rest of my life.

"So what made you decide to come to Hayhurst?" Kent asks, thankfully breaking the silence and the chaotic ramblings of my inner thoughts.

I wanted to go to a school far enough away from home that no one here would have any idea who I was. But it turns out me and my friends are so codependent, that we all secretly applied to the same schools so we could stay together, I think, but thankfully don't say aloud.

"We made a pro/con list for all the schools we got accepted to, and Hayhurst came out on top. We actually took a road trip out to see the campus and we all fell in love with the place." I tell him.

"A road trip sounds fun. I came and did the campus tour with my folks. We toured like eight schools."

"Are you close with your parents?" I ask.

"Really close. They hate that I'm so far away, but Hayhurst is my dad's alma mater so he was pretty stoked that I decided to come here."

The easy conversation makes me relax and by the time the server brings our food I'm starting to enjoy myself.

"Is Emmy short for anything?" Kent asks, cutting into his steak.

"Nope, it's just Emmy. My brother's name is Phoenix, so although Emmy is a little unusual, I'm kind of glad I got the relatively normal name."

Kent laughs and I take the moment to enjoy how cute he is in his white oxford, blue tie and blue cardigan. I'm not sure I've ever seen a real-life guy in a cardigan before, but with his preppy style he totally pulls it off. Kent is put together in a way I'm not used to. Zeke and Griffin are hot in an athletic, rugged way, and Valentine exudes angry bad boy. My family are all about the biker chic and the guys I went to school with were more country than country club. But I think I like Kent's look, it's definitely different and different is exactly what I'm looking for.

The food is good, the company better, and when our dessert plates are empty, we agree to split the check and get ready to leave. As I place my cash down on top of Kent's, a frisson of excitement rushes through me.

To some girls going Dutch would feel like an insult, but to me, a guy not insisting he pay is kind of awesome. Even when we go out as a group, the guys almost always pay for everything, refusing any money that Nova and I try to put in, and it drives us crazy. I have my own money; I definitely don't need a man to pay for me, and honestly it just feels like an archaic tradition that annoys the crap out of me.

If I was in a relationship, like a serious relationship, then it wouldn't matter who put the cash down, because our money would be ours, not mine or his. But this is a first date, and I refuse to start anything, even a friendship, with someone who thinks they have to coddle me because I'm not capable of looking after myself.

We leave the restaurant and Kent motions for me to lead the way. The smile that spreads across my face is so wide I think I might hurt myself. This is exactly why I know that a biker isn't for me. No self-respecting Sinner would take his old lady out and not pay; no way would he walk behind, letting her potentially step first into danger—even though ninety-nine percent of the time there's no danger to worry about. My dad and every single one of my uncles worship the ground their wives walk on; they smother them with love and adoration and protect them with an intensity that's beautiful but also ridiculous.

My mom and aunts tolerate their caveman behavior and I just don't get it. How can they stand to have their guys turn up at every girl's night, just to make sure no one hits on them? How can they tolerate being told what to do and ordered around? How does it not make them want to run in the opposite direction of the insane claustrophobic love?

I asked Mom about it once and she just smiled and told

me that it drove her mad, but that she loved the intensity with which my dad loves her. That when I fell for someone, truly fell in love, I'd understand, and instead of resenting their obsessive possessiveness, I'd cherish that intensity. A part of me thinks she could be right, but the majority of me knows she's not, that I never want a man to feel that way about me.

When we exit the restaurant, Kent walks by my side, his khakis still unwrinkled. I watch surreptitiously as he lifts his hand, then lets it drop to his side, only to lift it again a moment later. My brow furrows as I try to decide what he's doing. Is he talking himself into something? Taking my hand maybe?

We reach the car before I can figure out what exactly it was he was doing and I open the passenger door and climb in while he walks around to the driver's side and settles into the seat. He glances at me and smiles shyly before he presses the engine start button and the car burbles to life. I've got nothing against Mercedes, in fact this one is very nice and still has that new car smell, but the biker's daughter in me internally weeps over the fact that the engine is so quiet you can barely even hear it. A wave of homesickness washes over me as I think about riding on my dad's bike or in my mom's beautiful Comet and listening to the rumble of the engine beneath the hot Texas sun.

It might not be what I want my future to look like, but it was a good life and sometimes I let my yearning for something more push those good memories aside. I lose myself in thoughts of the wind in my hair, asphalt rushing beneath me, and the freedom and adventure that's always there on the back of a bike.

Pulled back to the present, I take a moment to look at the boy driving the silent car and wonder if he plans to kiss me tonight. It won't be my first kiss, that went to Griffin when we were eleven. I smile unbidden at the memory that only feels like it was weeks, not years ago. We'd been at the club at a BBQ or some event, I don't really remember. He'd grabbed my hand and pulled me along, laughing as we ran behind the clubhouse to the yard at the back.

I'd let him drag me behind him, happy to go on whatever adventure he'd got planned. Only instead of climbing on the roof, or sneaking into the barn or Grandpop's office, he'd pulled me close.

"This is our future, Emmy. This place will be ours when we're older," he'd said.

I'd laughed, thinking it was silly to think about being grown up. Then he'd leaned in and pressed his lips to mine. I'd been so shocked I just stood there and let him kiss me, right up until he pushed his tongue into my mouth, then I'd tentatively kissed him back.

My cheeks heat as I think about that day, that kiss, the way he'd pulled back and looked at me with such intensity that I'd worried he'd never be my friend again. That's how Zeke had found us, our lips pressed together, Griff's arm holding me tightly. He shouted so loud, we'd lurched apart and I'd run away, confused and flustered as the boys yelled at each other.

Still to this day neither of them have ever told me what happened after I ran, but I know they refused to speak to each other for a week and both had cuts on their knuckles and bruises on their faces.

That was the first and only time I've ever been kissed. Until today… maybe.

The car journey goes too fast and I'm still lost in my memories when we pull up to the curb outside the house. I pause, waiting for him to turn off the engine and open his door, only he doesn't. I wasn't planning to invite him in, but the fact that he doesn't even plan to walk me to my front door irks me a little.

"I had a nice time tonight," I say, my voice laced with uncertainty as I unclip my seatbelt and reach down for my purse.

"I had a good time too." Kent says, barely glancing at me.

I smile, but it feels a little strained. "I should go in," I say, glancing over my shoulder at the house behind me.

"Okay."

Disappointment seeps into me. I like Kent. I thought he liked me too, but instead of kissing me, he's sending me on my way without even turning off the engine of the car. How did I get this so wrong? Twisting in my seat, I pull the handle and open the car door, climbing out as quickly as I can.

"Emmy," Kent calls.

A surge of something that feels a lot like hope bursts to life and I lean down into the car.

"Don't forget your cardigan," he says with a smile, pointing at my cardigan still on the car seat.

"Thanks," I say, barely holding in my grimace as I grab the soft wool and pull it to my chest, slamming the door behind me. Inhaling sharply, I roll back my shoulders and strut up the path to my front door, adding a little swing to my hips like I've seen my mom do a hundred times before.

What the hell just happened? I might be inexperienced with men, but seriously. After a rough start the rest of the date went well, then that. He didn't even turn off the engine, just sat at the curb with it idling and drove away before I even opened my door.

What a douche!

God, listen to me. I'm applauding that I got to pay for half my dinner, then moaning that he didn't walk me to the door; double standards or what? I'm the worst feminist in the world, but the truth is that I'm disappointed. I thought, oh I'm not sure what I thought, but obviously I was wrong.

For a moment I just stand and stare at the front door, actually questioning if I did something wrong. Then I mentally slap myself for assuming *I* did something wrong. *If he's not interested then that's his loss, I'm a catch*, I internally mock. A bubble of laughter spills from my lips as I push the door open and walk into the house. I can hear the TV on in the living room, so I kick off my shoes and walk toward the noise. Nova is in Valentine's lap, with Griff and Zeke at either end of the couch while they all watch some action movie on the TV. When they hear me, they turn as one and four sets of eyes stare at me with a mixture of excitement, intrigue, and… sadness?

Before I get a chance to question those looks, Nova jumps up from her spot and rushes toward me, an excited grin spread across her face. When she reaches me, she grabs my arms and shakes me. "So how was it? Tell me everything. Starting with why you didn't tell me you were going on a date and why none of us have ever heard you mention this guy before."

I sigh, wishing I could disappear and hide in my room with my book. In my books no one has bad dates that end in the guy practically running away at the end of the night. For a moment I resent her being here, all of them being here to witness this. If I'd gone to Dartmouth like I'd planned, they would never know about my disastrous date. They wouldn't know anything about my life.

"Oh no," Nova gasps, pulling me back to the moment and away from my mean and unnecessary thoughts. "What happened?"

Her eyes soften at my sigh and I remember why I'm in Alabama with my best friends and not on the east coast on my own. Nova experiences my highs and lows alongside me, just like I do for her and for the boys too. These people are my family and they celebrate my joy and commiserate my sadness as if it were their own. We're all here together because when it comes down to it, we don't want to be alone in the big bad world. We all crave the support and unending love we have always given each other.

Denying my first instinct to retreat into my own head and hide in my bedroom, I let her drag me to the couch and smile as she shoos Zeke over so she can pull me down to sit next to her.

"Was it bad? I'm so sorry, sweetie. In future you need to have a code word, then if it's terrible or the guy is a dud, you can just text one of us and we'll know to call you and fake an emergency so you can leave."

A laugh bursts from me. "That's not a real thing, people only do that in the movies."

She waves me off dismissively, "Stop stalling. What happened? Why was it bad?"

"It wasn't bad. In fact, it was good, or at least it was once I explained who the three meathead idiots circling him when he came to pick me up were."

"We're not meatheads," Zeke protests.

"Shush," Nova hisses at her brother. "So if it was good, why do you look perplexed and sad?"

"I'm not perplexed," I argue.

She silences me with an arched eyebrow.

"Okay, so maybe I am. After the showdown at the house it was super awkward. He drove us to dinner and when we got to the table, I really thought it was going to be a total disaster. I told him about you guys and our family. Obviously not who we are or the club or anything, just you know, that we're really close and that we decided to all go to school here together. Then it was good; we ate, we chatted, and it all seemed to be going really well. He's really sweet, an only child, a math major, and this is his sophomore year. We had dessert, then we split the bill."

"OHHHHH," Griff and Zeke hiss in unison, interrupting me.

"What?"

"He let you pay half the bill," Zeke says, outrage clear in his tone.

"Yeah, so? This is 2019, asshole, women pay their own way," I growl.

"Em, I get that. I'm totally a feminist, woman are powerful equals. I'd wear the t-shirt. But a guy asks you out on a date then he should pay. That's just how it is." Zeke growls.

I look to Griffin, then Valentine and find them both nodding in agreement. "You guys are cavemen. That's not how it should be. I'm more than happy to pay my share of the bill."

"Okay, whatever," Nova says impatiently. "What happened after that?"

"Nothing happened."

"What?" She squeaks.

"Exactly! That's the thing. Nothing happened. He drove me home, pulled up outside the house, and I got out and left."

Her brow wrinkles in confusion. "Did you freak?"

I scoff. "No, I didn't freak. I told him I had a great time, he agreed, then I got out of the car and left."

"He didn't try to kiss you?"

"Nope."

"Did you give him the chance, or did you bolt out of the car?"

"I gave him chance! He barely looked in my direction. He

kept the engine running and then drove off when I stepped onto the porch."

"Oh," she says, her lips falling into a frown, as sympathy fills her eyes.

Groaning, I let my head fall back against the couch. "This is why I don't date."

"Fuck him. If he's too much of an idiot to realize he should he worshipping at your feet, he's not good enough for you anyway." Valentine says, his voice sincere.

"Urgh, you have to say stuff like that," I moan, rubbing at my temples with my fingertips.

"He's saying it because it's true, shortcake. You're perfect, and if that preppy little motherfucker can't see that, then it's because he's not the guy for you." Griff growls.

GRIFFIN

What are the laws surrounding murdering stupid little assholes in Alabama? I don't give a fuck. Whatever the consequences, I'll deal if I get a chance to get my hands on the stupid fucking bastard who took out my girl and then ditched her at the curb like a fucking whore.

Hell no. Hell fucking no.

It was bad enough that we had no idea she was going on a date with this kid. She hasn't said a thing, and now this. He didn't open her car door, we watched; he didn't pay for their meal. He's so stupid, he doesn't even know how much a gem he just made feel like shit.

I'm going to kill him; I'm going to fucking kill him.

My anger is barely hidden beneath the surface of my skin and I'm two seconds away from losing my shit completely and kidnapping her to keep her in my room and away from jackasses who shouldn't be touching her anyway.

I'm losing her. I can see it happening in slow motion. The girls she's made friends with sound okay. She's been out with them a couple of times, although she still hasn't introduced them to us. But now this guy. He's skinny and he was wearing a tie for fuck's sake. It's a Wednesday night and he's wearing a tie.

His Mercedes was pretty sweet, but I bet it was an auto. Everyone knows real men drive stick if they don't ride a bike. I hate the stupid motherfucker.

He can't have her. I can't lose her. I won't lose her.

EMMY

My cell starts ringing and I lift my head from the couch, eyeing my purse on the coffee table. "I should get that," I say, dragging my purse toward me and pulling my cell from it. "It's Kent," I say aloud to the room.

Nova claps. "Answer it."

"Don't answer it," Zeke spits. "He had his chance, he blew it. Block his number, he's a pussy."

"I should answer it, right?" I ask.

"Yes," Nova says, at the same time the guys all say, "No," in unison.

I stare at my cell for a long moment, then on impulse I hit answer. "Hello."

"I'm sorry," Kent says, before I even finish speaking.

I swallow, not entirely sure what to say.

"I'm so sorry. I panicked and I was an asshole and I'm so fucking sorry."

Swallowing, I lift my gaze and find four sets of eyes watching me as they listen intently.

"Emmy?" Kent asks and I realize I haven't actually spoken yet.

"I'm here," I say, turning away from my audience and walking into the kitchen.

"Did I ruin this?" He asks and his voice is so earnest that I soften a little.

"I'm not sure. You're kind of giving me mixed signals here, Kent."

"I panicked. I haven't really ever dated and I wasn't sure if I was supposed to kiss you, or if you wanted me to kiss you, so I panicked. God, I didn't even walk you to your door," he says, mortification clear in his voice.

A giggle escapes me before I can stop myself.

"Are you laughing at me?"

"A little, yeah." I admit.

"Can you come outside?"

"Why?" I ask, darting to the kitchen window that looks out over the street and spotting his car at the curb with him leaning against it.

"I'd like to try that goodnight again, if that'd be okay?"

I pause, unsure what to do. Kent's cute, but tonight, him driving away, hurt my feelings a little and I don't like that feeling.

"Please, Emmy."

The sadness in his tone melts my resolve and my feet move without my permission. A moment later I'm at the front door, pushing it open and stepping onto the porch. His eyes lock with mine and a hint of a smile graces his lips. He watches as I take a couple of steps toward him, my feet bare, my cell gripped tightly in my hand at my side.

I walk a few more steps, then wait, unwilling to make all the effort. Kent looks up at me and smiles shyly, closing the distance between us and reaching for my hand. His fingers wrap around mine and he lifts my hand up to his lips and kisses it lightly. "I had a really great time tonight with you, Emmy," he says against my skin.

"I had a good time too," I confess quietly.

"I'm so sorry for leaving before. Hopefully, this good-night can eradicate the last one from your memory, because I'd really like to take you out again, if you'll let me?"

"I think I'd like that," I whisper.

Still holding my hand, Kent leans in and kisses my cheek. It's sweet and chaste and kind of perfect.

"Goodnight, Emmy."

"Goodnight, Kent," I say, pulling my hand free when his grip loosens and turning and heading for the house. Stepping inside, I pull the door closed behind me and rest my back against it, letting a small smile spread across my lips.

"That was so sweet," Nova says, her head appearing around the doorjamb.

I nod, still smiling.

"Are you going to go out with him again?"

I nod again.

Her lips spread into a wide grin, her shoulders lifting up as she squeals excitedly.

Rolling my eyes at her behavior, I shake my head as I push off the door and move past her. "I'm going to bed."

"Sweet dreams," she singsongs, giggling.

My steps feel light and my smile hopeful as I climb the stairs to my bedroom. Stripping out of my clothes I slide on a tank top and loose flannel shorts then climb into bed, flopping down on my back, my head nestled in the pile of pillows I sleep with.

Staring up at the ceiling above me, I allow my smile to get a little wider. That goodbye was so much better than the first one. He didn't kiss me properly, but what he did was almost better. A knock sounds at my door and I drop my gaze from the ceiling. "Yeah?"

"It's me, can I come in?"

"Sure," I call, shuffling a little further up my pillow pile until my shoulders are propped up.

The door slowly pushes open and Griff walks into the room, crossing to the bed and flinging himself down onto my comforter with enough force that I bounce. "Hey," I cry, shoving at his shoulder as he wedges his huge body next to mine, unbalancing me and making me fall into his chest.

"You okay?" He asks.

"I was until you and your huge ass jumped onto my bed."

Griff chuckles but doesn't move; he only lifts his arm and motions for me to snuggle into him. I pause for a second, then rest my head against his chest as he wraps his arm around me. "What did *Kent* want?" He asks, saying Kent's name with an edge of anger.

"To apologize."

"I hope you told him to go fuck himself, the kid seems like a dick."

"He's hardly a kid. He's older than us, he's a sophomore," I say against his chest.

"He looked like a pussy and from what you said he behaved like a pussy."

"He's not a pussy, he's just not like you. Normal guys are like that, normal guys aren't bikers," I say, rolling my eyes even though he can't see from my position pressed against him.

"We're Sinners, no point pretending to be something we're not," he says quietly.

"Don't you ever want anything else? Don't you want to see what the world's like when you're just you? When you're not Griffin the Scion, the Sinner prospect; when you're just Griffin Bennett?"

"I know who I am, Emmy. I don't need to play pretend and try to be something I'm not or hide the separate parts of me. I'm Griffin Bennett when I'm on the field playing football, I'm Griffin Bennett when I'm at the club with my brother and when I'm at your house talking to your dad about prospecting. I'm the same person right now, lying in bed with you. Distance doesn't make you a different person, or at least it shouldn't."

I stay quiet, because I don't know how to respond to that. I wish I felt that way, that I was the same person back home as I am here, but I don't know how to be that at peace with myself. I need to split myself up into little sections, so I know how to deal with the different aspects of my life. Here at Hayhurst I can't be a Scion because no one has any idea who the Sinners are and I'm glad of that. Back home I'm the daughter of the president of the Doomsday Sinners MC. I'm feared and revered, but I don't really know how to play that part either.

It dawns on me that I don't really know who I am in either part of my life, and if I don't know who I am, how do I know when I'm pretending?

Griff's grip on me tightens and I respond by snuggling a little deeper into the nook of his arm, needing his familiar, reassuring presence.

"Why didn't you tell us about him? Even Nova had no idea."

"I don't really know," I admit.

He sighs and I feel his chest rise and fall beneath me. "I know you struggle sometimes with being..." He pauses as if he's choosing his words carefully, and I stiffen, unsure where he's going with this. "I know that sometimes you just want to be on your own, and I respect that, we all do. We get that you probably find being a Scion the hardest out of all of us, even Nova. But I'm not going to let you push us away because you want this fancy new life where everything is the opposite of how we do it back home."

"That's not what I'm doing," I cry, pushing up from his chest and locking my eyes with his.

"It's exactly what you're doing, but I'm not going to let you. Every time you try to change who you are, your roots, I'm going to remind you of the Emmy I know and the world we thrive in." His eyes are blazing, his lips pulled into a firm line.

I shake my head and open my mouth to deny his words, but before my lips have fully parted, he flips so my back is against the mattress, his huge body hovering over me.

"College boy said goodnight with his lips on your hand and a chaste peck on your cheek. But Sinners say goodnight like this." Then his lips descend to mine.

For a moment I'm too shocked to do anything but lie there and let him kiss me, his mouth pressed against mine, his fingers tangled in my hair. His hand slides along my ribs, grazing the side of my breast and I gasp. Teeth nip at my lower lip and I open my mouth, not pushing him away when his eager tongue tangles with mine.

Without thought, I kiss him back, my hands gripping his strong shoulders and clinging to him as he devours my mouth with his. This is nothing like our first kiss all those years ago, but I feel as dizzy now as I did back then. His tongue slides along mine, caressing it before sucking on it lightly and forcing a moan to slip from me.

The sound is feral and raw and if I hadn't felt it escape me, I'd deny I could ever make that noise. Griff's lips move against mine one last time before he pulls back and ends the kiss, leaving me breathless and dazed.

"That's how we kiss back home, shortcake. Like the world is ending and it might be our last chance. When a Sinner kisses his woman, he wants her to know whose lips were pressed against her, he wants her to feel that kiss for hours so when she climbs into bed no one else is on her mind or in her dreams." Griffin growls against my ear, then he lifts off me, climbs off my bed and walks to the door.

Opening it, he turns back, his arms braced against the doorjamb. "We're Sinners, Emmy. The next generation, the future. You can try to change, be someone different, but when it comes down to it deep inside where the real you lives, you'll always be one of us. You'll always be a Sinner," he drawls, winking at me with a roguish grin on his face before he steps into the hall, closing my door behind him.

Exhaling a ragged breath, I stare at my closed door with my heart racing in my chest. Griffin just kissed me.

Why would he do that? Why would he kiss me? My mind feels like a jagged mess, but my lips are still tingling. I shouldn't have enjoyed it. He's my family, my best friend. But the way he kissed me felt nothing like I've ever imagined, and if it was wrong, why is my heart still beating erratically in my chest, and why do I want him to kiss me again?

GRIFFIN

I shouldn't have done that. Fuck, I shouldn't have done that. But I can't even regret it because nothing has felt so right to me since I was eleven years old and kissing her for the very first time. I stole her first kiss that day all those years ago, I stole her next kiss just now, and I'm not even slightly ashamed.

Emmy Grace Devereaux is it for me. My perfect other half, my soulmate. I knew it the very first time I met her at eight years old and I know it now. All those years ago Zeke caught me kissing her and he told me she could never be mine; that she was Prez's daughter, off-limits in the most extreme way, and I accepted that. She's too good for me, always has been. But I've never moved on. How do you move on from perfection?

Fuck, I can feel her lips against mine, the taste of her still in my mouth. I shouldn't have kissed her, but now I've done it, now I've touched her like she's mine, I'm not sure I can stop myself from doing it again.

Pushing through my bedroom door, I close it behind me

and turn the lock. I need that barrier between us, a physical reminder that I can't go back in there and really make her mine. As the reality of what I just did dawns on me, I slide down the door until my butt hits the floor. My head falls into my hands and a wave of panic rolls through me as I clutch at my hair.

I want her so much my heart aches for her, my body longs for her, and my soul breaks over and over every single day that she's not mine. A part of me is missing. It was lost when my parents died. I'm incomplete and empty, until I'm near her. When she touches me, it's like the world is brighter, louder, more impactful. She's the sunshine on a cloudy day, the moon in the black of night; she's everything and she should be mine, she's always been mine.

It's been getting harder and harder to hide my feelings for her since we came away to school. Back home she didn't look at other guys. She was so introverted, so suspicious of everyone that she went through life with blinkers, assuming that because she wasn't seeing them that they weren't seeing her.

But they saw her, they all did, and when they looked twice, I threatened to beat the shit out of them. Keeping assholes away from my girl has become my life's work, and in Archer's Creek every single fucker who even thought about looking at her knew she was untouchable. I might not be able to claim her, but I sure as shit wasn't letting anyone else have what's mine.

I never anticipated that college would be a whole new world. No one here knows who we are, they aren't scared of us, and I can't keep them all away. The night of the frat party, when she came down wearing those clothes, so different from the stuff she normally wears, I lost my fucking mind. I went full blown caveman on her and if Zeke hadn't have walked in, fuck knows what would have happened.

Growing up in a biker club is all I've ever known. My parents were bikers and I was raised in the club. When they died, I moved in with Duke, and the Archer's Creek Sinners all took on the role of parents. I might have lived with my brother until we came to Hayhurst, but I have my own room at Zeke and Nova's place and between them and my other unofficial aunties and uncles, I was surrounded by family.

The Sinners saved my life. They took me in, made me family, and kept me on the straight and narrow. I owe them everything. I'm a Sinner to my very fucking core and Sinners look after their own.

A wry laugh slips from my lips and I lift my head up, letting it fall back against the door with a thud. I'm not sure they'd all think of me as family if they knew I was jonesing for Prez's baby girl. I found my perfect woman when I was eight years old, and since that day I've been pretending that she's nothing more than a friend.

I've kept myself under control for a decade; the only time I've ever slipped was the day I kissed her, until now. I can stop myself from touching her, I can stop myself from acting on my feelings for her, or at least I always could. But seeing that guy here for her tonight, seeing him touching her, kissing her, it snapped something inside of me, broke my resolve and destroyed my control.

I'm not good enough for her, I'm not the future she wants, but I can't lose her. I'll become a black hole of nothingness without her. So maybe it's time to fight.

Emmy thinks that people don't see her, that they overlook her to look at Nova, but she couldn't be any further from the truth. I love Nova, she's my sister, and she's gorgeous. But Emmy, she's more than just a pretty face, she's ethereal. She's the kind of outrageously stunning that makes you blink and look again to make sure she's actually real.

Emmy draws people in, but the moment they meet her they know that she's destined for bigger and better things. Maybe I'm an asshole for keeping guys away from her, but I know that if they had a chance, if they had even one taste, took one step too close, they'd be ensnared, captured in her thrall and never want to leave.

Emmy's a siren and she caught me when we were only kids. I'd been living with Duke for a few days, barely coping with the fact that both of my parents were dead. I remember her finding me sat on the porch of Duke's shitty little house. The moment her tiny yellow sneakers had appeared next to me I'd tried to wipe the tears from my cheeks, not wanting the pretty girl to see me cry. She hadn't said anything, hadn't asked me if I was okay; she'd just sat down next to me on the step, a huge book clutched to her chest and rested her head on my shoulder.

At eight years old I'd thought girls had cooties, but this girl, she took my breath away even back then. I can still remember the way her hair had tickled my cheek when I'd rested my head against hers, the way she smelled like cotton candy. She didn't say anything, she just sat next to me, her head on my shoulder, while I silently cried. I think I fell in love with her that moment and I've been in love with her for every moment since then.

Another laugh slips from my lips, but it changes to a raw broken noise that comes from the back of my throat when I think about losing her to some other guy. I can't watch her make a life with someone other than me. I can't watch her fall in love with someone else. I just can't.

Covering my lips with my hand, I stifle the animalistic growl that's bursting from me. I'm not this guy, I'm the happy-go-lucky joker. I'm the light-hearted, doesn't take anything serious guy. Only I'm not that person. That's who I want to be. But in reality, I'm the guy who is still grieving the loss of my parents. I'm the guy who will never be whole, who will never be truly happy, because they're gone and I don't know how to move on, to move forward.

I'm not saying I'm a broken, fucked up mess, because I'm not. I have a great family; without them I have no fucking clue what kind of nightmare I'd have become. But Duke's just as lost without Mom and Dad as I am. The two of us are adrift, anchorless, and it sucks, but at least neither of us are alone with our unending grief.

The Archer's Creek Sinners are nothing at all like the club Duke and I grew up in; the club my dad was the president of. They weren't a family like the AC chapter are and I'm so fucking grateful for the life I've had, but it will all be completely worthless if she isn't in it.

Emmy's my tether, my anchor, my axis, and she has no idea.

The summer between junior and senior year I thought I was losing her. She hid herself in a world of make believe, making elaborate plans for a new life for herself. What I'll never admit to anyone, is that as she was making plans to run as far from us as possible, I was making plans to chase her.

I've never been Ivy League material, but I applied to every school that was close to the schools she dreamed of. She might have been planning to leave us all behind, but I was never going to let her.

Since the day I realized what love was, I've known that Emmy is it for me and a part of me has always hoped that she might feel the same way. She's never dated, never had a boyfriend, never kissed, never snuggled with anyone but me.

But now there are guys pouring from every fucking nook and cranny and they want her, they all want her.

First there was that guy at the frat party. I couldn't even look at the way he was dancing with her, dancing with my girl. I'd been on the verge of killing him when I just couldn't take it anymore and I had to touch her, to claim her and make sure everyone there knew she was mine. Now there's this guy: the preppy, weedy little motherfucker who stole her first date from me.

I want to hunt him down and beat the living shit out of him. Pound his fucking face until he understands that she's mine and he can't have her. But instead of beating up assholes who think they can make a play for my girl, I'm here on the floor of my room wallowing in self-pity.

Did I miss my chance to make her mine? The thought hits me like a tsunami and pain lances through my heart. I don't know how to see a future where she belongs to someone else, where I belong to anyone but her.

My door ricochets when a fist hits the wood. "Open up, asshole." Zeke demands, his voice a growl.

Forcing myself up, I turn the lock, then step away from the door, retreating to my bed and slumping down onto it, loss and empty fucking broken heartedness making my body wilt.

The door swings open, hitting the wall behind it with a bang, as Zeke stomps into my room, taking in my pathetic appearance. "Jesus fucking Christ," he snarls. Turning, he slams the door shut, strides over to me and yanks me upright by the front of my shirt. "Snap out of it, asshole."

I don't speak. What is there to say?

"Is this it? You think you deserve her if this is how you are?" He yells, shaking me as he speaks.

I shrug, too annihilated to even respond.

Zeke's fist plows into my face, snapping my head back and jolting me out of my grief filled stupor.

"What the fuck?" I cry.

"You gonna watch her get with some pussy ass little motherfucker who drives a Mercedes?"

I don't speak. What the fuck does he want me to say? He's the one who told me I couldn't ever have her.

He punches me again and I feel my skin split, blood pooling on my lip before dripping down my chin. "You gonna let her leave us, ride off into the sunset with some asshole who can't even open a fucking door for her? You gonna let that fucker in the tie and cardigan climb between her legs and take her virgin pussy?"

A growl comes from the back of my throat, bursting out in a warning that sounds feral even to my own ears.

"She'll leave us. She thinks she wants something different, something other than the Sinners. She wants to be invisible, but we both know she's all most people see." Zeke hisses, baiting me.

Pressing my lips together, I fight the words that want to get free, the words that will claim her, tell the entire fucking world that she's mine and that no one will ever take her from me.

Zeke smiles, an evil, chilling smile. "Maybe you're not man enough to claim her. Maybe I should show her what her life would be like if she embraced her heritage instead of hiding from it. I could be the one to make her mine."

Ripping myself from his grip, I tackle him to the ground, my fist meeting his face again and again. "You touch her, and I'll fucking kill you. I'll rip your fucking dick off and shove it down your throat if you even look at her as anything other than a sister. She's mine, she has been our entire fucking lives. Mine."

His laugh breaks through my anger, and my fist pauses midair as I look down at my best friend. Blood coats his teeth, his lip's split, and his nose is bleeding. Pushing off him, I roll to the side and sit beside him, wiping at the blood on my own face with the back of my hand.

Zeke sits up and pulls at the hem of his t-shirt to dab at the blood running freely from his face. "You ready to admit you're in love with her now?" He asks, turning to look at me.

"How did you know?"

He laughs. "You're a fucking idiot. I've known how you felt about her since we were eleven years old. You're not exactly discreet."

I snap my head to the side, my eyes wide with horror. "She knows?"

He shakes his head, chuckling beneath his breath. "She hasn't got a fucking clue."

"I kissed her tonight," I admit, not sure why I'm telling him.

"Finally."

"She doesn't want me," I say, exhaling wearily.

"She tell you that?"

"No."

"She kiss you back?"

I nod once, brisk and assertive.

Zeke smiles and the blood from his lip makes his teeth look pink. "So what you gonna do?"

"I have no fucking clue."

EMMY

I stare at my closed bedroom door long after he's left.

Griff just kissed me.

Griffin just kissed me.

Griffin Elijah Bennett just fucking kissed me.

I wait for my brain to process it, for my mind to figure out what the hell just happened and tell me how to feel about it, but ten minutes later, my eyes are still fixated on the door he just left through and all I can hear and see and feel is static.

Logically, I know I should be horrified that he kissed me, because he's my friend, my best friend, my family. Right?

Logic, yep, that's the way I should be feeling, logical. Only right now, logic feels like something other people have. My mind feels… fuzzy, distorted, like the way your vision gets after a few too many drinks.

I know how I should be feeling, but instead I'm blurred and conflicted and dazed.

Launching myself off my bed, I stomp forward, intent on storming into his bedroom and insisting to know what the hell that was, what the hell he thought he was doing kissing me. Why he just pressed his mouth against mine, why he pushed his tongue between my lips, why he made my heart race, my breath pause. Why he just obliterated my clear logical world into a cascade of chaotic psychedelic mayhem.

When my fingers touch the door handle, the rest of my body freezes, refusing to move forward. I don't know if it's fear or hope or apprehension, but something prevents me from going any further.

Confronting him is a risk. Do I want to know? What if his answer's good, or bad, or something that I just can't handle right now? So instead of plowing forward I step back, my fingers sliding from the door and falling to my sides as I retreat.

The back of my knees hit the bed and as I sink down onto the comforter a blast of Griff's familiar scent fills my nose. Rolling to my side, I curl into a ball and pull my knees up to my chin as tears fill my eyes, slowly rolling down my cheek until they fall onto my pillow. I don't understand what happened tonight, my emotions are so tremulous I have no idea what I'm feeling.

Griff told me that he'd pull me back if I started to pull too far away. Was that kiss his way of reeling me back in? He said that was how a Sinner kissed. Was he just giving me a piece of home, reminding me of my roots as I spread my wings with a guy so far from a Sinner it's ridiculous to even try to compare the two?

Pain stabs behind my ribs and I clutch at my chest over my heart. He wouldn't play with my emotions like that, he wouldn't manipulate me like that, would he? But if that kiss wasn't his way of reminding me of my heritage, or my home, what was it?

Anger builds inside of me, but I push it away. What do I

do if this is all just him manipulating me? Or worse, what do I do if he isn't trying to manipulate me?

Another tear falls from me, adding to the growing damp patch beneath my cheek. I remember the first time I met him; he'd been sat on the porch steps outside his brother's house. Duke had been living in a tiny little place that Nova and I had thought looked like a witch's house, with flaking paint and sagging wooden shutters.

Phoenix had stayed with Mimi, but Mom had said that I needed to go with them because there was a kid the same age as me that they wanted me to meet. They told me he was really sad because his parents had gone to live with the angels. When we'd pulled up outside the house, Griffin was just sat there, staring straight ahead, looking lost.

I remember climbing out the car and just walking straight over to him and sitting down next to him. We didn't speak. I just sat there, then I snuggled a little closer and rested my head against his shoulder, the way I did with my mom when I was sad.

I think I knew even back then that we'd end up being friends, but I had no idea that he'd become one of the most important people in my life. Closing my eyes tightly, a flurry of tears rolls down my face and I lick my lips, tasting the saltiness.

What do I do if this ruins everything? What happens if one kiss changes us all?

I wanted something different, something new, but I can't live in a world where he isn't my friend. The thought of losing him over a stupid kiss makes me want to run back home and hide from this stupid new life I so desperately wanted.

My mind spins from Griff, to Kent. From possessive Sinners kisses to chaste pecks, from bossy dominant men to sweet feminists and back again. How has my first date morphed into all this confusion?

Rolling onto my back, I stare up at the ceiling above me, blinking through gritty eyes. What do I do when I see Griff in the morning? Do I ignore him? Yell at him? Leap into his arms and kiss him again to see if it's as hot as it was tonight? Or do I pretend nothing happened and hope this was all just a blip that neither of us will allow to affect our friendship?

Uncertainty barrels through me so fast I feel dizzy. What about Kent? I like him. He's sweet and nice, really nice and that's good. Right?

I lay awake, just staring at the ceiling for hours. When I finally fall asleep, my dreams are full of conflicting thoughts. My home, my family and Griff; versus a new life, a new home, and maybe Kent. I was so sure that I wanted something new, so why does something so entwined with the life I'm running from feel so right?

Rolling out of bed the next morning, I make my way to the bathroom Nova and I share and quickly shower. I'm the only one of us who has an early class on a Thursday morning, so the house is quiet and still. Nova's official bedroom is next to mine on the top floor of the house, but in reality, she's only spent one night in it after her and Valentine argued back when we first moved in. The rest of the time she stays in Valentine's room, even going as far as moving most of her clothes into his closet.

The pair are disgustingly in love and while I'm happy for them, I can't help feeling a little bit of jealousy too. The way Valentine looks at her, like he worships the ground she walks on, is on the verge of throttling her and is desperate is rip her clothes off all at the same time, makes me a little wistful.

I don't want Valentine, that's not the issue, but I want a guy to want me with the intensity that Valentine wants Nova.

Perhaps Kent could feel that way about me, although he doesn't strike me as the type of guy to be bold and demanding and intense. Kent is shy and sweet and nice and falling in love with him would be easy. A relationship with him would be easy, or at least I think it would. But would it be satisfying? I've always been adamant that I didn't want a guy who would boss me around or be jealous and possessive, but if that's true why does growly caveman Griffin make me feel so confused?

God, I sound ridiculous. I've known Kent for a week; I don't know him anywhere near well enough to be thinking about falling in love with him. I've never even kissed him, and a peck on the cheek definitely doesn't count.

Then there's Griff. He's not nice, or sweet, and falling in love with him is impossible, isn't it? 'Like the world is ending and it might be our last chance. When a Sinner kisses his woman, he wants her to know whose lips were pressed against her, he wants her to feel that kiss for hours so when she climbs into bed no one else is on her mind or in her dreams'. That's what he'd said to me after his lips had been on me, his tongue in my mouth.

Inhaling sharply, I try to banish the image from my head and the words from my mind and think about Kent instead. About how he didn't insist on being the man, how he treated me like an equal. Deep down I know the men in my life don't truly think women are lesser individuals, in fact I'm confident my dad knows my mom is superior to him in most ways. But actions speak louder than words and spending time with Kent made me feel independent and powerful in a way I haven't ever experienced before.

To an outsider, being charmed by a guy who didn't offer to pay, who didn't open doors for me, or behave like a traditional gentleman would seem a bit dumb. But when over the top alpha male behavior has been shoved down your throat your entire life, the alternative is refreshing and charming. Others might long for what I'm so easily dismissing, but this is my life not theirs.

Shaking my head, I try to clear my mind and focus on the present. My cell beeps, signaling that I need to get ready for class, so I walk back into my bedroom and open my closet pulling out my favorite ripped skinny jeans, a white cami, and an oversized check shirt. I get dressed quickly, pausing in front of my dressing table to twist my hair into two braids and slick on some mascara and a little lipgloss, before heading downstairs to our quiet kitchen.

The coffee machine is prepped and ready to go, so I turn it on and eat a quick bowl of cereal while it whistles and glugs, filling the glass pot with rich dark caffeine infused goodness. Every creak and groan the silent house makes has my eyes snapping up to the kitchen doorway. I'm not entirely sure if I want Griffin to come downstairs or not. I'm not ready to talk about the kiss, but I don't know if I can just pretend like nothing happened last night either.

I'd hoped the morning would bring me some clarity, but instead I feel more confused than ever. On one hand I'm starting to find the life I've craved and coveted. I'm here, meeting guys and making new friends, I'm even going to a sorority mixer tonight with Avery. But on the other hand, is the comfort of home, so achingly familiar that it's easy and natural. I'm stuck in the middle, torn between two worlds, two lives, two versions of myself. I thought choosing the new would be easy. I want it, I've wanted it for years, so why am I starting to second guess everything?

How can one kiss be so impactful? The moment I allow my mind to think about Griffin's lips against mine, visions fill my head and butterflies swarm to life in my stomach. I never thought I'd kiss him again, not after that day all those years ago when I gave him my first kiss. He's my constant, my safety net, my roots and I can't imagine any life without him in it.

Clenching my hands into fists, I force the thoughts away. I shouldn't be thinking about Griff, our kiss, or how it might change things. That's a slippery slope, a path that I can choose not to traverse, because changing our status quo could mean risking losing him and that's too great a risk and one I'm just not prepared to take.

Filling my travel mug with coffee, I add creamer, then twist the lid firmly into place and hurry to leave. I'm not late, but the longer I stay in the house, the higher the chance the others might wake up. I can't deal with them right now; I need to center myself just in case I blurt out everything that happened last night the moment I see them.

Pushing through the front door, I allow my smile to break free as I take a deep breath of the crisp cool air. Fall is on its way and I'm excited to experience the seasons in a brand-new place now that the stifling heat of summer is starting to fade.

I wish I had the time to hide in my room and lose myself in a book. It's what I'd normally do when I'm feeling this conflicted. But I'm so busy living and studying and fighting off Griff's constant attempts to stop me from reading that my Kindle has barely been turned on the last couple of weeks. Suddenly, immersing myself in someone else's life feels like exactly what I need and I quickly download the audiobook of a new release I've been looking forward to reading. Sliding my earbuds into place, I close the door behind me and start the short walk to campus. When the first words flow into my ears, I feel some of the tension start to seep from my shoulders. Back home our high school was about five miles out of town and the novelty of actually walking each day hasn't wore off yet. Pulling my backpack a little higher on my shoulders, I drink my coffee and listen to the story start to unfold as I enjoy the peaceful morning.

My cell beeps with an incoming text message, so I slide it from my pocket and click in to read it.

Kent

Good morning :)

A smile spreads across my lips. Kent is just so damn cute.

Emmy

Good Morning

Kent

I had a great time last night. If I promise not to be an idiot will you go out with me again? There's a slam poetry night at the coffee shop on campus this weekend. I'd love for you to come.

I almost choke on my coffee. Slam poetry? Surely that doesn't actually exist outside of Dawson's Creek and angsty arthouse cinema? Is he being serious with his invite? I mean his look is totally hipster, so I suppose a poetry night is kind of appropriate, but still 'slam poetry'? I love books, but I just don't get poetry. It's too highbrow and too open to interpretation for my tastes. A giggle slips from my lips. Maybe slam poetry is really a code name for party or something and I'm just not cool enough to realize it.

Maybe I misread it and it didn't actually say what I think it did? Lifting my cell up I reread the message, concentrating on the screen and not looking where I'm going as I step into the street to cross the road.

I don't see the car until it's almost on me, the blaring

sound of the horn forcing my shocked body into action just in time. Leaping back onto the sidewalk, I stumble, falling backwards onto my butt a second before the car screeches to a stop on top of where I was standing a millisecond before.

My hand snaps up to cover my racing heart and I blow out a shaky breath. There's no doubt in my mind that the car would have hit me if I'd reacted even a second slower. I could have been killed because I was too distracted by my cell and a damn text message to see the car coming.

My vision goes black at the sides, like I'm in a tunnel, and my limbs start to shake. I vaguely hear a car door closing and then someone is in front of me, crouched down and staring at me, concern etched across their face.

He pulls my headphones from my ears. "Shit, are you okay?" The voice sounds vaguely familiar, the tone a warm caress that has me blinking and trying to focus. "Can you hear me? Hey, fucking answer me, now."

The demand finally forces my attention back to the present and my vision clears, the colors of the morning seeping back into my consciousness. "You?" I say, when the person crouched in front of me, his hands cupping my face, finally comes into focus.

"Oh, thank fuck," he growls, relief filling his voice.

Blinking up at him, it takes me a moment to realize why he seems familiar. It's the guy I danced with at the Fresh Meat party, the frat guy that Griff pulled away from me. "You," I say again.

"Van," he says, his brows pulled together, his expression angry.

"Van?" I repeat, still not really processing.

"What the fuck are you doing, stepping into the street without even looking? Are you trying to get yourself killed?"

He shouts, his Alabama accent becoming thicker with his anger.

"I…" I have no idea what to say, because it was stupid and dangerous. "I'm sorry, I'm sorry."

His angry expression softens a little and he stands up, holding out a hand for me to take. I place my fingers in his and he slowly pulls me upright. My knees buckle, still a little shaky. He curls his arm around my waist and pulls me forward until our chests are almost touching. "You okay?"

I nod, each breath in and out building my strength, as the heat of his body starts to filter through my shock.

"Did you hurt yourself when you fell?"

"No, I'm just a little shaken, that's all. Thank you for stopping to check on me."

"I didn't stop to check on you. I stopped to yell at you for almost getting yourself killed," he snaps, his voice becoming angry again. "You need a warning sign hanging around your neck or something. Where the fuck is your merry band of protectors? They were quick enough to step up at the party, but they're not here when you almost get yourself killed."

"Protectors?" I ask dazedly.

"Yeah, the three big dudes you and the other chick were with at the party."

"They're my friends. I don't need protectors."

Van's laugh is low and dry. "Sure as shit acted like your bodyguards… or your boyfriends."

I wrinkle my brow, starting to get annoyed with his tone. "They're not my boyfriends either; they're my friends and they're protective that's all."

He smiles and my stomach flips. "Sure thing, Little Red, whatever you say," he drawls, amusement lacing each word.

The sound makes me bite my lower lip to stop from sighing in response. What the hell is going on with me lately?

Between Kent, Griffin, and this guy, it's like I'm in heat. In the past nineteen years, guys have barely made it onto my radar and now all of a sudden, my body has decided to sit up and take notice.

"Get in the car. I'll give you a ride to school," he orders, squeezing me a little tighter before releasing me completely and taking a step back.

My brow furrows and I shiver a little now I'm no longer engulfed in the warmth of his body. "I'm not going to get in your car."

"Don't argue. I could have killed you and you're still trembling. Get in the car."

I shake my head again. "I'll be fine."

Van growls, then drags his hand through his dirty-blond hair. "You're impossible; just get in the car."

"No," I snap. "I don't know you; you could be a stalker or a serial killer or something."

"Red, if I was a serial killer don't you think instead of rescuing your ass I'd have just let you walk out in front of the car?" he says with an exasperated laugh.

"Look, I appreciate your concern, but I'm fine. I'm sorry I stepped out in front of you. I'll be more careful from now on."

I hear him grumbling beneath his breath as I turn and start to walk away, glancing over my shoulder as he loudly stomps around to the driver's door of his car. For the first time I actually look at his car and my step falters. It's an original Chevrolet Camaro Z28. It's beautiful, absolutely perfect and I want to stroke it or lick it.

My dad might be a biker, but my mom loves vintage and she loves cars. When her business was first successful, she restored a Mercury Comet and even as a kid I fell in love with it. That started my love of cars and this car in front of me is like porn.

The red paint is polished to perfection, shining gloriously in the morning sun. I can't help taking a step toward it and peering in through the window at the black leather seats, the simplicity of the dash and the smooth wooden steering wheel.

As I gawk at the car it takes me a moment to realize that instead of getting in, he appears to be locking it. The keys jangle loudly as he circles the hood and walks intently toward me, reaching down to grab my hand as he unceremoniously pulls me forward.

"What?" I say as he checks for traffic, then tows me into the street and across to the other sidewalk. "What are you doing?" I ask, shocked, but not pulling at his hand to get free. Heat is radiating up my arm from where his fingers are wrapped around mine and it's… nice. No, it's more than nice.

"I'm walking you to school, Little Red, seeing as you don't have any of your harem of bodyguards with you. It looks like the only way to keep you out of trouble is to take care of you myself," he replies flippantly, both amusement and annoyance lacing his voice.

"Why do you keep calling me Little Red? This is hardly a fairytale."

"Because it suits you better than Emmy," he drawls, his accent thick, syrupy, and delicious.

"You remember my name?" I ask, a little shocked considering the party was weeks ago and we only danced for one song.

Sighing, he tilts his head to the side and stares at me. "You're not easily forgotten."

My mouth falls open and I gawp at him. What the hell is happening here? "Err, I'm fine. I can get to school on my own. I mean, don't you need your car?" I mumble.

His smile is indulgent and a little smug. "I can fetch my car later."

"Why are you driving anyway? The frat house is only just off campus?"

"I don't live at the frat," he says, his hand tightening around mine a little as he guides me along the street.

"Oh," I say, not really knowing what else to do.

He slows his pace until it matches mine and he's walking next to me instead of pulling me along. I know I should make him let go of my hand, but walking beside him, his huge hand holding mine and his massive body sheltering me, fills me with a feeling that's both achingly familiar and excitingly new.

We fall silent and I glance up at him, noticing how confident everything about him is. He's not unsure of who he is; he's not a kid who's just figuring himself out. Van seems older, but he can't be that much older than me if he's still a student.

"How old are you?" I blurt.

He stops walking and I realize that we're already at the campus, just outside the main faculty building. He doesn't release his hold on my hand, but he turns to look at me, his stubbled face and amused grin doing nothing to distract from how ruggedly beautiful he is.

"I'm twenty-one. You're what, eighteen, nineteen?"

"Nineteen," I answer.

He nods, lifting his free hand up to stroke my cheek with a single finger. "So young," he whispers.

Then he leans forward and for a moment I think this virtual stranger is going to kiss me. Instead he pulls my cell from the pocket of my jeans and I watch shocked as his fingers move quickly over the screen and a second later music starts to play from his pocket.

"Did you just call yourself from my cell?" I ask incredulous.

"I wanted your number," he answers succinctly, like it's the most obvious thing in the world.

Snatching my cell from his hands, I hold it protectively to my chest. "That's such a dick move," I say scowling at him.

He shrugs, cocking an eyebrow at me without an ounce of remorse. "I'll see you around, Red," he says in his lazy Alabama accent, then turns and stalks back through the entrance gates and out of sight.

What the hell was that? For a second I really thought he was going to kiss me, and I was going to let him. What's happening to me? Back home if a guy, regardless of how hot he was, had leaned in to kiss me, I'd have kneed him in the balls.

How can I go from the girl who hasn't been kissed, hasn't been interested in any guy ever, to the girl who went on her first date, kissed her best friend, and somehow caught the attention of another guy all in the space of a couple of days?

I stare at his retreating back, my confusion warring with the desire to chase after him and ask him if this is all a joke. First Kent, then Griff, and now Van. This isn't my life. I'm not the kind of girl who has two guys interested, and I'm definitely not the girl whose best friend suddenly starts kissing her.

Someone clips my backpack that's loosely hanging from my shoulder as they walk past, and I realize I've been standing in the middle of the path having a crisis while the rest of the world walks around me. I glance one last time in the direction Van walked in, then turn and force myself to move on slightly unsteady legs to my class.

My economics class is just as dreadful as the others have been. If it wasn't a Hayhurst requirement to graduate, I wouldn't be taking it. I try to concentrate on Professor Clarey, but my mind refuses to cooperate and instead I find myself thinking about Griffin.

The more our kiss plays on a loop through my head, the more I convince myself that it was just him playing a mind game with me, reminding me of home and of the lifestyle we grew up in. If it had been him kissing me, just because he wanted to, he wouldn't have said all those things about the Sinners or about how they want their women to feel; he would have spoken about him, and how *he* wanted to leave me feeling.

Him kissing me to remind me of how 'real men' behave makes so much more sense than him suddenly having feelings for me, because even though he tries to, I know he doesn't really understand my need for new people and experiences. Griff wanting me as more than a friend is absurd and it makes no sense. He's never been short of female attention and I know he's just waiting for the right woman to come along and capture his heart. He needs a strong, beautiful girl who will become the center of his universe because he has so much love to give. When he does give away his whole heart, it'll be forever and whoever she is will be the luckiest girl on the planet.

A pain ricochets through my chest and I lift my hand and cover my heart, pressing down on the raw void that feels like it just appeared. I love my friends, I truly do, but when they grow up and meet people, I'll lose them. It's different with girl friends, but with the guys, the women they fall for won't understand our relationship, or who the Scions are and I'll be pushed aside. Maybe if I'd been the one to drift away the pain would be less, but the idea that my time with them is counting down hurts so much more than I ever would have thought. But this is life, people grow up and the frivolities of childhood and childish notions like friendship above everything else fade.

I'm jolted from my internal musings by class ending and the screech of fifty chairs all moving at once. Reaching forward I hit save on my meager notes, then shut the lid of my laptop and lift it off the desk, sliding it into my backpack. Hoisting my bag onto my shoulders I slowly follow the mass of students out of the classroom and toward fresh air and freedom. My next class isn't for an hour, so I pause for a moment, debating if I should head to the library like a good little student, or go find somewhere I can sit and read until my next class starts.

"Emmy."

Spinning at the sound of the voice, I find a stern-faced Zeke striding toward me. I wave and his expression softens a little. "Hey," I say when he reaches me.

"Hey, you got time for a coffee? I'm jonesing for some caffeine."

Laughing at his pained expression I nod. "Why didn't you just bring a coffee with you? I made a pot before I left this morning."

"I did make one, but I left it on the counter and didn't remember 'til I was already on campus," he whines grumpily.

My shoulders shake as I chuckle silently.

"Don't laugh," he chides. "I'm still getting used to remembering my own shit."

"Come on, I have time for coffee," I say.

Zeke curls his arm around my neck and turns us in the direction of Brew Me Up Buttercup, the small kitschy coffee shop that's hidden in the corner of campus. Unlike the cafeteria that sells burned, chewy coffee, Brew Me Up sells delicious richly roasted caffeine goodness and sugary treats. The place is full of bleary-eyed students when we push through the door and Zeke shoos me over to a table and heads to the counter to order our drinks. He returns a couple of minutes later with a tray laden with a frothy latte for me, a dark roast Americano for him and two Biscotti muffins.

"I hate early morning classes," he says, yawning.

"My class started an hour ago," I remind him.

"I know. Thank God none of mine are that time. There's no way I'd make it if I had to be here for eight. I had to set ten alarms to get here now."

I roll my eyes at him, then we lapse into silence as Zeke drinks his coffee and I pick at my muffin.

"So what's going on with this Kent guy?" Zeke asks, his expression suddenly serious.

"Nothing yet. Last night was our first date," I say with a shrug.

"I don't like it, Em. I don't want you going out with anyone who isn't going to treat you right," Zeke growls.

"You don't even know him. He could be the perfect guy for me," I argue.

"Exactly. I don't know him. I never even knew he existed until he turned up on our doorstep yesterday. What the fuck is up with that?"

"I don't have to tell you about every guy I meet. You sure as hell don't tell me about every girl you fuck," I snap, sitting up straighter in my seat and crossing my arms pointedly across my chest.

"Do you want to know about every girl I fuck? 'Cause I got no problem telling you."

"No," I cry. "Of course I don't want to know. I'm making a point."

"And what point's that exactly?" Zeke asks, raising an eyebrow at me imperiously. "If I met a girl who meant anything to me, I'd talk about her. I'd tell you guys, because you're my family, my best friends, and I'd want you to know."

"It was a first date, Zeke. If things had gotten serious I'd have told you all, but I only met him last week," I cry in exasperation.

"See that's the thing though, Em. You don't date. Have you even been on a date before?"

Avoiding his gaze, I focus on my muffin, pulling a piece off and shoving it into my mouth.

"You're not like me. For you to agree to go out on a date with that guy, you must already think he's important. So, I'll ask again, why didn't you tell us about him?" Zeke growls, his eyes boring into me and demanding answers.

"I don't know," I cry, throwing my hands into the air dramatically. "I don't know, okay? He asked me out and he's cute and different and I just—"

"Do you wish you'd gone to school on your own? The Ivy League one you had your heart set on." Zeke asks, his eyes watching me warily.

"No," I say immediately. "No, I'm glad we're all here together. It's just that you guys are all so certain of how your future looks. You and Griffin want to be Sinners. You plan to get your degrees, then go home and start your life. Nova wants Valentine and he wants her; they're going to be blissfully happy no matter what they end up doing, and then there's me."

"What about you?" He asks.

"I think about my future and it's just this big, black empty space."

"That's okay, we're only nineteen. It's normal to not know what you want to do with the rest of your life," he says, leaning across the table toward me.

"I know that, but I feel like what I do now, who I date,

what classes I take, they're all forging a path that if I'm not careful will just lead me right back to Archer's Creek."

"What's wrong with Archer's Creek?" he asks quietly.

"Everything and nothing," I answer. "But I want something else, something more than just being the kid of the Sinners Prez. Kent is different, and he doesn't look at me like I'm anything more than just me. It's nice, to just be me for a change, to have something that's just mine."

I expect Zeke to argue, but he doesn't. Instead he inhales, then exhales slowly and nods. "I get that. He's not like us and that's what you want."

The sadness in his expression almost has me denying it, but what's the point? It's the truth.

"Why are you here, Em?" He asks, his tone serious.

"What do you mean? You came to find me after my class and asked me to come get coffee," I say, confused.

"I mean here, at Hayhurst. You had your something different all ready for you. You had your get-out clause, a brand-new life just waiting for you. So why are you here?"

My lips part and I stare at him. He's not joking around; his eyes are narrowed slightly at the corners and his lips are pressed together in a tight line. He looks daunting and intense and I inhale sharply, shocked at how serious he's being.

"Because."

"Don't give me the bullshit stock answer. I want the real reason." He demands.

A lump forms and I clear my throat. "I…" I pause, swallowing again. "I wasn't ready to be alone."

I expect his face to soften, but it stays the same. "Why else?"

"I didn't want to leave Nova."

This time, there's a glimmer of something in his eyes. "Why else?"

"Does it matter?" I snap.

"Yeah it does. The summer before Valentine showed up, we barely saw you. You were distancing yourself from us, withdrawing more and more. You were getting ready to leave and we all saw it. Then Nova lost her shit and suddenly you were back, you were one of us again, you were present, but we all still expected you to leave. I need to know if the only reason you're here is because you feel some kind of fucked up sense of obligation to Nova."

I start shaking my head even before he finishes speaking. "No. No, I love Nova and yeah maybe her illness is what made me change my mind, but it's not the only reason."

"Explain it to me then, Em. Because right now, you're here, but you're not. You're in, but not all the way. You're you, but you're trying to be someone else. Tell me what the hell is going on," he begs, his voice softening.

"I don't know," I admit, my eyes dropping to my fingers that are wrapped around my mug. "The plan was always to use college to get as far away as possible from home and the club and this fucked up world that somehow made us royalty when all I've ever wanted to be was normal."

Lifting my eyes, I implore him to understand, to really hear me. "You and Griffin, you like the way people revere *The Scions*," I say making quotation marks in the air with my fingers. "But I never wanted the attention. I don't want to be someone that people have expectations of. I just want to be normal. I thought getting into a good school, where no one thinks about bikers, where I could reinvent myself, I'd be happier."

"So if that was the plan, the dream. What changed?"

"Nova," I say simply. "I had no idea she was falling apart. I knew she played the role of the mean girl because she thought that's what people expected of her, but I had absolutely no idea that she was literally battling with her own head every single day. She's my best friend, we've known each other our whole lives, and I was completely oblivious. That day in the gym when I saw that video of you and her, I realized that I'd been so fucking selfish. I'd been so busy trying to forget who I was, to plan my escape, that I actually did forget who I am. I forgot who my friends are, who in my life is important."

"But," Zeke interrupts.

"No, let me finish," I say. "You guys are my best friends and I realized that if I ran away and made myself into a whole new person that I'd end up just like Nova. I'd end up fighting a battle of who I am and who I think I need to be, and I don't want that. I don't want to pretend to be someone new, but I don't just want to be Emmy, the Sinners kid either. Here I can try to be different, but still have you guys, my family, to make sure I don't lose sight of who I really am. Does that make any sense?" I ask, my eyes blurred with emotion and unshed tears.

Zeke nods slowly before getting up and rounding the table. His strong arms wrap around me and he lifts me out of my chair and into a tight hug. "Love you, Em," he whispers against my ear.

"Love you too," I whisper, hugging him back just as tight.

When his arms loosen, he drops me into my seat and walks back around to his side of the table, sitting down in his chair. "I don't want to lose you, but I understand, or at least I think I do. We'll be here, when you need us, but just because you want to try new things and experiment with who you are, that doesn't mean that you have to hide things. You don't have to pretend; you never have to fucking pretend. Hell, if everything Nova's been through has taught us anything, that should be it. Be you, meet new people, reinvent yourself, but don't push us away; don't move on without us because you're part of us and we love you and we want to celebrate the good shit and help you when things are fucked up. We're Sinners, Em. No matter if that's not your future. Sinners look after their own."

I nod, too choked up to speak and Zeke smiles and nods back at me, because nothing else needs to be said; we're family and that's it.

Finishing my coffee, I pop the last bite of my muffin into my mouth, leaning back in my chair and watching as Zeke drains the last dregs from his cup. He sighs, staring down at the mug as if he's hoping that looking at it longingly will make it full again.

"You want another coffee?" I ask.

"I really do," he nods.

"I'll go."

"Nah, it's fine. You want another?"

Sighing, I fold my arms across my chest and glare at him. "I'm more than capable of waiting at a counter and ordering coffee, Zeke."

An annoying smile spreads across his face as he pushes himself out of his chair. "I know you're capable, but my dad raised me to treat a woman right, so stay put and let me take care of you." With that he leans down and presses a kiss to the top of my head before walking to the counter and returning with two more coffees. "Okay, so explain to me what's so bad about a guy being a gentleman?" He asks.

Rolling my eyes, I exhale. "There's nothing wrong with it, it's just so antiquated. I don't need a guy to look after me. I don't need one to pay and maybe, just maybe I'd like to be looked at like an equal and not treated like I'm going to shatter to pieces at any moment."

Zeke throws back his head and laughs. "You think we

were taught to act this way because we don't think you're equal to us?" He laughs again, loud enough to draw the attention of the other people in the coffee shop. "Emmy Devereaux, for a smart girl, you're an idiot."

"I'm not an idiot," I cry.

"Baby, you're an idiot. Our daddies taught us to treat a woman right, so that's how we act. But they behave that way because they're so fucking grateful, so fucking obsessed with their old ladies that they literally worship the ground they walk on. My dad doesn't exist without my mom. He knows that, so he protects her, shelters her, cossets her, because he knows that she's the most important thing in the world to him. He pays for everything because all of their money is *their* money, so who cares if he's the one who's carrying the cash. He opens doors, because it's respectful and she pays a fortune for her nails and she'd be upset if she chipped one. He orders at bars, because he knows how fucking beautiful his woman is and he doesn't want other guys to hassle her. My dad knows how much of a lucky bastard he is to have convinced my mom to marry him and he shouldn't ever forget that. But I'll tell you what, Em. Never, not fucking ever, has my dad or any Sinner guy thought that a woman was less than him. It's the complete fucking opposite. Sinners guys, hell, all fucking guys should know that women are so much more and that's why we behave the way we do. It's not us diminishing who you are, it's us being so fucking aware of how amazing you are that we want to protect it."

Zeke sits back in his chair and lifts his coffee cup to his lips and takes a sip, just like that, like he didn't just blow my freaking mind.

"Do you get now why I don't think that kid's good enough for you? Him not opening your car door, not offering to pay, driving off the way he did without even making sure you were safe in the house. All of that says to me that he has no fucking clue of your value, that he is so fucking blind that he doesn't deserve you. Because if he saw you, the real you, Em, he'd know that you're a fucking gem, priceless and irreplaceable. A Sinner; he'd see that in you."

Swallowing thickly, I stare at my best friend, shocked by his words and the passionate way he delivered them. This wasn't him placating me. He feels and truly believes everything he just told me. Goose bumps pebble along my arm. All my life I've believed that the guys in our world behaved the way they do because they're overprotective chauvinistic assholes but hearing what he just said somehow changes everything. Is everything I thought about the men I grew up with wrong?

Zeke's laugh is low and full of smug amusement. "Em, the look on your face right now is priceless. Come on, we're gonna be late if we don't get a move on."

Waving goodbye to Zeke, I take the path across campus to my next class as he heads in the opposite direction to his. Talking to him has left me rocked and off balance. What he told me somehow changes everything and I need time to process his words.

I don't understand why I've never asked the guys about this before, and why it's taken until now for one of them to speak to me about it either. Have I been wrong about the role women play in the Sinners world all along? And if I am wrong what does that mean? Balancing my past with my future has always felt like an impossible task, but maybe if I'd just talked to my friends and family about it, I'd have realized before now that it doesn't have to be so hard.

So much has changed in the last year and right now my present looks nothing like I pictured it would, but that's not a bad thing. Instead of being alone, I'm trying new things and experimenting, but I'll never lose who I am, because my friends will always be my anchor, my roots, and now that I understand, it's seems obvious that without them I'd be adrift.

Staring at my reflection in the mirror, I turn from side to side assessing myself from the different angles. Tonight's the night of the sorority pre rush meet and greet. Honestly I still can't believe that I let Avery talk me into attending with her, but she's so much more persuasive than I expected and before I realized what I was doing I'd agreed to go with her.

Avery and I are going out to dinner before the mixer, so I'm hoping to be out of the house before the others get back from their last class. I know I shouldn't be avoiding them, but I don't know what to say to Griff about last night and I don't want to explain what I'm doing tonight either.

Zeke met Avery back on the first day of school and they know I'm friends with Veronica too, but I haven't exactly introduced my two groups to each other. I'm not sure why I'm so hesitant to let my two worlds meet, but I am.

The clothes I have on are much more conservative than I'd ever wear back home and I'd definitely stand out if I turned up dressed like this to the club. Looking down at my pastel green chiffon slip dress I bite at my bottom lip and cringe. I'm definitely not a fashionista, but this dress is much more country club than I'd normally wear. Most of my closet is full of cute fashionable comfort with a vintage twist and right now I feel a little weird.

Maybe college Emmy is a Sorority girl? This is what I wanted right? To experiment with new experiences and Greek life is definitely something new. Sliding my feet into nude pumps I run my fingers through my hair that I've flat ironed so its straight and glossy, then I grab my tiny purse and leave my room, feeling strange and uncomfortable.

It's only a short walk to the restaurant we're meeting at, but the heels on these shoes are too tall for me to want to walk in, so I call an Uber and greet it at the curb all before any of the others make it home.

"Oh wow, you look so cute," Avery gushes when she sees me, rushing over to me and hugging me tightly.

"I feel ridiculous," I say, grimacing. We'd gone shopping for outfits a few days earlier and I'd let her talk me into this dress.

"Don't be silly, you look gorgeous," she says. "How do I look?" she asks, doing a twirl in front of me, the hem of her white dress swirling around her thighs as she moves. The dress is fitted around her chest, then flares at her hips into a cute skater skirt that makes her look curvier than her slim frame actually is. Her blonde hair looks even blonder against the white and she looks stunning, like a beautiful, tanned angel.

"You look amazing," I say sincerely.

"I'm so excited, the Sigma Gamma Phi's are the best sorority on campus."

I smile, trying to look at least a little enthusiastic but failing miserably. "Let's eat, I'm starving."

She nods, then drags me into the bar.

Swallowing thickly, I lift my foot and place it on the first step that leads to the Sigma Gamma Phi house. The place is gorgeous: red brick, double-fronted with white windows, a huge dark wood front door and a beautifully landscaped front yard. A smiling brunette in white shorts with a pink t-shirt with the Sigma Gamma Phi logo on the front smiles brightly at us from beside the door, a clipboard clutched tightly to her chest.

"Welcome to Sigma Gamma Phi, ladies. My name is Cora-Lee, could I take your names and I'll get you a name tag."

"I'm Avery Richards and this is Emmy Devereaux," Avery says excitedly.

"Well, it's a pleasure to meet you both, could I just check how you spell Emmy. It'd be awful to send you in there with a typo on your tag," Cora-Lee says, laughing brightly.

"E-M-M-Y," I say spelling my name.

"Fantastic, here are your tags. If I could just take your room numbers too, so we can let you know about our other rush events." Cora-Lee asks, her grin firmly fixed in place.

Avery quickly offers up her room number, then Cora-Lee turns to me.

"Oh, I live off-campus. You can just put me down at Avery's room too, if that's easier."

"Oh, okay, well that's fine for now. We don't usually have many freshman who don't live on campus. Why don't you two head inside, our president Mallory and our vice president Alicia are both inside and they can tell you more about our little family. Have a great night and all us sisters are in pink shirts so feel free to say hi and I'm sure any of them can answer any of your questions."

"Thank you so much, Cora-Lee," Avery gushes, hooking her arm through mine and pulling me into the house.

The house is so beautiful I have to blink twice to make sure I'm not seeing things. The décor looks like it came straight from a homes and gardens magazine spread with whites, creams, and the odd pink highlight dotted here and there. There are probably twenty girls in pink shirts and white shorts, then maybe another thirty girls in dresses alarmingly similar to mine. In fact, all of the potential rushee's look so much alike I could swear they all bought the same dress just in different colors.

Lustrous pearls and sparkling jewels adorn necks, and there's a sea of nude heels. We look like clones. I wonder what these girls would say if they found out my dad wore leather every day and rode a Harley. A giggle bubbles up my throat but I swallow it down when a smiling girl glides toward us, a double row of pearls peeking out of the neck of her pink shirt. A pinbadge that says 'President' rests over her heart and when she reaches us she immediately reaches out and engulfs me in a hug.

"Hello, I'm Mallory Bryant and I'm the President of Sigma Gamma Phi. We are so delighted to welcome you into our home."

"Hi," I say a little awkwardly when she releases me. "I'm Emmy."

"Emmy, that is such a pretty name." She turns and pulls a delighted looking Avery in for a hug next. "And you are?"

"Avery Richards," Avery says proudly.

Mallory tilts her head to the side, assessing Avery with a little more interest. "Any relation to Eliza Richards?" She asks.

Avery blushes a very pretty pink color. "She's my mom."

Mallory's face light up. "A legacy," she cries with so much excitement it's a little unnerving.

Two more girls appear at Mallory's side and one hooks her arm through Mallory's. "Did I hear we have a legacy in the house?" the petite girl with a mane of black hair that's shining beneath the room's lighting asks.

"Elle, this is Avery, she's Eliza Richards daughter,"

Mallory introduces. "And this is Emmy," she says, gesturing to me.

"It's so lovely to meet you both. You guys are going to love Sigma Gamma Phi, we are the oldest and most prestigious sorority at Hayhurst."

She proceeds to launch into the sales pitch and after a few minutes I zone her out, letting my attention move around the room to all the other girls in here. Everyone is so perfect, so polished. Nova would fit in perfectly, but me, this isn't me. I might be trying to find myself, but I'm fairly sure I won't be discovering anything new about myself here.

I force myself to rejoin the conversation, realizing that Elle has moved on from how old and important the sorority is, to how hot the guys are in their brother fraternity Omega Neu.

"Our brother fraternity my freshman year was Kappa Kappa Epsilon, but those guys were the worst. I went on a date with this guy called Ben and he took me a pizza place, then expected us to split the bill. God, he even turned up in a wrinkled shirt and ripped jeans. Yuck. The guys in the frats are great and all, but I want a guy like Jason Momoa, huge and ripped and super possessive," she giggles.

The night is quite possibly the longest of my life and by the time my Uber parks outside our house I am just so ready to go back to living in books because this real-life stuff is not for me.

Pushing through the front door, I shout a hello, then go straight upstairs without even poking my head into the living room. I don't want whoever's here to see me in this dress, or ask me about my night, so instead I let cowardice rule my actions and rush to my room, pulling the dress over my head the moment I get inside.

Not considering my actions I head to the closet and pull

out my Sinners tank top, pulling it on before I grab some pj shorts from my dresser and twist my hair up into a messy bun. The exhale that falls from my lips is pure relief. I like Avery a lot, so far she seems like a nice girl without a bitchy bone in her body and I'm lying to her.

She has no idea who I am. All she knows is what I've told her, this lie I've perpetuated about myself to allow me to reinvent myself into the person I think I'm supposed to be. Why is growing up so confusing? I don't want to be high school me, the person who kept to a small circle, but the truth of the matter is that we kept to ourselves because we have so much in common.

Tonight I witnessed my first experience of Sorority life and it really isn't that bad, but just like the Scions, the sorority girls stick together in a tight knit group, because they share common experiences and because they understand their 'sisters' lives in a way only people in the Greek system can.

Greek life isn't for me, but it's made me appreciate my friends a little more. Sighing wistfully, I let my body fall back to my comforter and close my eyes. I thought doing new things, finding myself would be easy. That moving away from home was the key to everything but changing myself is so much harder than I thought it would be.

Maybe you should stop trying so hard, I think. My subconscious is obviously much smarter than I am, because when I think about it, it's obvious. I need to stop trying so hard to be different and just see what happens. I can choose new experiences but it doesn't have to be at the cost of who I am at my core. A smile drifts to my lips just as my cell beeps, then beeps again in my pocket. Grabbing it, I lift it up, sliding my fingertip across the screen to bring it to life.

Clicking into the message app, it opens on to the text I was reading from Kent this morning when I stepped in front of Van's car. I click out of his slam poetry invitation and see that I have a new message from an unknown number and I select it, assuming it'll be a promotional text or something.

Unknown

Hey, Little Red.

My heart skips a beat, then starts to thud a little too quickly. Van. Somehow, I'd almost forgotten that he'd called himself from my cell this morning. It feels like so much has happened since then, but a vision of his beautiful rugged face pops into my head and I feel a blush fill my cheeks. I don't know anything about him, except that he's part of a frat, gives girls SipChips at parties to keep them safe, and drives a sexy as sin car. So why is my skin alight with excitement just thinking about him?

My fingers move across my screen and I'm typing out a reply before I can consider how stupid engaging with him might be.

Emmy

Stealing girls' cellphone numbers and then texting them is kind of stalkerish behavior.

I stare at my screen for a minute expecting him to reply, but nothing comes through. A pang of disappointment hits me, but I ignore it and click out of the message thread and into the message from Kent this morning.

Kent

I had a great time last night. If I promise not to be an idiot will you go out with me again? There's a slam poetry night at the coffee shop on campus this weekend. I'd love for you to come.

A smile spreads across my face and I can't help giggling a little. He can't be serious with this poetry stuff. But Kent is just so adorably sweet and geeky in the most endearing way, so maybe he actually does go to poetry nights. Despite everything Zeke said this morning about him not understanding my worth, I can't help thinking about how nice and refreshingly different he is and my fingers are typing out a reply without thought.

Emmy

I take promises seriously.

His reply comes through almost immediately.

Kent

Me too. Is that a yes?

Emmy

Yes.

Kent

Fantastic, let me work out the details and I'll call you later.

Emmy

Ok, ttyl.

Kent

:)

Closing my message app, I bite at my lip to stop my smile from getting any bigger. I'm excited to go out with Kent again. I'm excited to see him and spend time with a guy who isn't uber macho and bossy. Laughing to myself, I wonder how many other girls would be excited to be dating a guy who doesn't treat them like they need to be looked after and protected.

Van doesn't strike me as the kind of guy who would sit back and placidly let me take care of myself. The thought comes from out of nowhere and I chide myself for even thinking about the guy that is a little too much like a Sinner. Why am I even thinking about Van at all? He's just another person who seems to think that I don't know how to look after myself, and I don't need another overbearing guy in my life. I have enough of them at home and with the guys I live with.

My cell beeps in my hand and I look at the screen, expecting to see a new message from Kent. Instead there's another message from the unknown number.

Unknown

Not a stalker, but you can call me your knight in shining armor after I saved you this morning, or maybe just savior for short.

Emmy

Wow!

Unknown

No?

Emmy

Definitely not

188

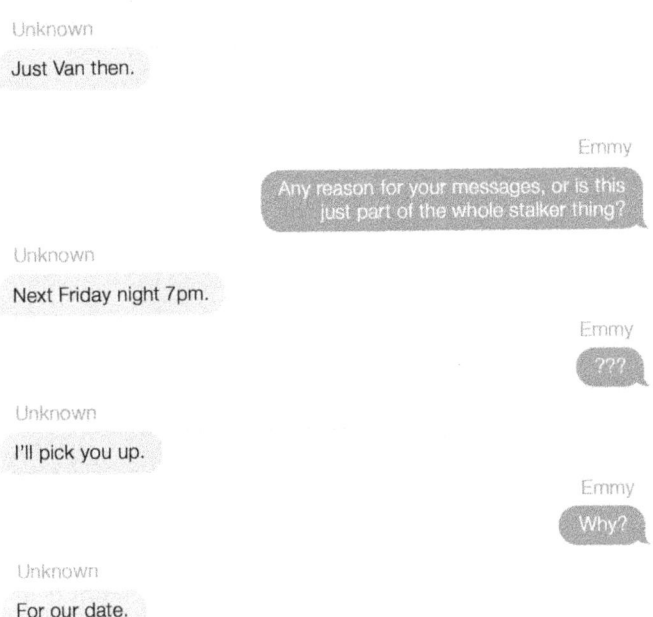

Unknown
Just Van then.

Emmy
Any reason for your messages, or is this just part of the whole stalker thing?

Unknown
Next Friday night 7pm.

Emmy
???

Unknown
I'll pick you up.

Emmy
Why?

Unknown
For our date.

What the hell? Van is asking me out? No, he's telling me he's taking me out. Annoyance flares to life inside of me. Who the hell does this guy think he is? He can't just tell me he's picking me up, we don't even know each other and he stole my cell number. I definitely didn't give it to him.

My cell beeps again, but I don't look at it, instead dropping it to the comforter as I crawl up the bed and climb under my comforter. It beeps again as I'm pulling my Kindle from my nightstand, but I ignore it, refusing to look at the message, no matter how much I want to. Turning on my Kindle I click into the book I was listening to on the way to school this morning and wait for the eBook to sync to the current page. Exhaling a slow tired breath, I try to focus on my book, waiting for the story to engulf me and for me to lose all concept of time and anything except the story, but my brain refuses to co-operate moving back to my cell and the message I know is waiting for me.

Gritting my teeth I try not to, but before I even realize I've done it, my cell is in my hand and I'm clicking into the new message.

Van

Red. Ignoring people is rude.

I wish I could ignore him, but I can't and my fingers are flying across the screen as I reply.

Emmy

No thanks, not interested.

Smiling to myself, I lift my head from my cell and try to focus my attention on my book until my cell buzzes again.

Van

You're interested and so am I, but we can discuss that next Friday night on our date.

The tone of his words instantly annoys me. The confident arrogance sets me on edge and for a minute I consider replying, but I don't. Engaging with him will only make it worse, so instead I ignore him burying my cell under my pillow and forcing myself to read instead.

GRIFFIN

The front door slams closed and Emmy yells a hello, before disappearing upstairs. She was out tonight with her friend Avery, but I have no idea what they were doing, not that it's really any of my business. I haven't seen her since I kissed her, then walked away like the fucking idiot I am.

I told Zeke I had no fucking clue what I'm going to do about my feelings for her and I still don't. Part of me wants to march up to her room and kiss her until we're both panting and breathless, but I know I can't. The other part of me wants to pretend it didn't happen, that I don't know what she tastes like on my lips, what she feels like under me.

Nova and Valentine are out watching a band at a local bar with some people from one of his classes and Zeke is off getting his dick wet, and I'm here, waiting for her to come home and praying that she didn't bring that fucking Kent guy with her.

I have no idea where her head's at. I don't know if she's pissed at me, horrified that I crossed a line, or if by some miracle she actually feels the same way. Most of the time I consider myself a pretty brave guy, but when it comes to her I'm a chickenshit. So instead of being upstairs with her, I'm down here overthinking everything and wishing I was with her instead.

When the movie I was watching, but barely paying attention to finishes, I turn off the TV and make my way upstairs. My room is on one side of the house, hers is on the other, but instead of my feet taking me to my own bed, I find myself standing outside her room, my fist raised and knocking.

"Come in," she calls, her voice distracted.

I already know what she's doing. I've heard that tone in her voice a million times and when I push through her door she's exactly where I expected, curled into a ball with her Kindle in front of her face.

A smile spreads across my face. This is my girl in her natural environment and despite all the unspoken words between us, I act on instinct, closing the door behind me, climbing onto her bed and stealing the Kindle from her grasp. I lower my hand off the side of the bed and slide the Kindle along the floor, til it slides to a stop just in front of her closet door.

"You asshole," she cries, fire burning in her eyes. "If you broke my Kindle I'm going to kill you."

I laugh, I can't help it. "I didn't break it. I slid it, I didn't throw it."

"Go get it. NOW. I was just at a good bit in my book," she demands.

"Nope, you owe me snuggles. Put a movie on and get over here," I cajole.

"I'm reading," she snaps, moving to climb out of bed.

I snatch her before she gets a knee off the bed and roll her beneath me, hovering over her, my arms on either side of her head caging her in. Leaning down I press a kiss to the side of her neck. "You owe me, shortcake, and Sinners always pay their debts."

"That's not a thing. Isn't that from Game of Thrones or something," she says rolling her eyes.

"Em," I growl, warning her that I'm about to do something even when I have no idea what it is I'm warning her I'm about to do.

Her eyes widen slightly and she visibly swallows. I can't help myself. I lean down and press another kiss at the base of her neck, then another a little lower, then lower again 'til my lips are resting on the swell of her full fucking tits and all I want to do is dip down a little further and taste one of her nipples.

Lifting my head up, I lock my eyes with hers and wait for her to tell me no, to show me her disgust or anger, but all I can see is surprise with a hint of want, or maybe that's wishful thinking. Slowly, so slowly I feel like I'm going insane I lean down and press my mouth to the outline of her nipple through her shirt. Her Sinners shirt. I hadn't noticed it before, but somehow kissing her nipple through the Sinners logo makes this so much hotter.

Her lips part and a silent gasp falls from her mouth. I kiss her hard and fast, then I force myself to pull back and roll to my side, pulling her with me so her head is rested on my chest. Without another word she reaches for the remote and turns on her TV as we lay wrapped in each other's arms.

Chapter 20

EMMY

I don't know what time Griff left my room last night. I have a sleepy memory of him carefully moving from beneath me and kissing my forehead before he left.

Now I feel more confused than ever.

Forcing myself to get up, I drag myself to class, but I barely hear a word any of my professors say to me. Everything is swirling around in my head and I need to get it out. I need to tell someone about my talk with Zeke; my date with Kent; Van almost running me down, then asking me out; and everything that's happened with Griff, because I have no idea how to process everything that's going on.

My cell buzzes in my jean shorts pocket and I carefully pull it out and click into the new message.

Nova

Morning, do you want to meet for lunch?

Relief fills me as I read the words. I know I could probably talk to Avery or Veronica, but they don't really know me and Nova, well she knows everything about me, she's my best friend. I need some girl time to talk about what Zeke told me, and about the new guys in my life. More than anything I need to tell her about Griffin. I need to see her face when I tell her that he's kissed me twice now. I need her to tell me what it means. I need to talk to someone who can understand and then tell me what the hell I'm supposed to do now.

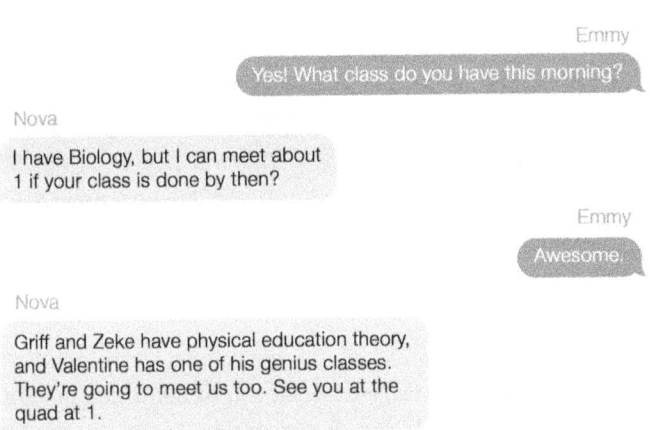

Emmy

Yes! What class do you have this morning?

Nova

I have Biology, but I can meet about 1 if your class is done by then?

Emmy

Awesome.

Nova

Griff and Zeke have physical education theory, and Valentine has one of his genius classes. They're going to meet us too. See you at the quad at 1.

Disappointment hits me hard. I want to talk to Nova, just Nova, and tell her about everything that's going on. For months now we've all gone on and on about talking about our problems instead of bottling them up, but no matter how many times I've heard myself say it to her, I haven't been taking my own advice. My come to God moment with Zeke has made me realize that I can't expect Nova to be the only one who puts all her shit out there. I have to do it too. Zeke already knows about Kent. He wanted to know about him to make sure I'm okay, so maybe I can talk to the others about him too. Right? Oh God, *can* I talk about Kent and Van to Griff? Did our kiss change that? If Van my maybe stalker is about to become a problem, I'd rather the guys know about it, so I can tell him about that, can't I?

What I can't do is talk about Griff, in front of Griff, so that will have to wait until I can get some time alone with Nova, because I need to tell someone and my best friend, my sister, is exactly who I need.

Emmy

Can't wait, ttyl xo

Clicking out of the text chat with Nova, I force my attention back to my boring professor and his droning monotone voice. Scanning the room, I spot several people with their heads on the desk and even one guy with his eyes closed and mouth open, very obviously asleep. Maybe that's why the TA always posts lecture notes in the online bulletin board for this class.

Forty minutes later, I slide my laptop back into my backpack and drag my bored, weary self out of the room, inhaling the warm, fresh air deeply the moment I step outside. The huge, old lecture theater with no air conditioning and the lingering smell of damp, coupled with a terrible professor and a boring subject makes me grateful that this class is only once a week.

My stomach growls as I head in the direction of the quad and the one decent place to eat on campus. The food in the main cafeteria is worse than the coffee and I shudder at the thought of having to eat there every day like most of the kids in the dorms.

"Emmy," Nova calls, waving from a wooden picnic table at the side of the enclosed courtyard.

Smiling, I walk a little faster, sliding in next to her on the bench and lowering my backpack to the ground at my feet. "Hey, how was biology?"

"God, so interesting. We were looking at human cell structure and the chemical foundations of life. I can't believe I hated it at high school because this course is fascinating," she gushes.

"Where are the guys?" I ask.

"They went to grab food. I'm guarding the table," she says on a laugh.

Looking at the doorway that leads into the café, I check for any signs of the guys reappearing, but I can't see anything except a line of people waiting to order. "So, something happened, and I need to tell you about it."

Her eyes light up with intrigue and she twists around to face me, crossing one leg beneath her. "What?"

"Do you remember that guy from the Fresh Meat party, the one I danced with?"

"Ohh the hot one that my brother lost his mind over?"

"Yes, his name is Van."

"Ohhhh good name," she says, leaning forward and resting her chin on her hand.

"I know," I agree, then shake my head to refocus. "Well yesterday morning on the way to school I almost got run down by his car."

"Oh my god," she cries, "Are you okay, what happened? Why did you wait 'til a full day later to tell me?"

Reaching out, I grab her arm. "I'm fine. It was my fault. I wasn't looking where I was going and stepped into the street. He honked at me and I managed to jump back onto the sidewalk, well fall is probably a better description."

"Oh my god, Emmy, you need to be careful."

"I know," I say, then squeeze her arm. "But that's not what I need to tell you."

"Okkayy," she says.

"So after I fell on my butt to stop myself from getting hit by his car, he stopped and got out to come tell me off for almost stepping in front of him. He was all growly; then he got sweet, and then he tried to get me to ride with him to school."

"Tell me you didn't get in a car with him?" Nova demands.

"Of course I didn't. I'm not an idiot. But when I refused, he just left his car on the side of the street and walked me to school."

"He walked you to school," she cries and I can practically see the hearts forming in her eyes. Her lips tip up into a teasing grin and she opens her mouth to speak just as the guys crowd around us, dropping three trays of food onto the bench and loudly climbing into their seats. Valentine lifts Nova up and sits in her place, lowering her back down onto his lap and pressing a kiss against her neck while Zeke and Griffin slide onto the bench opposite us.

"Hey, shortcake," Griffin says, a smirk etched across his lips.

"Hey," I say, my gaze falling to his lips, the lips that were pressed against mine last night. My heart misses a beat. I expected to feel different, awkward around him, but I don't. Griff feels like home, familiar and comforting. Only now there's something more, something that's simmering just beneath my skin, reminding me that I know how it feels when he kisses me. That I know how it feels when his body is on top of mine, his weight pinning me down. I know how it feels to have his raspy voice against my ear, telling me how it would be if things were different between us. If Griff was mine would he feel about me the way Zeke said his dad feels about his mom? Would he want to protect me to shelter me, cosset me, and worship me?

How did I go from thinking about how awkward things could be, to thinking about how it would feel to be his? We're friends, only friends. The kiss was just an aberration and nothing more, only he's kissed me twice now, and once is a mistake, twice is deliberate. No, I internally scold myself. I'm dating Kent, nice, sweet Kent; and then there's Van, who's bossy and demanding, but thoughtful enough to give out safety advice to girls at parties.

How did this happen? How did I end up being kissed by one of my best friends, going out on my first date with one guy, and being asked out by a third guy all in less than twenty-four hours?

"Emmy's starting her own harem," Nova announces loudly with a giggle.

"Nova," I cry.

"What?" All three guys say at once.

"It's hardly a harem," I mumble, not making eye contact with any of them.

"Explain. Now." Griffin demands, all of the playfulness gone from his voice.

Sighing, I glance down at the trays full of food before lifting my eyes and facing him. "Do you remember the Fresh Meat party?"

"Yes," he growls, and I can feel both Zeke and Valentine's attention focused on me too.

"Well, you remember that guy I danced with? The one that Zeke pulled me away from?"

"Yes," Griff snarls, his voice terse and hard.

"Well, I saw him again yesterday morning," I say, then explain about stepping out into the road and him stopping.

"So this guy almost runs you down, then walked you to

school? Was he creepy with you? Why didn't you call one of us?" Valentine asks.

"No, he wasn't creepy, and I didn't call you because I was fine," I say quickly.

"What happened after he walked with you to campus? Why didn't you tell me about this last night?" Griffin demands.

My eyes flick to Nova, whose expression is alight with excitement.

"He, err, he grabbed my cell from my pocket and called himself from it," I say quickly.

"Has he called?" Nova asks. "Oh my god, this is so romantic."

"No," I say quickly.

"Good," Griffin growls.

"But he texted me," I mumble.

"Give me your cell," Zeke demands, holding out his hand expectantly. "Why didn't you tell me any of this yesterday morning? We had coffee after all of this happened."

"Because he hadn't texted me then," I snap back, annoyed by both his and Griffin's condescending tones.

"What did he text you?" Griffin growls.

"He asked me out," I say, rolling my shoulders back and lifting my eyes to glare at him head on. All of the confused, excited, scary, bewildering feelings that were lingering from our kiss last night evaporate beneath his domineering, alpha male tone and the urge to bait him rises unbidden to the surface.

"Delete his number and block him. He sounds like a fucking creep," Zeke says coldly.

"He's cute." Nova says, the only one of the five of us who seems oblivious to the tension.

"Nova," Valentine warns.

"What? Emmy has two guys interested in her. I've been waiting for years for her to find one guy she gives a second look to, and now she's got two. This is amazing," she extolls excitedly.

A giggle bubbles between my lips and I try hard to stifle a grin.

"Two?" Griff asks.

"Yeah, Kent who she went out with last night; and now Van, the sexy frat guy," Nova singsongs.

"You're going out with that nerdy kid again?" Griff asks.

"He asked me out again," I say, my voice softening a little.

Something flashes across his expression, but it's gone so fast I think I might have imagined it. His eyes harden, and as I watch, his lips tighten into thin lines. Why is he so pissed? I know he's not a fan of Kent and that he doesn't think he's the right guy for me, but what could he possibly have against Van? He doesn't even know him. Is he...? Could he be jealous?

"Hey, Emmy." A voice calls from behind me and I twist around to find Kent stood behind me.

"Kent, hi," I say, my voice coming out a little shrill.

"Sorry, I know I said I'd call you later, but I saw you from across the way and thought I'd come say hi."

"No, it's fine. Are you on your way to class? Do you want to join us?" I ask, taking in his navy-blue chino shorts and adorable pale-pink polo shirt.

Kent's eyes scan the others at the table and he swallows visibly.

"Here you go, dude. You can sit here," Valentine says, lifting Nova up and grabbing a chair, before sitting back down at the end of the table and pulling her onto his lap.

"Are you sure? I don't want to intrude." Kent says warily.

"No, sit," Griff says, a mischievous glint in his eye.

Tentatively, Kent slides into the open spot on the bench next to me, placing his bag at his feet and pulling out a sandwich.

"What did you get me to eat?" Nova asks, prompting the guys to hand out the food I'd almost forgotten about.

"Em, I got you a turkey club," Zeke says, sliding the wrapped sandwich across the bench toward me.

"And they had that sweet tea we had the other day that you liked, so we grabbed you that too," Griff adds, dipping his head toward the paper cup with a red and white striped straw poking from the lid.

"Thank you," I say opening my sandwich and taking a quick bite. "As these knuckleheads didn't make the best first impression the other night, let me introduce you again. This is Zeke, Griffin, Valentine, and Nova," I say, motioning to each person in turn. "And guys, this is Kent."

Everyone smiles and nods between bites of sandwich. "So, Kent, are you a freshman like us?" Valentine asks, before taking a pull of his soda.

I smile gratefully at Valentine, glad to have someone at least trying to make small talk.

Kent shakes his head. "Sophomore."

"Cool, you picked out a major yet?"

"Yeah math. I'm a number geek," Kent admits with a slightly embarrassed smile.

"I'm taking a few math classes. Which ones do you have this semester?" Valentine asks, seeming genuinely interested.

Kent tells Valentine about the statistics and linear algebra courses he has, and I use his distraction to glare at Zeke and Griffin, mouthing 'be nice' at them. The guys look at each other, then smirk, and I narrow my eyes in warning at them.

"Oh, I took linear algebra as a summer course," Valentine says.

"You took a sophomore algebra course over the summer?" Kent repeats, shock clear in his voice.

"Yeah, I did all my AP classes in high school, then I took some summer classes so I could jump straight into the good stuff," Valentine says nonchalantly.

"He's a genius. We just ignore it," Nova says dryly, smiling at Kent.

"Okay," Kent says slowly. "So where are you all from?"

"A small town near Houston," Griffin answers. "What about you?"

"I grew up near Washington, DC."

"Was that sweet Mercedes yours?" Valentine asks.

"Yeah, it was a graduation gift from my parents, but I don't really use it that much. I have a motorcycle."

Shocked, I turn to Kent, catching Nova's surprised eyes as I do.

"Nice, what do you ride?" Zeke asks, real enthusiasm in his tone.

"A Vespa," Kent says, grinning proudly.

"A what?" Nova asks, clearing her throat.

"A Vespa. It's an Italian scooter. It's really cool," he says, completely oblivious to our horror.

No one says anything as I try really hard not to make my internal cringe a visible one. A scooter is not a motorcycle. Our dads ride proper bikes: Harley's and Honda's and Triumph's, huge vintage bikes, shiny and covered in chrome. I'm pretty sure my dad would kick the shit out of anyone who said they had a motorcycle and turned up on a scooter.

"Nice," Valentine says, and I can tell he's actually trying to make this whole situation better, but it doesn't work.

The rest of lunch is a little forced. Everyone is polite and nice, but it's awkward. Zeke and Griffin manage not to do any more obnoxious male posturing. I'm not sure if that's because they've figured out that Kent is a nice guy, or just because they assume, I could never be interested in someone who says he has a motorcycle, then tells you he rides a Vespa.

I see the way they're glancing between themselves, laughing behind their eyes at him, at me, and a wave of anger spreads through me. How dare they be so narrowminded, so judgmental. Valentine isn't a biker, he's a genius rich kid with a fucked up tragic past, but they never laughed at him. They never considered him an object of ridicule just because he's different to us. In fact, from the day he turned up outside Auntie Brandi and Uncle Sleaze's house they welcomed him, included him. Why does that only extend to him? Is this what it's going to be like for every guy I date? Are they going to laugh behind his back, laugh at me?

The last hour has shown me more than ever that my friends truly don't understand my desire to experience something different than the narrow world we grew up in. Sweet, geeky, scooter riding Kent is as much an enigma to them, as he's a world of possibility to me. I'm craving the chance to try new things and see how they fit into my future, where my friends already know what they want and like and refuse to consider things that are outside of our usual norm.

"My class starts in ten minutes, so I need to get going," Kent announces, standing from the table.

"Oh, okay," I say, standing up too.

"I'll call you later," he says, leaning in and sweetly pressing a kiss to my cheek. "Bye, Emmy."

"Bye, Kent."

As I watch, he looks over my shoulder and tips his chin up at my friends. "Nice to see you guys, bye."

"Bye," Nova calls, while the guys just grunt.

With a final adorable wave, he leaves, and I sink back down into my seat. I wait until he's far enough away that he won't hear me before I speak. "You narrowminded, bigoted assholes," I seethe, looking between Griff and Zeke. "Do you seriously think you're so fucking special that it gives you the right to look down on other people because they're different?"

Zeke opens his mouth to argue with me, but I lift my hand into the air and stop him. I shake my head, my anger fading into sad disappointment. "Who are you?" I ask. "You laughed at him, just because he rides a scooter. Do you know how pathetic that is? Do you laugh at me too because I want something different to the Sinner way of life? Do you laugh at the books I read, the new experiences I dream of? Is that who you are now? Assholes who think anything different than what you know or believe is something to poke fun at?"

I pause, taking in their horrified expressions and shake my head again. "Valentine, thank you for trying, I appreciate it. Nova, I'm gonna go. Are you staying or coming?"

She kisses her boyfriend on the lips, then slides off his lap, grabbing her bag from the floor. "Coming," she says quietly.

Without another word, I spin around, giving the guys my back and walk away from them, my head held high, Nova at my side. Her fingers slide between mine as a show of solidarity as we head in the opposite direction.

GRIFFIN

As I watch her stalk away from me, Nova's fingers entwined with hers, I can feel my body rising from the seat without me consciously deciding to follow her. Zeke's hand lands on my shoulder pushing me down and I spin around to look at him.

"Nope," he says, his lips pressed together in a firm, hard line.

"I need to go after her."

"No you don't. She needs to calm down, else one of you will end up saying something that will only make this whole mess worse."

"Why don't you just tell the girl you're in love with her?" Valentine says dryly.

My head twists in his direction so fast I'm surprised I don't give myself whiplash. "What?"

He laughs lowly. "Dude, the only person who doesn't know how you feel about her is her. You're not exactly hiding it; it's written all over your face every time you look at her."

I sigh, lifting my hand up to rub at my throbbing temples

with my fingertips. "She doesn't feel the same way about me."

Both Valentine and Zeke burst into laughter.

"What?" I demand.

"That girl would be yours in a hot second if you just grew a big enough pair of balls to tell her how you feel," Zeke says, between amused chuckles.

"She doesn't want a Sinner or the Sinner way of life. She's told us this over and over. I kissed her last night. If she felt anything for me, she wouldn't still be saying yes to dates from all these assholes. Look at this fucking guy she's dating; he couldn't be any less Sinner if he tried. He rides a fucking Vespa for fuck's sake. He doesn't treat her right and she's lapping that shit up, loving that he's a fucking pussy and that she feels like an equal or some shit."

"I explained a few things to her yesterday morning. I thought she understood things a bit clearer now," Zeke says.

"What the fuck did you say to her?" I demand, my hand gripping Zeke's shirt tightly.

"Calm down," Valentine snaps, shocking me. "Emmy isn't your average girl. You can't treat her like she is or expect her to behave like she's just the usual pussy wanting to hang off a Scion."

"Don't fucking call her pussy," I growl.

"I didn't," He smirks. "That's what I'm trying to say. Emmy is a Scion, *The* Scion, if you think about it. She's the Prez's kid and her dad is one scary motherfucker."

"What's your point?" Zeke asks, his head tilted to the side thoughtfully.

"She thinks she wants something different than Archer's Creek and the family, but that's just because she's never known anything else. Let her experience what guys are like outside your world, let her experiment with that Kent kid;

he's harmless. But while that's happening, show her what it's like to belong to a Sinner too. Be her guy, treat her like the Sinners treat their women. Treat her like a woman, like a Scion, like Emmy deserves to be treated. I'd lay money on the fact that she wants you just as much as you want her, but right now home is the familiar and she wants new, so let her do her thing." Valentine says with a shrug.

"I can't let that pissant Kent touch her, I'll fucking kill him," I growl, my fingers curling into fists just thinking about his hands on her.

"So make sure she's getting what she needs at home, then she won't go looking for it elsewhere," he says conspiratorially.

For a moment I mull over his words. She didn't pull away when I kissed her; in fact, she kissed me back. Could Valentine be right? Could Emmy feel the same way about me as I do about her? Just the thought of watching her date someone else makes me feel violent and out of control, but maybe I could threaten Kent, warn him to keep his hands to himself? Then she could date him and I could be staking my claim behind the scenes. He might get her for a few hours, but I live with her, I have all the rest of her time.

My brother doesn't have an old lady, but I've spent enough time around the club and my friend's families to see how Sinners men treat their women. I've had girls. I'm hardly a fucking virgin, but I've always known that Emmy is the only woman I've ever wanted to own me, heart, body and soul. She's had all of me since we were kids, she just doesn't know it yet. Maybe the guys are right? Maybe it's time to step up and stake my claim.

Standing, I pull my cell from my pocket and step away from the table, not bothering to look back at the others. I'm pretty sure they know what I'm about to do. My hands are shaking as I scroll through my contacts until I find the one I'm looking for, hitting dial before I can talk myself out of doing it.

"Griffin, you okay?" The deep, gravelly voice asks as he answers my call.

"Yeah, I'm fine, we're all fine. But I need to talk to you about something."

A low laugh reverberates through the line and my heart kicks up a notch, beating hard beneath my chest.

"I'm in love with your daughter. Have been pretty much since the day we met. I know I'm not fucking good enough for her, but I still want her. You gonna kill me if I try to make her mine?"

"Does she want you?" Prez asks.

"Honestly, I have no fucking clue, but she's started dating this little prick and I can't wait any longer. I'm gonna lose her for good if I don't try to show her how I feel."

"She's dating?" He roars.

I flinch, knowing I probably shouldn't have told him that, but Emmy's dad scares the fucking shit out of me and my default setting when I'm around him is total fucking honestly. "Yep, she went out with him the other night and he asked her out again."

"You know I can rip off your dick and balls, beat you to fucking death with them, then get rid of your body where no one will ever find you if you hurt my baby girl, right?"

"I know that. I love her," I say simply.

"Good, bout fucking time you told her," Prez says, humor dancing through his voice.

"You knew?" I ask, shocked.

"Kid, the only person who doesn't know is my daughter. I've been waiting for this conversation for the last eight years. Took you fucking long enough."

"Well, fuck."

"Take care of her. I'll see you when it's parents' weekend," he says, his voice laced with amusement. Then he ends the call, leaving me staring at my cell in shock.

Turning back to the table, I lower myself back onto the bench, too stunned to really process what just happened.

"Prez gonna kill you?" Zeke asks.

I look up at him, surprised to see worry on his face and shake my head.

Valentine sniggers. "So, he knew too?"

I nod.

Zeke slaps his hand against my shoulder. "Come on, we need to get to class, then we need to figure out how to make peace with Emmy, so you at least stand a chance of showing her how you feel about her.

EMMY

My anger follows me through the rest of my day and by the time I open the front door of the house I'm seething and thoroughly pissed off. The smell of Mexican food hits me as soon as I step into the house, followed immediately by Griffin's familiar scent as he scoops me off the ground and holds me to his chest in a tight hug.

"We're sorry," he whispers against my ear. "We're assholes and we're really, really fucking sorry."

I didn't realize how much I needed his apology until I heard it, and some of my anger bleeds from me as I melt a little into his embrace.

"Forgive me. I hate it when you're pissed with me. Please don't be mad at me anymore. I haven't had my snuggles in days and I was just pissy because I missed you," he drawls into my neck, pulling me in even tighter.

With a sigh, I free my arms and wrap them around his back, hugging him. "You're a dickweed," I say against his chest.

"I know, but I'm your dickweed," he whispers. "Will you come snuggle with me properly on the couch? We made you enchiladas just the way you like them and Zeke went and got you a gallon of that sweet tea you like so much."

"I'm not sure you really deserve snuggles," I goad him.

"Don't say that, Em, never say that. I need them and you promised me." His voice is almost desperate, frantic, and even though I'm annoyed with him and Zeke, I feel awful for suggesting I won't give him the comfort I promised him I'd always be there to give him.

"I didn't mean it. You know I'm always here for you, even when you're behaving like an unmitigated asshole," I say, gripping him a little tighter.

My feet leave the floor and Griffin carries me into the living room, sitting down on the couch and positioning me on his lap. His hold on me is a little too tight, like he's afraid I'll leave him, even though I'm snuggled into his chest the same way we've done a thousand times before. The way we were last night after he kissed me. My core heats at the memory and I wonder what he'd do if I kissed him.

Zeke slinks into the room, his eyes downcast, his expression repentant. "I'm sorry, Em. You know we would never laugh at you, ever. We shouldn't have been jackasses about Kent either and I promise it won't happen again. He's not what we're used to, but for you we'll try to be better."

I nod and he steps closer, pulling the hand from behind his back and revealing the clear plastic cup holding my favorite sweet tea. A small smile forms on my lips and I reach for the cup, taking it from his outstretched hand and bringing the straw to my lips.

"We made your favorite food and we're taking you out tonight to apologize. It's Karaoke night at the bar, so we're all going, we thought you could see if Kent wanted to come too," Zeke says, sitting down on the coffee table in front of the couch.

"And you'll be nice?" I ask, my brows arched in question.

"Scouts honor," Griff says from beneath me.

"You were never in the scouts," I say with a laugh, rolling my eyes. I know I should probably still be mad at them, but they're my best friends, my family, and as much as I might try, I can never stay angry with them for long. "Karaoke sounds like fun," I concede.

"Karaoke!" Zeke sings out loudly, jumping up from where he was sitting.

Shaking my head resigned, I can't help but laugh, and shove at Zeke's arm, as he breaks into a booty wiggling dance in front of me, then bursts into a very loud and very off-key rendition of 'Oops!...I Did It Again'.

Nova and Valentine are both back by the time the food is ready, and we all sit and eat together as one big dysfunctional family. I'm reminded once again why I don't want to pull too far from them, because as loud and obnoxious and insular as we can be, we're still family and I love them all.

When we get to the bar, I flash my fake ID at the huge stern looking bouncer, then let Griffin take my hand and pull me along behind him as he makes his way into the busy bar. Zeke spots an empty booth, so we all rush toward it and I slide into one side as Valentine steers Nova into the other side, nodding pointedly at Zeke before he leaves to go get drinks from the bar.

"Is Kent coming?" Nova shouts over the noise of a very bad rendition of a Bon Jovi song.

I nod. "He's at work until eight, but he said he'd come after he'd got changed."

"What does he do?" She asks.

"He works at the bookstore on campus."

"That's cool," Nova replies.

I nod, shuffling along to the edge of the booth so Griffin can slide in next to me. Valentine appears a moment later carrying a pitcher of beer and a smaller pitcher of something pink which he places down in front of me and Nova. "What's this?" I ask him.

"It's called Bubblegum Dream. The guy behind the bar says it tastes like candy," Valentine says with a shrug, disappearing again and returning a moment later with five glasses.

Nova looks at me, then to the pink drink. She shrugs, then pours us a glass each, sliding mine toward me and lifting hers into the air to make a toast. "To the Scions," she says.

I lift my glass up and the guys follow suit. "The Scions," we all say, clinking our glasses against each other. Until Valentine came into our lives, I'd never heard the nickname the kids at our high school had given our group, but somehow we've adopted it and we celebrate it, because whether we like it or not, we are the Sinners Scions.

Bringing the glass to my lips, I take a tentative sip, then moan in happiness when the sweet, candy flavored drink fills my mouth and coats my tongue. "Oh my god, that is so good," I cry.

Nova eagerly nods, taking a longer sip, then handing her glass to Valentine so he can try. His face is hilarious as he pinches his lips together and screws his nose up in obvious disgust.

"That's revolting; it's like drinking pure sugar," he spits out, taking a long pull of his beer.

"It's delicious," I argue, taking another drink. Nova and I finish the jug quickly, laughing as we peruse the songbook to decide what Karaoke song we want to perform. I wobble a little as she drags me onto the stage and as the first notes of 'Sweet Home Alabama' start to play, we receive raucous applaud from the crowds filling the bar. Tipping my head back, I sing loudly along with the music, dancing around with Nova until the song ends and sweat coats my skin.

Laughter falls from my lips as Nova holds my hand, skipping as she pulls me back to our seats. "Kent," I cry, spotting him sat uncomfortably next to Griffin in the booth. He looks tiny, his shoulders slim and narrow compared to Griffin's wide, muscular, athletic frame.

Kent slides off the seat and steps toward me, leaning in to press a kiss against my cheek. "Hi," he says, his sweet smile eliciting an equally sweet smile to spread across my own lips.

"Hi," I say back, suddenly feeling a little shy. Glancing over to my friends, I watch as Nova climbs onto Valentine's lap, wrapping her arms around his neck and whispering in his ear. I have no idea what Kent would do if I tried to sit on his lap. He'd probably run away from me. Unsure how to behave around him, I stand awkwardly for a moment then say. "Err, we need more pink drinks, or maybe purple drinks because I saw someone with a jug of something purple. I'm going to go see what they have at the bar," I announce. "Do you want a drink?" I ask Kent.

"No, I just got a beer, thanks." Kent says, lifting the glass bottle in his hand to show me.

"Stay here, I'll go to the bar," Griffin says, sliding out of the booth toward me, amusement lacing his tone.

"No." I cry. "I can go to the bar. I'm a Scion for fuck's sake."

"The Scions," Nova cheers, reaching for her glass to toast and finding it empty.

"What are the scions?" Kent asks.

I freeze, unsure what to say or even if I should say anything at all. I mean the truth is a slippery slope, admitting one thing could lead to him knowing everything and I'm not ready for my two worlds to implode.

"Just an in-joke, don't worry about it," Griff says, slapping Kent on the shoulder playfully.

It feels like my entire body sags with relief, but I do my best to cover it. "Do we need more beer, or just pastel colored drinks?" I ask.

"We're good for beer," Valentine says, laughing.

"I'll go with her," Griff says, but I'm already moving away from the table and making my way to the bar.

"What can I get you?" The girl behind the bar asks me, when I step up to the sticky wooden platform.

"What's the purple drink in the pitchers called?" I shout.

The girl eyes me, her head tilting to the side as she assesses me. "I'm gonna need to see some ID."

I hand over my fake ID, feeling Griffin's presence behind me as his arm snakes around my side and lands on the wooden surface next to where my own hand is resting.

The bartender nods at me and hands back my ID. "It's called Purple Haze. It's vodka, grape soda, peach schnapps, and lemonade. Tastes like a grape popsicle."

"Perfect," I shout over the loud wails of someone attempting to sing a Katy Perry song. She nods, then turns away, grabbing bottles and mixing liquids together. "I'm more than capable of getting drinks on my own," I say loudly, addressing Griffin without turning around to look at him.

The hand he had rested on the bar winds around my waist and he pulls me back into his chest, his fingers spreading across my stomach. The heat of his body presses into my back and I feel his breath against my ear a moment before he speaks. "You're drunk, in a busy bar, and that pussy you're dating wasn't putting his hand up to come keep an eye on you, so I'm making sure no one hassles you."

His words are harsh, but the tone of his voice is soft, almost cajoling. A flashback of the way he kissed me last night jumps into my head. I'm still expecting him to mention it, but he hasn't, and I don't know what that means.

"Kent isn't a pussy. He just gets that I'm an adult and don't need to be babysat," I hiss.

"Taking care of you, isn't babysitting you, Em. Wanting you to be safe isn't suffocating you. But that's the bit that you don't get, that you don't ever seem to have got," Griff says, his hot breath warming the side of my neck.

"But I'm not yours?" Even though I intended on making a statement, it comes out like a question, my voice raspy.

"Aren't you?" he says, his lips pressing a kiss against the pulse point in my neck.

Something sparks to life inside of me and I feel my skin heat beneath where his lips are touching me. Suddenly everything else becomes obsolete and all I can feel is his hard body pressed against me. I take in the strength of his huge arm wrapped around my waist; the way he's curved around me; how his body is towering over me, huge, strong and powerful. My breath catches in my lungs and I'm not sure if I want to run from this or push my ass back against him just to see what he'd do.

"Little Red, fancy seeing you in here."

The new, yet familiar voice startles me, pulling me from my Griffin induced haze and I look around to find Van leaning against the bar a few feet from us. His eyes take me in, running up and down my body, lingering on where Griff's hand is spread across my belly still touching me.

"Van," I say, my voice sounding husky and a little breathless. I refuse to think about if it's his sudden appearance, anticipation of spending time with Kent, or the way Griff's touching me and the memory of our kiss that's affecting me.

"Van?" Griff growls.

"Am I just in time to rescue you again, little one?" Van asks, amusement flashing in his eyes.

"No," I snap out. "I don't need to be rescued."

Griffin's grip on me changes and in the blink of an eye he moves me from in front to behind him, his body hiding me.

"Ahh," Van drawls. "I thought you looked familiar. You're one of Red's protectors."

Forcing my way forward, I step to Griffin's side and glare at him. "Griffin, this is Van. Van, this is Griffin."

"Boyfriend?" Van asks coldly.

"You're the asshole from the frat house?" Griffin says smiling, ignoring Van's question. He glances back to our booth for a second, before his arm snakes around my waist again and I'm pulled back against his body.

"Van Torres," Van says, holding out his hand.

Griff's hold on me tightens as he leans forward and takes his outstretched hand. "Griffin Bennett."

I roll my eyes and consider reminding them that I already made introductions a few moments ago, but before I get a chance to open my mouth, Zeke ambles up to my other side smiling widely, even though I can sense the tension in him.

"What's taking so long with the drinks?" He asks, his voice light and amused, or at least that's how he sounds to someone who doesn't know him as well as I do.

"Nothing, go back to the booth, the bartender is just mixing it," I say.

"You making friends?" Zeke asks, nodding to Van. "Introduce us."

"Oh my god," I groan.

"We've already met," Van says, glaring at Zeke.

Zeke's laugh is low and dangerous. "So we have. Zeke Stubbs," he offers, reaching his hand out to Van.

Van takes it, his eyes hardening as he glances between the guys before his gaze rests on me. I sigh, rolling my eyes as I try to push Griff's arm out of the way and lean forward to hand the bartender some money when she places a jug full of purple liquid on the bar in front of us. Griff's grip tightens on me and he holds me firmly in place, dropping a twenty onto the bar before I get a chance.

"Looks like you collect protectors. Are these two my competition?" Van asks, ignoring the guys and looking at me.

"We're her family," Zeke says, still smiling despite the coolness in his voice.

"There's no competition," Griff drawls, his palm spreading wide, his fingers disappearing beneath the bottom of my shirt.

"Is that right?" Van drawls, his eyes dropping to the possessive way Griffin is holding me.

"Oh my god!" I cry. "This is why I want to date a guy like Kent, who for your information is sitting right over there," I say, pushing Griffin's hand from my waist and grabbing the pitcher of purple drink as I turn on my heel and stomp back over to the booth without a backward glance at the three infuriating alpha males at the bar.

When I reach the table, I exhale a sigh of relief, placing the pitcher down. Kent is animatedly talking to Nova and I force away my frustration and smile, glad that at least one of my friends is being nice to him.

"We need glasses," Nova says. "You sit, I'll go grab some."

I wave her off. "I'll get them, I'm already up."

Reluctantly, I head back to the bar hoping to find Van

gone, but instead, he, Zeke, and Griffin are still facing off, all of them wearing matching hard looks. Determined to break up the standoff, I push between them and ask the bartender for two glasses, before I spin back to face them.

I allow my eyes to rake over the three men, all of which are giving off eerily familiar vibes. Van seems older, but still sexy and oozing confidence. Zeke is beautiful but intimidating, and Griffin is intense like the quintessential alpha male. Looking at the three of them, so different, yet so similar, I get why women throw themselves at men like them. Men who want to protect and covet their women, just like my dad does for my mom, like my uncles do for my aunties. For the first time I really do get it, and it scares the shit out of me. In this moment I understand completely why women lose their minds over possessive dominant men.

"I have no idea what the hell this is about, but it's really not necessary," I say. "I don't need any of you to defend me. My daddy is the biggest badass y'all will ever meet and I have at least twenty uncles who would help him kill all of you for pissing me off and dispose of your bodies somewhere no one would ever find you. But I don't need them either. I'm Emmy Devereaux, and I'm more than capable of looking after myself, so why don't you all back the fuck up and go find someone else to rescue, because I have no use for any of you."

My little rant has all three guys' attention fixed on me. Zeke and Griffin are smiling widely, while Van looks shocked with a hint of admiration.

"Every time I think you've forgotten, you do something like this to remind me exactly who you are, shortcake," Griff hoots, scooping me into the air and twirling me around, making me hold the glasses tightly to stop from dropping them.

Instead of putting me down, Griff holds me off the ground as Zeke laughs and the three of us head back to the table, leaving a bemused Van behind us. Despite the noise of the bar I swear I hear him say, "See you soon, Little Red," as he watches us disappear into the crowd.

Griffin doesn't lower me to the ground until we reach our booth and I slide in next to Kent, while he slides in next to me still smiling widely like the confrontation with Van never happened. Nova arches her eyebrow at me, flashing me a questioning look, but I subtly shake my head, letting her know that I don't want to talk about it.

She takes the glasses from me and fills them with purple stuff, pushing one toward me. Lifting hers into the air, she winks at me and I laugh then tap my glass against hers, taking a healthy pull of the liquid. Swallowing, I inhale raggedly, trying to hide how shaken I am by every bizarre thing that's happened tonight and the way Griff's touch is affecting me.

All I wanted was to be invisible, not have the weight of my family's legacy pressing down on my shoulders. I've done all the right things. I made friends, I've tried new things, I've kept my new college life separate from my best friends and everything that reminds me of home. I had a plan, this was all supposed to make me normal, just a face in a crowd, but it hasn't worked.

What did I do wrong? Avery and Veronica are great, but I feel like I'm lying to them, because I'm so desperate to be new and different that I don't want to be honest and let them see the person I am at my core.

I met a nice guy; Kent is someone so different to anyone I've ever known, and I'm lying to him too, pretending, and it's not fair. Then there's Van. I like him too, but because he reminds me so much of the guys I grew up around, I'm lashing out and being every bit of the Sinners Scion I'm pretending not to be.

And Griffin, the person who normally grounds me and keeps me together is kissing me and making me feel things I'm not supposed to be feeling for my best friend.

Confused, I lift the glass full of purple cocktail to my lips and down half of the contents in one long gulp. The sugar and alcohol coat my tongue and throat and I shudder as I swallow, feeling a burning warmth in my chest.

"Woo hoo," Nova cries, throwing one hand into the air and lifting her own glass to her lips with the other. She downs her entire glass, then lifts her gaze to me, arching her eyebrows as she shakes her empty glass at me tauntingly.

With a laugh I drink the remaining liquid, then lift my glass into the air and toast her with it. The guys all hoot and holler, all except for Kent who just looks bemused. His arm brushes against mine and I'm dragged back to the present and the sweet and entirely different guy sitting next to me. He's everything I thought I wanted. A smile forms on my lips and some of the tension dissolves from my shoulders. "Hey," I say, nudging his arm with mine.

"Hey," he replies.

"So, what's your Karaoke song?" I ask.

He laughs. The sound is light and easy and I instantly love it.

"Maybe we should do a duet? You sounded pretty awesome up there with Nova."

"I like this plan," I say, looking up at him from beneath my lashes.

"Dibs on Genie In A Bottle," Zeke announces loudly.

"Oh my god, not again. I swear that's the only song you ever pick," Nova bemoans.

Griff's low chuckle beside me draws my attention and I

turn to look at him. His big body is angled slightly so he can lean against the side of the booth, one arm draped along the top of the seat behind me, his fingers absentmindedly toying with the ends of my hair. All of the tension from only a couple of moments ago is gone and his expression is relaxed, his smile happy.

His gaze meets mine and he nudges my knee with his. I can't help smiling back. Despite everything, Griff is my best friend and he always will be. I nudge him back and his smile widens. "Em and I are gonna do our usual," he says to the group, his eyes not leaving mine.

"You guys do Karaoke a lot?" Kent asks, pulling my attention back to him.

Nova chuckles sweetly. "Emmy begged her mom and dad for a Karaoke machine one Christmas when we were like, what? Ten or eleven? So all we did for like a year after that was sing Karaoke on that thing. I swear we used to take it to the club every time there was a family day."

"The club?" Kent questions, smiling.

Her eyes widen and she glances at me for a split second. "Just something our families are all members of back home."

Kent nods. "Oh, like a country club. My parents are members of our local one. But I'll be honest it was more golf tournaments and less Karaoke when I was growing up."

I don't correct Kent's assumption about 'the club' being a country club. Yet another lie of omission. What's one more on the ever-growing pile? A clawing feeling of guilt flares to life in my stomach. I'm not ashamed of my heritage, my family or the Sinners; it's just that Kent isn't the type of guy who would understand and take it in his stride, or at least I don't think he is.

Not five minutes earlier I was mouthing off to Van, Zeke, and Griff about coming from a family of badasses, yet here I am letting Kent believe that my family are members of a country club. I'm so confused, so at odds with myself.

Maybe just staying away from boys like I did in high school might be the smarter option. I need to spend some time figuring out who I am, perhaps then I might be able to make sense of all these guys who have suddenly burst into my life.

Something touches my arm and I look down to find Nova pushing my now full glass toward me. She winks again and I smile back, lifting the glass and taking a healthy pull from it. "Let go pick our songs," I announce, pushing Griff in the ribs to get him to move.

Hours later, I step through the bar's door and out into the evening air. Goose bumps pebble across my skin and I wrap my arms around myself trying to stay warm. Kent steps out behind me, a sway in his step as he traverses the sidewalk to move to my side.

"Emmy," he slurs. "I like Karaoke."

I giggle, although I'm not sure why it's funny. Kent must think it's funny too, because he starts to laugh and Nova quickly joins in, shoving me in the shoulder playfully.

"Purple drinks are fun," she whispers, lifting her finger to her lips. "Shhhh," she says, then breaks into another bout of giggles.

"I gotta go," Kent says, spinning on his heel and pointing back toward campus.

"Nooo," I whine.

"Yep, gotta go to class," he mumbles.

Pushing out my bottom lip, I pout at him. "You're so different. I thought different was good. It is good. Come back to ours, different boy," I slur.

"Come on, drunk girl," Griff says, scooping me off the floor and into his arms. "Say goodnight to Kent."

"Goodnight, Kent," I call, laughing and waving.

Kent's eyebrows furrow together as if he intends to say something, then he blinks slowly, lifts his hand into the air and points at me.

"You gonna be alright getting back to the dorms?" Zeke asks, stepping in front of Kent.

Kent nods, but then his head keeps nodding, like it's moving of its own accord. "I'll be f- fine."

Zeke laughs, then turns to us. "I'll make sure he gets back okay; I'll see you guys at home." Turning back to Kent, he slings his arm over his shoulder and guides him in the direction of campus. "Come on, big guy, let's get you home."

I open my mouth, intent on saying something, but Griff spins us around and walks in the opposite direction. I blink, hoping to clear my vision, but instead, as my eyes shut, I struggle to open them again. Sighing, I rest my head against Griff's chest, enjoying the warmth of his skin and his delicious Griff smell.

"It's a good job you're such a tiny little thing, shortcake," he whispers.

"Uh huh," I mumble, sighing again, then yawning.

"You okay carrying her?" I hear Valentine ask.

"Yeah, she's light as a feather. You good with Nova?" Griff asks, his voice rumbling through his chest where my head is rested.

"I wanna piggyback," Nova giggles.

"Princess, you're a pain in the ass," Valentine moans playfully.

"Good job you love me," Nova singsongs.

"Good job I do," he replies.

Griff hoists me higher into his arms and I wrap myself tighter around his neck, clinging to him.

"You doing okay, Em?" He asks.

"Yep," I say popping the p. "I gotta tell Kent I'm too drunk to do poetry with him tonight," I slur.

"Okay, shortcake, whatever you want," he laughs.

I must fall asleep, because the next thing I know, I can feel the cotton of my comforter beneath me. "Griff," I call, disoriented.

"You okay?"

"Yeah, come snuggle with me," I say, lifting my arms into the air, my eyes still closed.

"I thought I got to ask you for snuggles, not the other way around?" He laughs.

"Griff," I whine, wiggling my fingers until I feel the bed depress at my side and Griff's big, warm body move next to me.

"Come here, shortcake," he says, indulgently.

I roll into his chest as he slides his arm beneath my neck, wrapping it around my back and pulling me closer. His lips press against the top of my head and he exhales softly against my hair.

"Griff," I whisper.

"Yeah?"

The words come before I even think about what I'm saying, "Kiss me."

His body stiffens. "You're drunk."

"I still want you to kiss me," I say, pressing my lips against the warm, soft skin just above the collar of his t-shirt.

His fingers hook under my chin and he tilts my face back. "Open your eyes," he demands.

Forcing my eyes open, I look up into his stormy, conflicted depths. Then he lowers his face and presses his lips against mine in a gentle barely there kiss.

He pulls back a second later and I suck in a gasp. "Kiss me again," I whisper.

"Why?" he growls, his voice so gravelly I barely recognize the sound.

"Because I need my roots right now more than I need wings and because I want you to."

As I watch, something flashes across his face a second before his lips meet mine again. Only this time our kiss isn't sweet and gentle. His lips dominate mine, claiming me like I'm his and this kiss is his brand. I kiss him back just as passionately, parting his lips with my tongue and deepening the kiss until I'm unsure where I end and he begins.

My fingers find their way into his hair, pulling at the strands as he drags me even closer to him, until I'm half draped across him, my breasts pressed against his heaving chest.

We kiss as if we'll never have another chance, as if we'll never see each other again, and I feel desperate with need, want, and desire. I'm not sure how I recognize the feelings, having never felt them before, but something old and instinctive has me clawing to be closer to him, willing this to never end.

Griffin pulls away first, tearing his lips from mine and turning his face until it's buried in my neck. "Fuck." The single word is an angry snarl.

"Griff?"

"Fuck," he snarls again. "We need to stop. Not now, not like this."

He pushes me gently off his chest, but I reach out and grab his arm. "What's the matter?"

"You're drunk, Emmy."

"So? You're drunk too."

"No, I'm not. I had three beers, I'm not even slightly drunk. I haven't been all night," he says, sitting on the side of my bed, his feet on the floor, his hands scrubbing at his face.

"Griff," I say, his name a desperate moan as I move beside him.

"You should go to sleep."

Sliding my hand along his chest, I lift it until it's cupping his jaw and he turns into my touch. Pushing up onto my knees, I move closer and press my lips to his. For a moment he freezes and I wait for him to push me off, but instead he wraps an arm around my back and pulls me off the bed and into his lap, my hips straddling his waist, my core pressed against his.

Something hard rubs against my sex and a cry falls from my mouth. His hands grip my waist, but he doesn't stop me from moving as I tentatively roll my hips. A needy pulse blooms to life in my stomach as I move against what I think is his hard cock and I feel a gasp form on his lips that are still pressed against mine.

He inhales deeply as I move again, grinding a little harder into his lap, then his lips press against mine, kissing me punishingly hard for a split second before I'm lifted from his lap and dropped to my feet in front of him.

Inhaling sharply, he closes his eyes and shakes his head. "Not like this, fuck, not like this," he whispers.

Shuffling forward, I try to get closer to him, but his hands on my waist stop me. "You should go to sleep," he orders, his voice raspy.

"Stay with me," I say, exhaustion settling over me now he's mentioned sleep.

"Emmy."

He says my name, like a warning, but I don't heed it, or understand it. "Griff, please," I beg.

"Get into bed," he demands and I do as he says without question, turning and crawling onto the bed, sliding beneath the comforter. For a long, painful moment I think he's going to leave, but then the mattress dips and he cautiously climbs onto my bed, settling himself behind me.

The moment he's beside me, my eyes close without permission. The last thing I remember before sleep consumes me are Griffin's arms wrapping around me from behind and his lips pressing against the back of my neck.

GRIFFIN

I'm a fucking idiot. A stupid, fucking idiot, but when it comes to her I just don't seem to be able to help myself.

The sun rose over an hour ago, and every single bit of self-preservation in me has been telling me to get the hell out of her bed since the sun pushed its way into the sky. But I'm still here, wrapped around her, spooning her tiny body from behind as she clings to my arms, holding me in place.

Last night was one of the best and worst nights of my life. I watched her own who she is, embrace her heritage and show the world and that guy who's sniffing around her how much of a Sinner she really is. Then I spent the rest of the night watching her share her smiles and her laughs with another dude. I hate Kent with every cell in my body, just because she was looking at him and not at me.

I want all of her smiles, all of her laughs, all of her attention, and last night she was his, at least as far as the outside world thinks.

Kent isn't a bad guy; he's just not one of us and he never will be. Emmy wants something different and she thinks he's it, but I can guarantee he's not enough for her. She's built up the image of a new life in her head, but when it comes down to it, she'll be miserable with someone who doesn't challenge her, and Kent doesn't have enough conviction to challenge anything.

A small sigh escapes her lips and I hold my breath. I can still taste her kisses on my lips, and I want to cling to this feeling, her in my arms, her wanting me, needing me for as long as possible. But it's not real, it's just a drunken fantasy and with every minute that passes I get closer and closer to her waking up and telling me we shouldn't have touched, that she was drunk, that she didn't know what she was saying, what she was asking me for.

Or worse, she won't remember it at all.

I want to freeze time, to stay in this limbo forever, but I know I can't. Real life wins over fantasy every time, so I silently slide my arm from beneath her and roll out of her bed. Slowly, I back away from the tiny sleeping body of the woman I am heartbreakingly in love with and leave her room before she wakes up and tells me the best night of my life was all just a mistake.

EMMY

I hear the soft click of the door and roll toward the noise. My bed is empty, but the warmth of the sheets where Griffin was until a moment ago makes my heart ache.

We kissed again last night. Worse than that, I begged him to kiss me. Heat coats my skin as I remember the way I clung to him, how I practically climbed on top of him, how he kissed me back.

Licking my lips, I can almost taste him on my skin and a pang of something that feels a lot like desire pulses through me. I want Griffin.

The thought makes my heart pound in my chest and my breath shorten until I'm gasping with the knowledge. I wanted him last night and I still want him now.

Kent is nice, sweet, and different, but as much as I like him, I don't want him. Not like I want Griffin.

Griffin, my best friend, and the boy I grew up with. My family.

A sob forms unbidden on my lips, breaking free and soundlessly bursting from me. I want Griffin. I've never wanted a guy before and now I want Griffin, someone I can't have, someone who doesn't feel the same.

My dad would never allow it and he'd punish Griff for it. He'd stop him from prospecting, he'd ruin his future. Another sob bursts from me and I slap my hand over my lips to stifle any sound that tries to break free.

I'm the daughter of the president of the Doomsday Sinners MC, my father's baby girl, untouchable, forbidden.

A tide of nausea rises in my throat and I dash from my bed, barely making it to the bathroom, before I vomit purple and pink cocktails until there's nothing left in my body. Crawling to the basin, I wash my face and swill my mouth out with water. My bladder takes that moment to remind me that it still exists and I use the bathroom, wash my hands, then drag myself back to my bed.

I lie back down and Griffin's achingly familiar scent surrounds me. How did I go from no guys, to three guys, only to realize that the one I can't have is the one I want?

Tears fill my eyes, but I bury my face into the pillow that smells like my best friend and eventually fall asleep, dreaming about kissing Griff, imagining that he was still here with me and that everything was going to be okay.

As my eyes flutter open, I'm filled with memories of the night before. For a moment I'm jealous of those people who don't remember all the things they do when they've had too much to drink, because apparently I remember every single embarrassing moment.

Visions of singing Karaoke, drinking far too many candy flavored drinks, and then letting Griffin carry my drunk ass home assault me.

Griffin.

A pain lances through my chest as I think about my best friend, my anchor, my roots. We kissed again, only this time it was me that instigated it not him. The pain in my heart is replaced with a pulse of desire so strong I actually flinch. I want him, I want to be his.

Lust, desire, call it whatever you want, crashes over me so violently that even lying down I feel knocked off my feet. I've felt childish crushes in the past, but I've never experienced the longing that crashes into my body as I think about the way he felt beneath me, the way his lips tasted, how I felt wrapped in his arms.

If this were a book, he'd feel the same way. We'd wake up in each other's arms, confess our feelings for each other and live happily ever after; but this isn't a story and I don't think there's a happy ending in store for us.

Griffin's gone, having skulked from my room just after the sun came up, and now I'm alone, rejected and foolish. Apparently drunk me is a lot bolder than sober me, because in the cold light of day my first instinct is to pretend last night didn't happen. To write off the way it felt to be close to him as just a by-product of the alcohol.

Only I know that would be a lie. The moment I woke up with him laying me down on my bed I'd felt sober again. I'd wanted him to touch me, to kiss me. Just him, just Griffin. Neither Kent nor Van had even entered my mind. I'd just wanted the boy who carried me home, who brought me to bed, who protected me, cared for me. The boy I've known almost my whole life.

For the first time ever, I wanted to be loved by him, worshipped by him, owned by him.

Closing my eyes, I bask in the memory of our kiss and for a moment I feel whole, centered and complete, then I allow my eyelids to flutter open and I remember that he left. He left me and now I have no idea what any of this means.

Did he just kiss me because I begged him to?

Was it just a drunken, indulgent kiss between friends?

Was Griffin just reminding me again what a taste of home felt like?

Confusion swirls with disbelief, leaving me sad and confused. If he were any other boy this would be so much simpler. If Kent had brought me home last night, I'd know how to process everything that's happened. If Kent had fled from my bed before I woke up, I'd know it was the rejection this feels like. But Kent and I are dating, and Griffin and I are family.

I shouldn't even be thinking about this. My dad would decimate Griff if he found out we kissed. He'd rip him limb from limb if he knew Griff slept in my bed. Our families just wouldn't be okay with us being more than family.

Our parents refer to us all like we're siblings and here I am lusting over my pseudo brother. Groaning, I roll onto my stomach, burying my face into the comforter. I thought I had all of this figured out. I wanted something more, something different from the men I grew up around. I thought I wanted Kent, or at least someone like Kent, only when I was drunk and needy it wasn't Kent I was begging to kiss me and stay with me, it was Griff.

Embarrassment washes over me and my cheeks heat. Last night I practically begged Griffin, then I molested him, kissing him like he was my man and I was his woman. Or maybe I just looked like one of the girls who hang out at the club, desperately clinging to any Sinner who will let them.

Jesus, how the hell am I going to face him?

I attacked him like some horny club slut, then begged him to stay the night. No wonder he sloped out of my room before it was even light this morning, he probably didn't want to face me.

But then he'd touched me like I was his in the bar. He'd been possessive, touching me as if he had the right to. Maybe my drunk brain was playing tricks on me? Maybe his lips on mine didn't make me crave more from him in a way I've never experienced before. Maybe it was all just a dream, but if that were true, I wouldn't be wishing he was still here.

I've spent my entire life wanting something different, only to realize that when I'm completely honest and raw, I want a Sinner. I want a guy who carries my drunk ass home from the bar after buying my drinks all night and keeping me safe from sleazy guys. I want a man who kisses me until no other guy in the world exists but him. I want a guy who holds me in his arms and shelters me from the world.

I want a Sinner. More than that, I want Griffin.

GRIFFIN

I've lost count of the amount of times I've walked past her bedroom door, tempting myself with pushing it open and crawling back into her bed.

I shouldn't have left this morning. I should have let her wake up in my arms, and told her I'm in love with her, because I am. I'm so completely and totally in love with her that apparently the only person who doesn't know is her.

Last night she wanted me, almost as badly as I wanted her, but I don't know if that was the cocktails talking or if it was actually real.

Before we left the bar she was with her date, dancing and flirting with him, and at the end of the night she wanted him to come home with her and the lucky fucking bastard would have if Zeke and I hadn't intervened. Then it wouldn't have been me waking up in her room, it would have been him.

Jealousy, hot and fast swells through me and the sudden urge to hunt down the bastard my girl is dating plows through me. He might be a geeky, skinny little fucker, but he's still a guy and he wants her. I saw the way he was looking at her last night, like he wanted to know what her skin tasted like all over.

I want to know that too, but the difference between him and I, is that one day he might actually find out.

Standing outside her door, I sigh wearily, lifting my hand up and resting it against the cool wood. I should knock, go into her room and confess everything to her, but when she rejects me, I won't just lose my soulmate, I'll lose my best friend too.

No, I need to play the long game like Zeke and Valentine suggested and then hope, just fucking hope, that one day she'll see if she just gave me the chance I could be her fucking everything.

Growling, I push away from her door and head for my own room a few doors down. Throwing myself down on my bed, I stare up at the ceiling, lifting my arm up and dropping it back down over my eyes. The faint smell of her perfume clings to the fabric of my shirt and I groan, my dick twitching in my pants.

The urge to grab my cock and imagine what it would feel like if it was her touching me is strong enough that my fingers are sliding beneath the waistband of my track pants before I even consciously decide to move.

When my fingers meet my rock-hard length, I hiss, my eyes fluttering closed as I wrap my fingers around my girth and slowly move my fist up and down. Precum coats my fingers as I glide them along my cock and allow my brain to wander to Emmy.

I imagine her above me, her thighs spread straddling me just like she did last night. Her hair is hanging over her shoulders, hiding her naked body from mine, but then she smiles and my dick twitches against her bare pussy, feeling the heat between her legs. Her hand pushes mine out the way and she wraps her fingers around me and squeezes.

"Fuck." The word slips from my lips on a gasp as her hand slowly begins to slide up and down, twisting at the top and pushing me closer and closer to release. Her hair tickles my chest as she leans forward and kisses me, her hands still on my cock.

I can't help myself; I grab her hair and hold her in place, devouring her lips as she jacks my length. Another groan slips from my mouth and she pulls back, gliding down my body until she's lying between my legs, my cock only inches from her mouth. Her plump bee-stung lips part and she dips her head, swallowing my cock whole.

Reality hits as my cock jerks in my hand, cum shooting from me, hitting my stomach in hot spurts. As my eyes snap open, I'm dragged back to the present, gasping for air, my chest heaving up and down as my body calms.

"Fuck," I hiss, my hand still slowly jacking my deflating cock.

That was fucked up, three seconds and a barely X-rated fantasy about my girl playing with my dick and I'm shooting my load like a preteen. But it's hardly the first time Emmy has been the center of my fantasies. Hell, if I'm honest with myself, she's been the star of every fucking wet dream I've had since I was thirteen years old. She turns me on more than anyone ever has, she's my ultimate perfect woman.

My muscles go lax, the adrenaline from my orgasm burning away, replaced by lethargy and dissatisfaction. A wistful sigh escapes from my lips. Is this all she'll ever be to me? A fantasy. Spank bank fodder that I'll jack off to in the dark of my bedroom while she lives her life with some other fucking bastard. The thought evaporates all of the happy chemicals my release produced and I'm back to being anxious and agitated.

Grabbing a discarded towel from the end of the bed, I clean myself up, tuck my dick back into my sweats and roll to my side, my gaze falling to the window. It's bright and sunny, a beautiful day, but I can't bring myself to find any enjoyment from it.

The urge to go to her, to confess everything, is so strong I actually roll to my back and start to get up. If I had any idea how she really felt, I'd have found my balls and told her I'm in love with her already. But if she rejects me it could ruin our relationship and I'll lose her completely and I can't risk it. If all I can have of her is friendship, I'll live with it. I'd rather have the dregs than not have her at all. I'm a fucking coward but at least this way I still have her in my life in some way, even if it's not in the role I so desperately want her to play.

EMMY

Somehow Griff and I manage to avoid each other for the rest of the day. The sun is high in the sky by the time I drag my hungover ass from my room, and I'm glad I texted Kent when I finished puking this morning to tell him I wouldn't be able to make our date tonight. When I get downstairs, the others are there with only one absence.

"Where's Griffin?" I ask Valentine, when he smirks at me dragging my heels through the doorway.

"Upstairs, I think. Haven't seen him."

I nod, then instantly regret the movement as blistering pain ricochets through my skull. Grabbing a coffee, I avoid food, then make my way back up to my room. When I wake again it's after seven in the evening and I finally feel almost human again.

Shuffling to the bathroom I empty my bladder, then pad downstairs, my stomach growling. As I pass the living room, I can hear the low murmur of the TV, but I don't go in, instead opting to head toward the refrigerator and the leftover Chinese food I'm hoping is still in there. Grabbing the carton,

I quickly reheat it in the microwave, then pull a fork from the drawer and head into the living room.

The room is dark and quiet, except for Zeke who is lazing languidly at one end of the couch, his feet resting on the coffee table.

"Feeling better?" He asks with a smirk.

I nod, shuffling over and dropping down next to him. "I swear I'm never drinking again," I groan.

His laugh is low and so full of amusement I reach over and shove him in the arm.

"Shut up," I scold. "Was Kent okay when you left him?"

"Yep, he was drunk off his ass too, so I made sure he got to his dorm okay then walked home."

"Thank you," I say, turning to look at him.

"It's fine. I might not be a fan of the guy, but if he's important to you, he's important to me."

A burst of something that feels a lot like guilt hits me. I wasn't thinking about Kent as I was mauling Griff and begging him to stay with me. In fact, I've barely given Kent a second thought. My thoughts, my everything, has been so wrapped up in Griffin Fucking Bennett that I'm barely aware of what's going on around me.

Digging my fork into the pot of noodles, I twist a pile up, then lift them to my lips. The salty, greasy goodness hits my tongue and I moan in pleasure.

Zeke laughs. "You should have had a greasy sandwich the moment you got up; it would have sorted you right out."

"God, no. I puked enough this morning without anything in my stomach."

"You were pretty badass last night, Em. You kinda blew me away with the way you handled that kid at the bar. Your dad would have been proud," Zeke says, nudging my knee with his.

Sighing, I lift another forkful of noodles to my mouth, chew, then swallow. "I don't know how I can be two different people and then just be me as well. Last night, I was annoyed with all your macho male bullshit posturing and I just lost my temper. But other times I have no idea what to say and I'm so meek and awkward."

"You're not meek, Em. You might be quiet, but you're strong. You've never taken any shit from us." He reminds me.

"Yeah, but I've known you guys my whole life."

"So what? That's exactly it. You haven't been pretending your entire life. The person you are with us is the real you. The way you behave with Griff and me, and Nova, and hell, even Valentine, is you. You saw what happened to Nova when she tried to play the roles she thought people expected of her. Don't fall into that trap, just be you."

My mind snags on the boy I've known forever, but who I think I feel a whole lot more than friendship for and sorrow washes over me. Zeke's right. Who I am with my best friends is the real me, but if the real me can so easily kiss and grope and want to be with Griff, then maybe pretending to be someone I'm not might be the best thing to do.

My best friend knows who I am. He saw how much I wanted him last night and he ran from me. He obviously doesn't feel the same way, because he's one of the only people who really knows what he'd be getting with me.

Tears fill my eyes and I duck my head to stop Zeke from seeing them. I can't explain to him why I'm crying right now, so it's better that he not see it. With my eyes lowered to my food, I quickly finish the rest as we sit in companionable silence.

"I should go find my cell, then text Kent to see if he's all right," I say, pushing up off the couch.

"You gonna go out with him again?" Zeke asks, his brows furrowed together.

I don't think. I just speak before I can convince myself otherwise. "Yeah, of course I am. It will be so much easier for me now I know you guys are going to give him a chance too."

"Oh," Zeke says slowly, his eyes narrowing slightly.

"Night, Zeke," I say, not giving him a chance to speak again as I turn and leave the room. Lead fills my stomach and I wrap my free arm around my waist to stem the tide of emotion I can feel coming. Saying that I want to date Kent feels wrong, but I can't exactly tell Zeke that I want to date Kent so he can help me get over my newly discovered crush on my best friend.

When I fall asleep later that night, my dreams are plagued with visions of Griff, and I wake up, hot and horny with a pulsing need between my legs. It would be so easy to slide my hand into my pajamas and release some of the tension that's thrumming through my body, but I refuse to get myself off thinking about Griffin no matter how much I want to.

Somehow using him as fantasy material feels like crossing a line I can never step back from and it will only make this need, this want I have for him even heavier.

For the entirety of Sunday, I waste the day lazing in bed, trying to lose myself in a book. But for the first time ever, the lure of another world and a perfect story don't appeal to me. Instead my head is full of my own fantasies of my own life.

When Monday dawns, I wake up full of fresh determination to ignore my new lusty feelings towards my best friend. Throwing my legs over the side of the bed, I pretend I don't feel the twinge of desire that courses through me when I squeeze my thighs together, and stomp purposefully to the bathroom. Turning on the water, I twist the control all the way to cold, then step beneath the torrent of icy water, letting it dissolve the lust I refuse to acknowledge.

Ten minutes later, I step out of the shower, dithering as I grab a towel from the rail and wrap my cold flesh in the fluffy cotton. Inhaling deeply, I exhale a relieved breath when I feel normal, calm, stable.

I quickly dry my skin, apply some lotion, then pull on the clothes I brought in with me. Rubbing my hair dry, I pull a brush through the strands and stare at myself in the mirror. There are slight black circles beneath my eyes and my skin looks a little dull.

Staring at my reflection, I scrutinize the way I look, pulling my hair back from my face and holding it with one hand. Tilting my head to the side, I turn one way, then the other, assessing my high cheekbones and freckles. My hair's still wet and the water darkens it to a brown color, completely different to my natural red. For a moment I wonder what I'd look like if I dyed it a different color and a thought jumps into my mind. Would Griff like me more if I were a brunette or a blonde?

Inhaling sharply, I drop my hair and turn away from the mirror, my breath coming in rapid pants. I don't want to be that girl; I don't ever want to be the type of person who would change themselves to get a guy to like them.

My hair is one of my favorite things about myself. I love the color, I always have. Yet one day after being rejected by a guy I like, I'm considering changing the way I look on the off-chance he might like me more.

Avoiding the mirror, I rush from the bathroom and down the hall to my bedroom, narrowly avoiding hitting Valentine as he passes me.

"Emmy?" He says. "You okay?"

The genuine concern in his voice makes my feet stop

moving. Valentine isn't as big of an asshole as I thought he was, but he's still not the guy who checks on a girl just to make sure she's okay. Lifting my eyes to look at him, I slowly shake my head. "No, I don't think I am," I say quietly.

His eyes widen as if he hadn't expected me to answer, or perhaps he only asked me because he assumed I'd tell him I was fine. "What time is your first class?" He asks.

"Err, nine thirty."

"Same. The others don't have any classes until ten. Go finish getting ready and we can talk on the way to class."

Then he turns and leaves, stepping into Nova's room as if he never spoke. What the hell? I'm not sure that I want to talk to Valentine about all the weird stuff I'm feeling, but I suppose he's the least involved of all of us; the one with the least history and perhaps the most rational perspective.

I find myself doing as he said and go back into my bedroom and get ready, leaving my hair to dry naturally and only applying a small amount of makeup. Quicker than I'm actually prepared for, I'm downstairs, a travel mug of coffee in my hands as I follow Valentine out of the front door.

We walk for a few hundred yards in silence, both of us drinking our coffees before Valentine speaks, "So, what happened to have you all freaked out?" He asks.

A sigh escapes my lips, sounding loud and weary. "This morning for a moment I became someone I never want to be," I confess.

I wait for him to laugh, or ask me to explain, but he doesn't, and when I look at him, I find him watching me thoughtfully. Squeezing my eyes closed, I grimace. "I was looking at myself in the mirror and thinking that maybe if I changed the way I looked a guy would like me."

Again I wait for him to say something, but he remains silent. "I don't want to be that girl," I say raggedly.

"You shouldn't be that girl." He says, his voice hard and unyielding as he stops walking, reaching out and stopping me. "Look, I know we're not close. I know it's gonna take you a long time to realize that I might be an asshole, but I'm an asshole that's in love with your sister and I will never do anything to hurt her. But regardless of who we are to each other, you should never be that girl. Guys think you're hot as fuck, Emmy, but even if you were butt ugly you shouldn't ever change yourself for some guy. We might not know each other that well, but I've spent enough time with you to know you aren't the type of girl that gets caught up in the hype of guys and all that shit. So what's happened? Whoever he is, if he's made you feel this way, I will happily hold the douchebag down while you beat the shit out of him."

A laugh bursts from my lips. "You don't want to beat the shit out him for me?"

He shrugs. "If you want me to, but I'm guessing you're just as capable of inflicting damage as I am."

"My daddy and every single one of my uncles taught me how to bring a guy down. Both Nova and I are pretty badass, but on this occasion there's no ass kicking needed, unless I'm bitch slapping myself for being an idiot."

We both start walking again and for a moment neither of us speaks. Eventually I say. "I like a guy and he isn't interested."

"It happens," Valentine says, taking a sip of his own coffee.

"I know," I say with a resigned sigh and that's it, we don't say anything else until we're inside the campus, my class in one direction, his in the other. Lifting my hand, I start to wave, but he shocks me by hauling me into a hug.

"Any guy that doesn't want you is blind, deaf, and dumb as shit. I'd like us to be friends, Emmy. I'm not good at that shit, I don't trust too easy and I'm an asshole, but I'm here for you, even if it's just to hold people down while you whale on them."

Then he releases me, peppering a soft kiss to my forehead before he pulls away and turns to leave.

"Valentine," I call.

"Yeah?"

"Thank you, friend," I say.

He nods, then leaves without another word.

GRIFFIN

I watch as Valentine and Emmy leave the house, then stare like the stalker I am as they walk down the street, neither of them saying a thing as they move side by side both drinking their coffees.

I didn't see her at all yesterday and I'm still trying to convince myself that I didn't hide out in my room to avoid her. But the truth of the matter is that I'm not ready to face her rejection or see the look in her eyes when she explains away her behavior and blames it on the alcohol.

Pouring myself a large cup of coffee, I sink down onto one of the stools at the breakfast bar and sulk. I know I'm being pathetic, but I just can't stop myself or apparently grow a pair of balls big enough to get myself out of this rut.

If I were giving advice to anyone else in my situation, I'd tell them to sweep her off her feet and claim her. Especially after the other night; the way she touched me, kissed me, clung to me and begged me to stay with her. But I'm too fucking chickenshit to take my own advice, so instead I'm nursing a fucking coffee and pining for her.

Hindsight is a fucking wonderful thing and I haven't stopped kicking myself since I crawled out of her bed. Why did I leave? Why the hell would I leave her when that night was the perfect segue into testing the waters and seeing if she feels anything more than friendship for me.

A palm bounces off the back of my head, jolting me forward and pulling me from my inner pouting. Twisting my neck, I find a smug looking Zeke smirking at me from the counter, pouring coffee into his own mug.

"Asshole," I hiss.

"What's eating you, brother?" he asks, lifting his mug to his lips and taking a sip.

"Nothing."

He nods condescendingly. "Looks like nothing."

"I fucked up with Emmy."

"Figured as much when I asked her if she planned to keep dating that Kent kid and she told me not only that she planned to keep seeing him, but that it would be so much easier for her, now that we'd all agreed to give him a chance."

"She said that?" I snarl, my lip curling in pure male fury.

"Yep, you had the perfect opportunity the other night. She was in your fucking arms. I got rid of the geeky kid for you. So, why the fuck didn't you make your move?"

"I did make a move, sort of," I hiss. "But she was drunk, and then things got a bit out of control."

"What happened?" Zeke asks, narrowing his eyes.

"We kissed."

"Ohhkkkayy…"

"But she was drunk."

"I know that. I'm not suggesting you take advantage of her, just be there for her."

"I was. She fucking begged me to stay with her. She fucking begged, brother."

"She begged you to fuck her?"

"No," I growl. "She begged me to stay with her, to snuggle with her."

"So, what'd you do?"

"I stayed, of course I fucking stayed, but then I left before she woke up."

"You did what?" Zeke roars, stepping toward me.

"I freaked. I knew she'd either regret it, or not remember kissing me at all, so I pussied out and crept out of her bed before she woke up."

"You're a fucking idiot," he says, shaking his head.

I nod in agreement. "I know, and now she's planning to keep dating that little jerk Kent, and I have no idea if she even remembers kissing me and I can't fucking bring it up."

"She's not that into that Kent guy, I'd lay money on it. You just need to keep reminding her why she's meant to be yours. Show her why Sinners are like fucking catnip to women. I know you have some charm, some fucking game, so stop being a pussy and use it."

I nod, re-energised by his words. "She's mine, has been since the day I stole her first kiss."

"Yes!" He says, slapping me on the shoulder.

"Time to act like a fucking Sinner. I'm a Scion and it's time to embrace my destiny." I cry. With a renewed sense of determination, I stand up from my stool and down the last of my coffee, then I pull my cell from my pocket and type out a text.

Griffin

Morning, shortcake. Hangover gone yet? Lunch at the quad today?

I stare at the screen for a minute but there's no immediate

reply, so I head back to my room to get ready for class. After a quick shower, I make my way into my room and grab some clothes for the day. I'm not one of those guys who plans his fucking outfits, so I grab the nearest, cleanest looking jeans, then throw on a Sinners t-shirt and some sneakers and call it good.

My cell beeps just as I'm pulling my socks on and I immediately abandon my task and leap for it.

Shortcake

Hangover is all gone, thank God. I'm never drinking again. Lunch sounds good. My class finishes at 12.15.

Griffin

Perfect. I have human anatomy in the building next to you, so wait for me and we can walk over together. PS I'm running low on snuggles, I'm gonna need to top up tonight.

The three dots appear, showing she's typing a reply, then they disappear, then reappear again. I wait with baited breath, hoping she'll remind me that I had plenty of snuggles on the night I spent in her bed.

Shortcake

Sounds good, class is starting, see you later.

My shoulders slump and I let my cellphone fall to my comforter. This was the perfect chance to talk about what happened this weekend and she never said a word.

EMMY

My hands are shaking as I type out a reply to his text message. Was he drunker than I thought he was? He said he hadn't had that much to drink, was he lying? We spent an entire night curled in each other's arms and he's pretending like it never even happened.

Anger pulses through me. I wasn't expecting him to declare his undying love for me or anything, but to pretend we didn't make out like horny rabbits then share a bed is just kind of insulting.

Before I can think better of it, I lift my cell back up and type out a text to Kent.

Emmy

> Hey, Kent, I had a great time the other night, although my hangover was an absolute beast. We're all meeting for lunch at the quad again today. I'm not sure what time your morning classes are, but we'll be there about 12.30 and it would be cool if you came x

I hit send before I can think any better of it, then force

back all of the doubts and guilt that hit me like a tidal wave. Am I just using him to get back at Griffin? Does Griffin even care? Will he even realize what I'm doing?

My mind swims with a thousand questions that make me wish I'd stayed completely oblivious to guys, like I was during high school. For years I've complained about how my family made me untouchable, unapproachable, but I never had to worry about my own motives when every guy in my school knew not to get involved.

"Hey, Red," a low gruff voice says.

Turning toward the voice I find Van lowering himself into the seat at my side, a wry smile curling at the edges of his lips.

"Hey," I say, unsure how to act around this guy after my outburst on the weekend. "Err, I didn't know you were in this class."

"Yep, I usually sit over there," he says, pointing to a seat a few rows back from where we're sat.

I busy myself with my cell, feeling self-conscious. Van seemed like a nice guy when I met him at the frat house, but the other morning when I almost stepped in front of his car and this weekend at the bar, he's been a little strange. I mean the guy is hot, big and muscular, with a presence that refuses to be ignored, but there's something about him that's making me feel cautious.

For a moment I consider apologizing for my outburst in the bar. Telling someone that your daddy could kill them then hide the body isn't exactly your average Friday night bar conversation. But something tells me that Van wasn't scared off by my attitude. In fact, the fact he's here sitting next to me, tells me that I might actually have intrigued him, rather than sent him running away from the crazy girl.

"So what time?" He drawls, his accent thick and syrupy.

"What?" I ask, turning to look at him, my brows furrowed.

"What time should I pick you up on Friday for our date?"

I can't help the smile that slips across my lips. His cock-sure attitude doesn't offend me like I expect it to. Maybe it's the way he's looking at me, like he isn't going to take no for an answer, or maybe it's the swagger he's exuding just by sitting in his seat. "How 'bout never," I sass back, biting my bottom lip with my teeth to stop my smile spreading even bigger.

"How 'bout eight," he sasses right back, without missing a beat.

"How 'bout coffee?"

"How 'bout happy hour?"

I pause, looking up at him from beneath my lashes. "Happy hour, as friends" I concede, then look away from him, turning toward the front of the class.

"I'm not looking for a friend," he growls.

"That's all I have to offer right now," I say.

"Ahh, let me guess, the bodyguard."

I want to deny it, I really do, but what's the point. He was at the bar; he saw the way Griff was touching me and that I wasn't pushing him away. I nod slowly.

"He gonna try to kick my ass just for talking to you?" He asks with an amused smirk.

"No," I laugh.

"You sure, he looks like one of those possessive types."

I shake my head. "He's more interested in playing body-guard than boyfriend," I confess, unsure why I'm talking about this with him at all.

Van laughs again, the sound so infectious I can't help but smile. "The way he had his hands on you at the bar says otherwise."

A cold scoff escapes my throat. "Trust me, he's not interested."

"So then you can go out with me, not as friends," Van says, challenging me with an arch of his eyebrows.

Our professor calls the class' attention, so I ignore his question and try hard to listen. An hour later, I stand from my desk, lifting my backpack up onto my shoulders and wait patiently for the people in my row to shuffle down the stairs and toward the exit.

A warm palm snakes around my waist from behind and Van's rough Alabama drawl fills my ears. "Let me pick you up from your place."

I shake my head. "I'll meet you at the bar, as friends."

His hot breath exhales against my skin and I can almost feel how much he wants to argue with me, but he stays silent, his palm sliding from around me. I try not to look, but curiosity gets the better of me and I glance over my shoulder.

Like he knew I would, his brow arches imperiously and he smirks. "See you Friday, Red," he says, then he steps over the row of seats in front of us and walks straight down the empty row and out of the door.

Van fills my thoughts as I shuffle out of the classroom and into the busy corridor. He's something new and different, while being alarmingly similar to the guys I grew up around. If I liked Griffin a little less and Van a little more, my life would be so much simpler right now. Van knows I'm seeing Kent, he knows I like Griffin, and that I have two other guy friends who are all willing to step in and cockblock me at every turn, yet none of that seems to be perturbing him at all. In fact, he actually seems more interested after my little hissy fit at the bar the other night. For the first time I can kind of see what my mom was talking about, when she said she loves how my dad pursued her. I've never had a guy come back to try again after I rejected him, and although maybe I should be a little annoyed with him not for backing off after I told him too, it's also kind of sweet, in a weird way.

When I finally breach the outside doors, the sun blinds me for a minute and I squint, trying to give my eyes a chance to adjust to the brightness, after being in the dim, windowless classroom for the last hour.

Blinking rapidly, the bright spots in my vision clear and I find Griffin a few yards ahead of me. Even with his hands buried in his pockets, he still cuts an imposing figure against the other students milling around us. Everything about him is big. He's tall, really tall, and built like a footballer. The black Sinners t-shirt he's wearing is stretched taut across his massive chest and his biceps are bulging beneath the sleeves. The armful of tattoos he got done this summer are clearly visible and even with a cap covering his mop of hair, he still looks… dangerous.

I can so easily imagine what he'll look like with his cut slid over the top of his shirt and it'll suit him, because he is a Sinner through and through even if he isn't an official prospect yet. My heart skips a beat and I feel my shoulder sag a little just at the sight of him.

How have I gone my entire life without realizing how sexy he is? I'm not blind. I know he's hot, but so is Zeke and if it was him stood in front of me right now, I wouldn't be thinking about running at him and pressing my lips against his.

Something changed the night he kissed me after my first date with Kent and now that I'm looking at him as more than just my best friend, I'm not sure I'll ever be able to see him as just Griffin, the boy I grew up with, ever again.

A sigh slips from my lips. In an ideal world he wouldn't have crept from my bed this weekend. In an ideal world, maybe I'd be spending lunch with just him, not all of our friends and the guy I'm sort of dating. In an ideal world, Griff would be taking me on a date on Friday, not Van. But this isn't an ideal world, this is the real world, and in the real world your best friends don't just decide one day that they want more than friendship with you.

Although that's exactly what I did.

Closing the distance between us, he looks at me from beneath the peak of his cap and flashes me a panty-melting smile that makes my core clench. I'm a virgin, I have zero experience with guys, but right now I want to do dirty, dirty things with Griff.

"Hey, shortcake," he growls, stepping into me and pulling me into a tight hug.

His familiar woodsy scent surrounds me, and I can't help the way my body relaxes into him. My head is telling me this is a dangerous trap that's only going to exacerbate my crush on him, but my body is acting purely on impulse. Griffin is home to me. He's familiarity, comfort. He's my roots and I can't help sinking into him and letting him embrace me.

His lips press against the side of my neck and I wrap my arms around him and hug him back, pressing myself into him and holding him just as tightly as he's holding me. Somehow in this moment we've become the eye of the storm; everything outside of our hug is chaos, loud and new and full of so many possibilities. We're the calm, the deceptively safe zone; only there's nothing calm and safe about us now, because my thoughts are pandemonium, anarchy, and dangerous enough to collapse even the most solid of foundations.

I pull away from him, needing to protect myself, to save myself. To save both of us from the fallout if I allow this crush of mine to develop any further. "I'm starving," I announce a little too brightly.

His brow furrows and he looks at me, confusion dancing in his eyes.

"Let's go and eat. I invited Kent to join us again," I say.

At the sound of Kent's name, Griff's expression shutters. He nods, dropping an arm across my shoulder. "Then let's go find your guy," he says, displeasure dripping from every word.

The walk to the quad is short and painfully quiet. I hate this, but I can't think of anything to say that will make this any less weird. The same bench we ate at the other day is free, so I slide onto it, taking Griff's backpack when he hands it to me.

"I'll go grab some food," he says, his lips tipping downwards, his displeasure obvious.

"I can get my own." The words come out with more barb than I intended and Griff's shoulders visibly tense.

He leans down, bracing one hand on the table in front of me. "Emmy, I have no idea what the fuck is going on with you, but I swear to fucking God, if you don't sit your ass down and wait while I go buy us some lunch, I will throw you over my shoulder, take you home and spank your ass until it's raw."

Pinching my chin between his thumb and forefinger a little too hard, he leans down and kisses me. Lust and love and joy and shock explode inside of me and I swear I can actually hear fireworks as his lips move against mine, his tongue forcing its way into my mouth and tangling with mine.

As quickly as it starts, it ends, and Griff walks away, leaving me panting and breathless, my whole body a mass of overly stimulated goo. My head is screaming at me to get up, to chase after him, and demand to know what the hell that was, what it means, but my body refuses to cooperate. My legs feel like limp spaghetti noodles and I'm fairly sure that if I try to stand right now, I'll collapse. So instead I watch his broad back and tight ass as he stomps into the café, eventually disappearing from sight.

He kissed me, right here, out in the open, not hidden away in my bedroom. But the more I think about the way he just behaved, the more confused I get. I don't understand. That wasn't a lusty, loving kiss; it was a punishment, a warning. He was annoyed with me, angry, and that kiss was his way of lashing out at me, but that's not a friend thing to do. Is it?

I've never kissed any guy out of sheer frustration. I mean that isn't a thing, so him kissing me has to mean something more. Right?

"Hey," Nova calls, sliding onto the bench opposite me. "How was your class? I feel like I've barely seen you this weekend. Hangovers are such a bitch."

Forcing a smile onto my lips, I nod at whatever she's saying, but I barely process her words.

"Hey," she says, snapping her fingers an inch from my face.

"What?" I say.

"What's up with you? You were totally spacing."

My eyes dart to the café door, then back to Nova. "Just tired I guess."

"Gah," she groans. "Me too. I swear I am never drinking again, or at least not for a few days."

Nova continues to talk, but I zone out again. My gaze is fixed on the doorway I know he's going to come out of soon, and then he appears, carrying a huge tray laden with food and my breath dies in my lungs. How in the space of a matter of days have my feelings for Griffin gone from best friend, entirely platonic, to something so far removed from platonic they might as well be from different planets.

When he reaches our table, he slides the tray along the wood, then sits down next to Nova, opposite me. Another tray slides in front of us and I glance up to find Zeke placing a second tray full of drinks down.

"Hey," he says, climbing over the back of the bench and sitting down next to me, opposite his sister.

A large paper cup, with a plastic lid lands in front of me, and Griff lifts a spoon from the tray holding it out to me. "Chili soup," he says.

Swallowing thickly, I take the spoon from him. "Thank you," I whisper.

He nods, and a hint of a smirk twitches at the edge of his lips, then he pulls an identical paper cup off the tray and places it in front of himself, before handing out a salad box to Nova, and a huge meatball sub to Zeke.

For a moment we all busy ourselves with our food and all I can hear is the rustling of sandwich wrappers and the ripping of paper, as straws are pulled from their packets and pushed into drinks. It's an easy quiet and the familiarity settles some of the anxiety that's swirling inside of me.

"Princess," Valentine says, appearing at the table and ignoring the rest of us while he greets his girlfriend. He kisses her deeply, his fingers tangling into her hair, then he pulls back and slides in beside her, his arm automatically reaching around to pull her closer to him.

Envy, an emotion I'm not overly familiar with hits me like a Mack truck. The effortless way he touches her, like he's one hundred percent confident in her reaction to him, makes me ache in a way I've never felt before. I've never had that; never had a boyfriend I was so in sync with and without thought my eyes move to Griffin.

He's looking at me and as our eyes meet something flares to light in his intense green depths. His lips part and I wait for him to speak, but instead his gaze moves to something behind me and the spark fizzles and dies. "Hey, Kent, nice to see you again, man," he says, with a forced politeness.

Snapping my head around, I find a smiling Kent behind me, looking adorable in a pale-blue shirt, tailored beige khaki shorts and brown leather sandals. "Er, hi," I say, hoping that I sound a little gladder to see him than I feel.

"Hi," he says, leaning forward and pressing a soft, closed mouth kiss against my lips.

Wrong, wrong, wrong. The mantra sings on repeat in my head for the two seconds his lips are on mine. Wrong, it feels completely wrong that it's Kent's lips that are pressed against mine and not Griffin's. I force a smile to my lips as I look up at the boy I'm dating and my heart softens a little. That tiny little kiss is the only other experience I have with kissing apart from with Griff. So maybe it's not wrong, maybe it's just different.

Kent slides onto the bench next to me and pulls a package sandwich and a bag of chips from his backpack. My soup is still in front of me, steam rising from the cup, so I turn my attention back to it and lift the spoon to my lips, stifling a groan when the hot, spicy soup hits my tongue.

Without thought my eyes lift to Griffin, but he's not looking at me. His cap is pulled low and all of his attention is on his lunch. I wait, hoping his gaze will lift, but it doesn't. After a while I give up and instead concentrate on my food.

"How was your hangover? Mine was the worst. My roommate is a total asshole and insisted on blasting music from like seven on Saturday morning." Kent says, twisting the top off a bottle of soda.

"You should move into a place off-campus, least then you'd get to pick your own roommate," Zeke says.

"Yeah, but most off-campus places don't look like your

place. Who the hell rented that house to a group of college kids?" he asks.

"I don't know. Our parents sorted it for us," I say quickly, before anyone can let slip that our families actually bought the house for us to live in.

"Nice. My parents insisted I stay in dorms after they saw what was available to rent, so you guys struck lucky." Kent says, as he lifts his sandwich to his lips.

"Our families know how close we all are, they understand how important it is that we all live together," Griff growls, then a malicious smile spreads across his face. He lifts his eyes to me, and I'm shocked by the anger I find in them before he turns to look at Kent. "Em's parents are going to be here for parents' weekend. I'm sure they'd like to meet you. Are your family coming in to visit?"

I feel my eyes widen and I kick Griff hard in the shin under the table, but he ignores me, his attention firmly fixed on Kent.

Kent twists his body toward me, his hand sliding onto my knee. "Emmy, I'd love for you to meet my parents. Maybe we could introduce our families to one another?" he says, a broad grin stretched across his face, like this is the best idea in the world.

"Errr, yeah, maybe," I say non-committal, going back to my soup and lavishing it with far more attention than it needs. The others carry the conversation for the rest of lunch and as we all put our trash in the garbage can, I'm more than ready to get away.

Kent reaches for my hand and I let him. Today he's touched me more casually than he has before. Nothing inappropriate, just those easy touches I'd been jealous of Nova and Valentine for earlier, but for some reason I don't enjoy them as much as I hoped I would.

I like Kent, I really do, but apparently liking him and *liking* him are two very different things. Waving to the others, I ignore Griffin's pointed stare and move to leave. Maybe that makes me a huge coward. Perhaps I should have stayed and asked him what the hell was going on with that kiss, but like the other times he's kissed me, maybe there's just nothing to say.

"Sorry, dude, but I need to talk to Emmy for a minute," Griffin's familiar voice drawls.

Spinning around, I look between Kent's sweet face and Griffin's dark, intense one. My eyes hold in place, staring at my brooding, confusing friend as I speak. "Err, Kent, I'll call you later."

"Oh, sure," Kent says amiably, pulling on my fingers until I look at him. Then he leans in and presses another kiss to my lips. This time he opens his mouth, kissing me gently and sweetly, letting me set the pace.

I kiss him back, moving my mouth against his, hoping to feel something, but all I get is that it's nice. It's a nice kiss, with a nice guy.

When I pull away, he lets me, his lips spreading into a contented grin. "See you later," he says, then waves to Griffin and the others and leaves.

For a moment I watch him go, not because I'm sad he's leaving, but more to prolong the moment before Griff and I have what I know will be an awkward and uncomfortable conversation.

The moment Kent is completely out of view, Griffin's hands cup my cheeks and he kisses me, his tongue forcing its way into my mouth. Shocked, I just let him devour me for a long moment and then I kiss him back, pushing all of my anger and frustration into my touch. He matches my intensity and pushes back with his own until it's as much a battle of wills as a kiss. When it feels like the air around us shatters, our kiss softens, and anger makes way for passion. Instead of clinging to him with my nails, I wrap myself around him, feeling the way his body responds to mine. His bruising hold changes to him pressing me as close to him as he can and I melt into his chest, wanting nothing more than to be near him.

His lips dominate mine and I feel marked, claimed, like he's letting everyone else in the world know that I'm his. All I can hear is the sound of my pounding heart echoing through my chest, and all I can smell is Griffin, a scent so achingly familiar that it's every good memory, eternal support, happiness, and endless love all rolled into his unique fragrance.

Then he's gone. His lips no longer touching mine, his hands no longer holding me to him, and I feel bereft, lost, and unmoored. When my eyes can focus, I look at him. His eyes are wild, his chest moving up and down with each ragged breath.

I open my mouth to speak, but no words come out. His lips part and I pray for him to say something, to do something, but instead he just lifts up his hand and drags his thumb across my bottom lip, touching the pad to his own mouth before he turns and walks away from me.

"What the actual fuck was that?" I say, as I watch him disappear around a corner, never even glancing back.

"Hot, that was seriously freaking hot," Nova says, appearing at my side and making me jump.

My eyes widen and I realize that he just kissed me out in the open, in front of all of the people still left in the quad including Nova, Zeke, and Valentine.

"I…" I start, then realize I have no idea what to even say.

"You guys are together! This is amazing. I always hoped it would happen, but I figured if it was going to, it would have by now. I'm so happy for you," she gushes.

I shake my head. "We're not together," I say dazedly.

"I'm pretty sure that kiss says you are," she laughs.

I look over to where Zeke and Valentine are standing; smug, amused expressions on their faces.

"He just walked off; he keeps walking off. Plus, I'm dating Kent, and Van too I think."

"You're what?" Zeke says, marching toward us.

"I…" I say, shaking my head as I struggle to process my thoughts. "I agreed to go on a date, a sort of date with Van, and Kent wants me to meet his parents."

"But Griff—" Zeke starts.

"He's gone," I snap. "He keeps doing this shit and then just leaving."

"He—" Zeke starts, but I interrupt him again.

"Isn't here," I say, my voice hardening. "I have to get to class."

"Emmy," Zeke calls.

"Em, you need to talk to him," Nova says, reaching over and squeezing my arm.

I nod, more to appease them, rather than because I actually plan to follow through. Then I wave goodbye and head in the direction of my next class. When I reach the door to the building my art history class is in, I stop, my feet refusing to move any closer.

He kissed me and then he just left, what the hell does that even mean? A wave of homesickness crashes over me, and for the first time since we moved to Alabama, I miss my home. I miss Archer's Creek and my parents. I miss knowing what to expect and how people will behave.

I craved something new, something different, but right now, different is scary and frustrating, and just too much and I want things to go back to the way they were.

Turning on my heel, I walk away from my class and head

back to the house. As I push through the front door, I kick off my shoes and run up the stairs to my bedroom, closing and locking the door behind me.

Lifting my comforter, I crawl underneath it, pulling it up and over my head as if the darkness will protect me from all these strange and confusing thoughts. Some days I feel like an adult, but in this moment I have never felt more like a child.

Pulling my cell from my pocket I dial the number I know by heart, my protector, my dad.

"Baby girl," he answers on the second ring.

"Daddy," I rasp, emotion clogging my voice.

Seven hours later with my backpack over my shoulder, I run across the arrivals lounge and throw myself into my dad's embrace. Strong arms lift me off the ground and the familiar feeling of home surrounds me.

"Hey, baby girl," he murmurs into my hair.

"Hey, Daddy," I say back, as he lowers me to the floor and pulls back to look at me.

"Come on, my bike's outside."

Following my dad, I climb on behind him, holding onto his waist as his bike roars away from the curb and onto the familiar Houston highway. I've always loved riding with my dad, the wind blowing through my hair and the sense of freedom that I've never experienced anywhere except on the back of a bike. Like a balm to my ragged soul, I block out all my chaotic thoughts and just focus on the ride, allowing it to soothe me until I feel calm and peaceful.

Before I'm ready, we're pulling into our driveway and mom is rushing out of the front door, our West Highland terrier puppy Norris scampering along excitedly behind her. "Sweetie, are you okay?" Mom asks, her hands pulling me in for a hug the moment my legs are free of the bike.

"I'm fine, Mom. I just got a little homesick that's all," I say, not ready to talk about Griffin yet.

"Oh, baby, that's okay, nothing a couple of days R&R won't fix. I already emailed the welfare office to say you'll be missing classes because of a family emergency, so you won't get marked down, and they'll be sending you all of your notes through on the bulletin board."

"Thanks, Mom," I croak, tears filling my eyes. "I missed you."

She hauls me in for another hug and I burst into tears, sobbing against her shoulder. After a minute, I pull back and inhale, trying to pull myself together. Her concern filled eyes meet mine and I sniffle. "I think I might go take a nap," I say.

"Okay, honey," she says, wrapping her arm around me and walking me into the house.

Stepping into my childhood home, I try to remember why I so desperately wanted to leave, when right now this place feels like everything good in the world. Leaning down, I scoop Norris into my arms and rub my cheek against the soft fur on his head. "Come on, dude, you can come nap with me, I missed you too."

The puppy licks my cheek, then settles against me as I head for the stairs and the solace of my bedroom. My cellphone feels heavy in my pocket. I switched it off when I got to the airport in Alabama and right now, I'm not ready to turn it back on again.

I sent a message to our group chat before I left, so they wouldn't panic, not knowing where I was, but I know they'll all still be losing their minds. Grimacing, I remember what I wrote and wished I'd worded it differently.

Emmy

Hi guys, don't freak out, but I'm headed
home for a couple of days. I'll be back
before Monday, see you later xoxo

That was it, all I said, then I turned my cell off and
haven't turned it back on yet. I'm an asshole.

Pushing into my room, I expect it to feel different and not
like home anymore, but apart from the air seeming a little
stale from where the door had been shut, it still feels like my
room. Crawling onto my bed, I place Norris down next to me
and he quickly spins in a couple of circles before collapsing
into a heap and yawning a puppy yawn.

A wave of exhaustion hits me and I lay down, resting my
head on my pillow, trying to sort through some of the
millions of thoughts that are running through my head. The
moment I'd spoken to my dad earlier all I'd wanted to do was
come home, to my real home, to Archers Creek, and because
my dad is my hero, he sorted it for me. An hour later I'd had
an email with an airplane ticket on my cellphone and the
option to run away from the new, different life I so desperately wanted, at least for a little while.

I know all the problems I have to deal with will still be
there when I get back, but at least for a couple of days I can
hide from them, until I can figure out how in the hell I'm
going to deal with everything.

The house phone starts to ring and I have a feeling I know
who it's going to be, so like the child that I am, I squeeze my
eyes shut and pretend that if I can't see my issues, they can't
see me either. Not the most mature attitude I know, but I don't
want to be mature right now.

A few minutes later I hear my door handle turn and my
door crack open. I freeze, keeping my eyes closed and my

body as still as a statue. I'm fairly certain my mom knows I'm not actually asleep, but I have never loved her more than when I hear her say, "I'm sorry honey, she's asleep." She pauses as whoever is on the phone speaks, then she says. "I will. I know. Okay, love you."

Then my door glides shut again, and I exhale a relieved breath. I must fall asleep for real, because the next thing I know Norris is whining and scratting at my bedroom door asking to be let out. Crawling from my bed, I open the door and he takes off like a rocket, rushing down the stairs so fast I worry that he'll end up tripping and gamboling all the way to the bottom.

Following him down, I open the French doors off the kitchen and he rushes into the blackness of the yard. I breathe deeply, inhaling the familiar scent of early morning Texas then pad barefoot into the yard and lower myself to one of the cushioned couches on the corner of the patio. Pulling my feet up, I rest my chin on my knees. I'm not sure what time it is, but the first rays of sunlight are peeking their way into the horizon, making the sky look like sparks are just beginning to smolder, before flames emerge.

I'm still wearing my clothes from yesterday. My jeans are clinging to my legs, my shirt twisted and falling off one shoulder. My cell isn't in my pocket, and for a moment I panic, until it dawns on me that it must have fallen out as I slept.

My feet move without thought and I'm halfway up the stairs before I make the decision to go and fetch it. I find it tangled in my sheets, the screen black and lifeless. Sighing, I make my way back into the yard, grabbing a bottle of water from the refrigerator as I pass, then sit back down on the sofa as more embers of daylight begin to spark in the sky.

Pressing the power button, my cellphone sparks to life

and nausea fills my stomach along with a healthy dose of guilt. I wait, expecting the chorus of dings and pings that tell me I have waiting texts, or WhatsApp, or Snapchat messages, but instead I get nothing, silence.

Confused, I click into our group chat first. I can see the last message I wrote before I turned my cell off, then nothing. Not one single message. Nothing asking if I'm all right or shouting at me for leaving, just nothing.

Swiping my finger across the screen, I move through my apps, but there are no new messages on anything. Disappointment, fear, and overwhelming sadness pool within me, swiftly consuming me until all I can feel is desolate isolation.

I didn't come home to provoke a reaction from Griffin or my friends, but I expected some messages of concern or support. I never even considered that me running away would get no reaction from them at all. Did I finally manage to push them away?

All of my breath evaporates, and I suck in a lungful of what feels like glass shards. My selfishness, my desire for something new, has finally pushed away the most important people in my life, right when I need them the most, and it's all my own fault.

Yesterday afternoon everything had felt so big, so overwhelming, that I'd reacted without thought. I needed to be saved, so I called my greatest protector, my knight, my daddy and he swooped in and saved me, just like he's been doing my entire life.

Everything had felt so out of control and I just had to get away. Griffin kissed me, right there in front of everyone and then just walked away and I still have no idea what any of it actually means. I should have stayed; I should have chased after him and insisted he explain what the hell he's doing. But instead I ran, because I'm so full of my own bullshit fantasies

271

of what my future should look like, that when I actually find something that's better than I even could have imagined, I don't know how to deal with it.

Norris paws at my leg to get my attention and I scoop him off the floor and into my lap. He yips playfully, then scrabbles from my grasp and disappears into the house. Following him, I lock the door behind me, intent on making my way back up to my room, when a flash of white fur barrels out of the family room, rushing around my feet in circles, before darting back off again.

Walking slowly forward, I peer through the doorway into the family room, wondering what had Norris so excited, and that's when I spot them. Nova and Valentine curled up together on one couch, Zeke asleep with his head thrown back in an armchair, and then Griffin fast asleep amidst a pile of blankets on the floor.

"Oh my god," I whisper, so quietly it's barely audible. They're here, all of them. I don't have a single message from them because they followed me home instead. I didn't get a hundred questions, they just acted and came for me, because that's what we do for each other. We're there for each other, we support each other, we love each other, and I feel like an idiot for questioning that even for a second.

My knees buckle and I sink down onto the arm of the chair beside me and a crashing realization hits me so hard that it steals my breath and stuns me. I was running from the world I grew up in, desperate for something bigger. But why? My world might be narrow, but what more than an amazing family and the best friends possible could I ever want?

My mom has made millions of dollars. We could be living it up in a mansion on Sunset Boulevard or sipping champagne in the Hamptons. But instead we live in a beautiful, but normal house in small town Texas. I always thought it was

Dad and the club that kept them here, that they were tied to the town, held tight by obligation. But that's not the case.

My parents have friends who became family and they are rich beyond their wildest dreams before they even think about what they have in the bank. It doesn't matter where I live, because it's who I am that defines me. How can something so simple have taken me so long to figure out?

Maybe I'm too young to have this kind of epiphany, or maybe everyone else figured this out when they were a little kid and I'm so far behind it's ridiculous, but that one simple thought feels huge and important and overwhelming in the best way possible.

A sigh falls from my lips, and it's relief and gratefulness and love. Instead of going back to my room, I slide down into the armchair I've been perched on, curl up into a ball, my head resting on the arm, and fall back to sleep, surrounded by my friends and richer than I'll probably ever be.

GRIFFIN

Several hours earlier

My fingers grip my cellphone so tightly, I swear I can hear the glass creaking and the plastic twisting. I read the stupid, selfish message she sent for the thousandth time since it came through and curse the fact that I'm stuck in class for the next fifteen minutes and can't leave.

Emmy

Hi guys, don't freak out, but I'm headed home for a couple of days. I'll be back before Monday, see you later xoxo

What the fuck kind of message is that? Did she seriously just take off, just like that? Who does that? I'm so angry my thoughts barely make sense. Ever since I kissed her in the quad, my body has been wound so tightly, I'm surprised I haven't snapped. Given the way the kids in my classes have been avoiding me, I guess I must look like as much of a psycho as I feel, but no matter how much I tell myself to chill out I just can't.

She brought that fucker to lunch, he kissed her on the lips. The fact that I didn't rip his fucking face in two is a miracle. He kissed her, right there in front of me and she let him.

She's mine and I just about lost my fucking mind. Maybe I shouldn't have asked to talk to her, I probably shouldn't have kissed her again, and I definitely shouldn't have just walked away. But in my defense, all I could think was that he touched her, he kissed her, and that she's mine: my girl, my Emmy, mine.

I have no idea what she feels, but every time I've kissed her, she's kissed me back with just as much passion and desire as I've been feeling for her, or at least that's what it feels like. Doubt wallops into me, and suddenly my brain fills with everything I don't want to think about.

What if she's just kissing me back because she doesn't know what else to do? What if she's going along with the motions, or using me for practice before she fucks Kent or that other guy who's sniffing around her?

What if she wants them more than she wants me? What if they take her from me?

If she were mine, I wouldn't let a guy like me near her. I'll be pushed out and become inconsequential while she falls in love with someone else.

People start moving around me and it takes me a moment to realize that class is over and that they're getting up to leave. Shoving my stuff into my backpack, I barge past the mass of shuffling people and push my way out, ignoring the annoyed, angry cries from the kids I shove out of the way.

Breaking through the front door of the building, I start to

run, my bag bouncing against my back as I sprint across campus, knowing that I need to get home, to see if she's actually gone.

"Griffin."

Nova's voice has me skidding to a stop, and I snap my head from side to side to find her.

"Hey," she says, her hand landing on my arm. "Come on, the others are all on their way home too," she says.

I nod, then let her tow me forward. We make it home first and I push through the front door and run straight upstairs and into her room. Her bed is rumpled as if she just crawled out of it, but nothing else seems out of place.

"She's not downstairs."

I jolt at the sound of Nova's voice so close behind me. "She fucking left," I snarl.

"Yeah she did."

"This is my fault."

"Yep," Nova says firmly. "What the hell were you thinking kissing her like that then just leaving? If you'd have stuck around and had an actual conversation with her, or I don't know, maybe manned up and told her how you felt, then maybe you guys would be the reason those sheets are all rumpled and your girl wouldn't be on the way to Texas on her own."

There's no anger in her voice, just mild censure.

"I know, it's just..." I start.

"She gone?" Zeke shouts up the stairs interrupting me, a moment after I hear the front door being thrown open.

"Yeah," Nova calls.

She grabs my arm, squeezing lightly. "Come on, let's go downstairs. We can talk about this later once we decide what we're doing."

I nod and follow her out of Emmy's room, taking one last look at her space before I pull the door closed behind me.

By the time we enter the living room, Valentine is walking through the door, his cell in his hand, all of his attention focused on it. "The next flight isn't until ten tonight, we won't get home 'til late, but unless we want to drive hours into Georgia to catch a flight that only lands an hour earlier than the one from Tuscaloosa, this is our best option."

"You booked flights?" I ask him shocked.

He lifts his attention from his cell and looks at me, his brow furrowed. "Yeah, I figured we were going after her. Aren't we? I mean this is what you guys do right? You're close, it's weird, but that's who you are. You're family."

"Thank you, brother," I say, crossing the room to him and pulling him in for a quick bro hug.

He pats my back awkwardly. "No worries, let's just get home, then we can make sure she's okay."

Turning to head to my room I take two steps and run straight into Zeke's fist. "What the fuck?" I yell, my head jolting back with the force of his punch.

Zeke grins at me. "Figured Prez might not kill you for upsetting his daughter if he thinks we already got a few hits in."

"Fuck you," I hiss, but I'm laughing too, my heart a little lighter now that I know we're going after her.

It's after midnight when we step out of the airport in Houston and Sleaze is waiting at the curb for us in his huge jacked up truck, smiling when he sees us. Valentine climbs into the passenger seat, while the rest of us get into the back. The others chat quietly as I stare at my cell, trying to distract myself from the fact that I'm going to see her soon. I'm so fucking pissed at her, but this is just as much my fault as hers. I should have talked to her, or maybe just not stopped kissing her until she accepted that she's mine and that I can't live without her.

"So, what did one of you do to piss Emmy off?" Sleaze asks.

All eyes turn to me and I lift my chin and meet Sleaze's gaze in the rear-view mirror. "I fell in love with her," I say simply.

Sleaze's laugh is low and rumbly. "Well damn it, you finally get the balls to tell her?"

"Nope, he kissed the shit out of her, then stomped off and left her standing there staring after him like an idiot," Zeke says, and for the first time I can hear the anger lacing his tone.

"In Griff's defense, she did bring the guy she was dating to lunch and then kissed him right in front of all of us," Nova says.

Sleaze whistles. "So Emmy's dating, but she knows you're in love with her and she still kissed the new guy in front of you?"

"She doesn't exactly know; I haven't actually told her how I feel. But there are guys coming from everywhere, this kid Kent and then a douche called Van and fuck knows how many more just waiting for their chance with her," I growl.

He laughs again. "You're gonna have to tell her, have a come to fucking God moment and tell that girl you love her, or be a man and let her go."

"Can't let her go," I say, locking my eyes with him again so he can see my resolve.

He nods slowly and smiles. "Figured as much. Just gotta hope Prez doesn't kill you before you get your girl."

I realize the truck's stopped and we're sitting outside Emmy's house, the lights still burning brightly inside.

"Good luck," Sleaze says, then turns to Valentine. "Make sure you come home, Brandi knows you're back and she'll tan your hide if she doesn't get to see you soon. We missed you, kid."

"I'll come around tomorrow, or as soon as we get Emmy sorted," he says. "I missed you guys too," he adds quietly.

"Thanks, Sleaze," I say, as I open the door and climb out, shouldering my bag and inhaling sharply as I make my way to the front door. It swings open before we reach it and a glowering Prez fills the doorway.

He looks past us and dips his chin to Sleaze, then focuses his attention back on me. "What the fuck did you do to her?"

"I fucked up," I admit.

"What. Did. You. Do?" He snarls slowly.

"Prez, you scare the fucking shit out of me, not gonna lie. But what happens between me and Emmy is between me and her. I fucked up today, I'll admit that, but we're all here because we love her, and if she runs, we run. We're Scions and just like Sinners we look after our own. If she chooses to tell you, that's up to her, but all you need to know is that I love her and I'm going to do whatever it takes to make things right."

Blade's expression hardens and I tense, expecting him to launch himself at me, but instead he offers me a single terse nod and steps back to allow us into the house. The others all pass me and head inside, but Blade grabs my arm stopping me. "Emmy do that to your face?" He asks.

I smile. "Nope, that was Zeke."

"I fucking love that kid," he laughs, releasing me and

shoving me forward. "Get in there, she's asleep so you're gonna have to wait 'til the morning. Don't even think about taking your ass upstairs. If I find you in my daughter's bed I really will kill you."

Nikki and Blade head up to bed just after we get there, leaving the rest of us sitting in the family room, unsure what to do. The urge to go upstairs and climb into bed with her is strong enough that I actually hold onto the arms of the couch to stop myself from moving.

My skin's crawling. Knowing that I'm in the same house as her, but that I can't get to her is eating me alive. It's only been hours since I last saw her, but I'm desperate to see her face again. I need her, I always have, and I'll do whatever it takes not to lose her from my life.

The TV's playing low, but none of us are watching it. "I'm exhausted," Nova says, her voice weary. "Airplanes always make me feel tired and I never know why, because all you do is sit there."

A soft smile tips at the corner of Valentine's lips and he pulls her closer to him, pressing her body against his. I want that. Not Nova obviously, she's like my sister, but I want that with Emmy. I want the right to touch her, to comfort her, and hold her and not because I beg for her attention, but because she gives it freely. Because she wants to touch me as much as I want to touch her.

"Do you think she's okay?" I ask no one in particular.

"She'll be fine. Knowing Emmy, she probably just needed some time to cool off and get her head around things. You both need to sit down and actually talk to each other. That girl is in love with you, just as much as you're head over heels for her, but the pair of you are idiots. So talk to her, tell her how you feel, it's all you can do," Zeke says, wiggling down in the armchair and sighing tiredly.

We fall into an exhausted silence and one by one the others start to fall asleep. Eventually, I pull the blanket from the back of the couch and lay down on the floor, my eyes fixed on the stairs, wishing I was in her room and hoping she doesn't hate me.

Chapter 30

EMMY

When my eyelids flutter open, I remember Norris waking me up and letting him out in the yard. My heart pangs when I think of my silent cell and then I glance around the room and see them all here. They all came home just because I had a hissy fit and ran away. They followed me, because they love me and want to be there for me, regardless of the circumstances. A contented sigh falls from my lips, then I let my eyes wander to Griff. He's still on the floor, his head rested on one of the throw pillows, but he's no longer asleep. His eyes are open and he's looking at me.

No, he's not just looking at me, he's devouring me with his eyes, begging me, and beseeching me and telling me something that I wish I could understand. There's something between us, there always has been, but I thought it was just friendship. Now it feels like more, but I have no idea what it is, and I don't know how to ask.

That kiss, all of our kisses, have felt like more than *just* a kiss, but we've never talked about it. In fact, beyond the obvious fact that we don't seem to be able to keep our lips away from each other, we've behaved like nothing has changed. We're friends, best friends, but it has to be something more than that, doesn't it?

His lips part, as if he's going to speak, when suddenly the house bursts to life. Phoenix's alarm screeches out, an obnoxiously loud heavy metal track that he swears is the only thing that wakes him up. Then the sound of Mom and Dad's feet move down the stairs, followed by the familiar gurgle of the coffee maker coming to life, the timer set for the same time each morning.

My eyes never leave Griff's, even as a small familiar smile graces his lips, even as the others start to stir and the quiet moment we're sharing is shattered.

Nova sits up, stretching her arms above her head and yawning loudly. "Emmy, I love you, but I'm gonna kick your ass," she says, her eyes still half closed.

"I can't believe you're all here."

"Where the fuck else would we be?" Zeke snaps, sounding surprisingly awake considering he was snoring like a beast a moment ago.

"You're here," Griff says quietly, as if that's all the answer I could need, and he's right. If one of them had run off, I'd have followed too. It's just how our group works.

"Morning, kids," Mom shouts, "I'm making pancakes if anyone's hungry."

"Pancakes, awesome," Zeke cries, ruffling my hair as he darts past me and toward the kitchen.

"Come on. I'll kick your ass after breakfast," Nova says, grabbing my hand and pulling me up from my chair.

I let her tow me to the kitchen, only looking behind me to Griff once, before the ritual of morning chaos descends. Mom bustles around, flipping pancakes, while Dad fills us all a cup of rich aromatic coffee, sliding them along the counter to us each in turn.

Phoenix stalks in the moment Mom drops the first pancake onto a plate, his eyes half-closed, his hair a wild mess. "Morning," he grunts, dropping onto a stool at the breakfast bar and pulling a plate full of pancakes toward him. After a moment he lifts his head and scans the room, eying us. "Why are you here?" He asks, squinting at us through tired eyes.

"Just feeling a little homesick," I say quietly, not wanting to get into everything that's happened between Griff and I in front of my family.

"Cool," he says with a nod, his attention dropping to his plate as he begins to shovel huge forkfuls of pancake into his mouth.

Breakfast passes quickly, with everyone eating Mom's delicious pancakes and only exchanging small talk beyond requests to pass the syrup and offers of coffee. Eventually Phoenix heads to school and my dad to the club. Then there are only Mom, me, and my friends left.

"Kids, I'm going to meet your Auntie Dove, you know where everything is," Mom says, leaning in to kiss my cheek and whispering, "Talk to him," into my ear before she disappears out of the room.

I haven't told my mom what's going on with Griffin, but she's always been intuitive and no doubt she had everything sussed out before I even got off the plane. I offer her a small smile as she leaves, then we all fall silent for a moment until we hear the sound of the front door closing.

"I think I'm gonna go see Brandi." Valentine says, clearing his throat.

I smile at him and he nods back.

"Yep, we need to go see Mom and Dad," Nova says to her

brother. "You know the telephone tree will have been engaged and everyone will know we're back. Mom will slaughter us if we see anyone else before going home."

"Griff can keep you company; Duke won't care if he has to wait a few hours to see him. You guys have stuff you need to talk about anyway," Zeke says pointedly as he gets up and walks around the counter. Stopping at my side, he leans down and wraps his arms around me. "We don't run, Em; we're Scions. You shout, you cry, you fight, but you don't run, especially not from us."

"I know," I say, my throat thickening with emotion. "I'm sorry."

"You don't need to be sorry. Talk, get this sorted out. We love you too much to lose you."

When he releases me, Nova takes his place, hugging me tightly before looking pointedly at Griff, then back to me. "Sort this out," she says and I'm not sure if she's talking to me or him.

Valentine presses a quick kiss to my forehead then leaves without saying a word and it's just me and Griff and a sea of uncertainty festering between us.

GRIFFIN

Silence stretches between us, but we don't speak, neither one of us wanting to be the first one to say anything, to admit anything.

"I fucking love you, Emmy," I blurt, unable to keep the words inside of me for another second.

"I love you too," she says softly.

This should be it. This should be the moment where she runs into my arms and kisses me, just like the heroines in those books she loves so much, but things with us aren't that simple. This isn't the first time I've said those words. I've been telling her I love her most of my life. Only what she doesn't know, has never known, is that when I said those three little words I wasn't just saying that I loved her, I was telling her I was in love with her, that she was everything, that she's always been everything.

Inhaling slowly, I lift my gaze until we're staring into each other's eyes. I need her to be looking at me. "Do you remember the first time we met?"

Her lips lift into a soft smile and she nods. "It was at

Duke's old house."

"I was sat on the steps crying, and you turned up with your mom and dad. You had yellow sneakers on, and you just marched straight up to me, all that red hair flying behind you and sat your little butt down next to me."

A small laugh bursts from her lips. "I was such a brat."

"No, you weren't. You were the first person I saw that day who didn't ask me if I was okay. You just sat next to me and put your head on my shoulder. I think I fell in love with you that day, but I didn't know it was love 'til the first time I kissed you."

I hear her sharp intake of breath, but I keep talking, worried that if I stop I'll never be able to force the words out. "I'd wanted to kiss you for months, but it was never just us, it was always the four of us, so when you took my hand and let me pull you away at the club I knew it was my chance. That kiss was the best one of my life, or it was until I kissed you in your room after your date with Kent."

"I don't understand," she whispers.

Reaching up, I rub at my forehead with the heel of my hand, never looking away from her. "Do you know what Zeke told me the day he found me kissing you?"

She shakes her head.

"He told me that you were too good for me. That you were Prez's daughter, completely off-limits, untouchable, and he was right. You are too good for me; you always have been. You're too good for all of us, for this town, this life, and we all knew eventually you'd leave, that you'd run. But then you had your chance and you didn't take it, you stayed, you stayed with us."

A sad laugh escapes me, and I run my tongue over my parched lips. "Do you know exactly what schools I applied to? Did you work it out the night we all opened our letters?"

She shakes her head, her eyes brimming with tears.

"I applied to every school within a commutable distance to the Ivy Leagues."

"What?" She gasps.

"I couldn't let you go, Em. I couldn't imagine a life without you being a part of it, and not just at holidays or when we both came home. I don't want any life where I don't get to see you every day."

"Griff."

Swallowing thickly, I shake my head, desperately begging her to let me finish. "Emmy Grace Devereaux, I am in love with you. I've always been in love with you and I will always be in love with you."

"You're in love with me?" She asks after what feels like an eternity.

I nod slowly.

"You've always been in love with me?"

I nod again.

"Why didn't I know?" She asks me, tears falling from her eyes and rolling down her cheeks.

"Because I didn't want you to, because we're best friends so it was easy to hide it, until I couldn't anymore." I admit.

Her face crumples and she lifts her hand and covers her mouth.

A lone tear falls from my eye and it feels like a weight settles on my chest. I've allowed myself to hope, something I haven't done since Zeke told me she would never be mine. But right now, when she's staring at me, her eyes full of tears, I realize that hope is a fickle fucking thing.

She doesn't feel the same way, and even though I always expected it, actually sitting here and listening to her tell me she doesn't want me is going to destroy me.

EMMY

He loves me.

He *loves* me.

He's in love with me.

It doesn't seem to matter how I try to process his words, they don't make sense. Griff is in love with me. He's always been in love with me.

I wait for the panic to hit, for the horror or relief or something to consume me, but it doesn't, and instead all I feel is this huge sense of rightness settle over me. There are tears running down my cheeks, and I want to say something, but the words I want to say are stuck inside. They won't come out and I reach up and cover my mouth with my hand, wondering if there's actually something covering it and I just didn't realize.

It feels like hours later when I drop my hand and open my mouth to speak, but before I can even make a sound, he's pushing the stool he's sitting on back with enough force to make it rock and standing up.

"Well fuck," he hisses, as he steps to the side and moves to walk away.

I feel my eyes widen and my body moves without thought; all I can think about is making sure he doesn't leave again. Jumping from my seat I spin around and scream. "Griffin Bennett, I swear to God, if you walk away right now, I won't let my dad kill you, I'll do it myself."

His feet stop moving and my heart thumps in my chest, beating so fast I swear I can see it pounding through my skin.

"That's a hell of a threat, shortcake. Do you even know how to kill someone?" he drawls, not turning to face me, his voice neutral and not giving away any emotion at all.

"Well I am the daughter of the president of the Doomsday Sinners, I'm pretty badass," I say, filling my own voice with a confidence I'm not sure I can even fake right now.

I can't see his face, but I don't need to. I can imagine his smile, the same one he always uses when I say something so ridiculous. Slowly, he turns around to face me, his expression guarded, his shoulders tense.

"I tell you I'm in love with you and you tell me you want to kill me, that's not exactly the reaction I was hoping for."

I take a step toward him, "You didn't give me a chance to reply. You were too busy walking away again. You've gotten pretty good at that in the last month."

He swallows visibly and I think he's going to say something as his lips part, then he presses them back together and just stares at me.

"You were my first kiss," I say. "It was perfect, and then Zeke found us and it took you seven years to kiss me again."

His nod is sad and full of resignation.

"Why did you sneak out of my room the other morning?" I ask.

"Because I thought you'd either regret what we did, say it

was a mistake, or not remember it at all," he admits, blinking slowly at me, his long lashes framing his eyes that tell me so much more than his words are confessing.

For a long moment I just look at him. I've been so blind, so stupid. I spent so long wanting something more, that I forgot to appreciate what I had already. "I'm in love with you too."

Griff's body actually jolts at my words. His lips part and he tilts his head to the side, staring at me like I've spoken in a foreign language. "What?"

"I'm in love with you too."

"You're in love with me?" Griff says slowly as if he's never heard the words before.

"I am completely and totally in love with you," I say, taking a step closer to him with each word until I'm pressed against him, my chest so close I can feel his heart beating in time with mine.

So slowly it feels like forever, he brings his hands up, cupping my cheeks as he lowers his lips to mine and kisses me. This kiss isn't like any of the ones we've shared before. This isn't possession, or anger, or manipulation. This is love: pure and sweet and forever.

EMMY

One Week later

"Oh my god, have you guys actually come up for air yet? It's been a week," Zeke says, faux annoyance lacing his words.

Lifting my middle finger, I flip him the bird without even pausing our kiss. Since we confessed our feelings for each other and came back to Hayhurst, it feels like Griff and I are making up for all the years we missed out on and we don't seem to be able to keep our hands off each other.

"Jesus, you have two rooms upstairs, go dry hump up there or something, your moans are louder than the TV and I'm sick of seeing Griff's hard-on through his jeans." Zeke whines again, turning up the volume on the movie he's watching.

I can't help the laugh that forms and I giggle against Griff's lips before wrapping my arms around him and burying my face in his neck. I'm sat sideways on his lap, his one hand kneading my ass, the other tangled in my hair.

I kiss up his neck, until my lips reach his ear. "Let's go upstairs," I whisper.

His whole body freezes beneath me. Since we got home, we've been hot and heavy, making out every time we're together, but he's been keeping everything else pretty PG-13, even though I can feel how much he wants me where his hard dick is pressed beneath me.

"Emmy," he says, my name a warning that I refuse to heed.

Blinking slowly, I climb off his lap and stand on shaky legs in front of him. "Come on," I whisper, reaching my hand out to him.

He looks at me, his gaze roaming over me, from my face down to my hand and back up again. A look passes over his face and for a moment I think he's going to refuse, then he places his hand in mine, only leaving it there for a second before he slides it up my arm and he scoops me off the ground.

I wrap my legs around his waist and press my lips to his for a quick, lust-filled kiss, before he pulls back and starts to move towards my room. Moments later, he lowers me onto his bed, dropping over me, but making sure that his weight doesn't crush me, as he leans down and takes my lips with his.

Our tongues move against each other in a sensual dance that only makes my body heat and my core throb with need. "Griff," I moan.

"Are you sure?" He rasps against my lips.

"Yes," I gasp, sliding my hands beneath his shirt and pushing it upwards to reveal his defined abs and hard chest. Running my fingers along his skin, I lift his shirt as high as it will go, until he balances on one arm and pulls it over his head.

If this were anyone else, I'd feel nervous, but this is my best friend, the boy I love, the one I've probably always loved without really knowing what it meant. His fingers dance along my skin, moving slowly as if he's giving me a chance to change my mind, but I won't.

Squeezing my thighs together, I moan loudly when his fingers glide over my bra, barely touching me, but making my back arch as my anticipation becomes almost too much to bear. "Touch me," I beg.

"Are you mine, Em? Is this all mine?" he rasps, his voice sounding almost as desperate as mine.

"Always," I say, my fingers fumbling with the button on his jeans.

"Wait," He growls, pushing my hands away. Then he rips my shirt over my head and drags my jeans down, leaving me in nothing but my bra and panties writhing with need beneath him.

I watch as he takes me in, his eyes raking over me, his pupils dilating as his dick becomes even harder against my leg.

"Fuck," he groans, dipping his head down to suck at my nipple through the satin of my bra.

I cry out, as his tongue laves and his teeth nip, then he changes side, lavishing my other nipple with the same torturous pleasure. My bra is ripped from me a moment later and he cups my breast with one hand and sucks on my nipple hard enough that I feel a gush of heat pool between my legs and I cry out. His other hand slides down my stomach and he cups my sex, circling my clit through the fabric of my panties. The sensation is almost too much and I close my eyes, fighting off the pleasure he's creating.

"I want to taste you," he says, his voice rough and low.

I nod, incapable of words and he slowly, so fucking

slowly slides down my body, taking my panties with him before he drops them to the floor. He gently rubs his hands over my thighs, sliding them inwards, parting my legs to make a place for him to lie between them.

"Jesus." I hear him say, a moment before his mouth is on me and my eyes roll back in my head. His tongue, lips, mouth, and fingers touch and lick me, pushing me towards pleasure I've never been able to give myself. When I climax, I cover my mouth with my hand to stifle the sound, as my core clamps down on his fingers that are still moving inside of me.

He rides out my orgasm with me, his tongue lapping at my clit, his fingers slowly pumping in and out of me until my body wilts, sagging into the mattress, my breath ragged. I watch as he crawls up my body, caging me in with his arms on either side of my head.

"Perfect," he whispers, leaning down to kiss me, his lips tasting of me.

I lose myself to his kiss, until my body demands more, and I wrap my legs around his back and grind myself against his dick.

"Em," he growls.

"I want you, all of you," I say against his mouth, pulling away from him so he can see the truth in my eyes.

"I don't want to hurt you," he whispers, his voice shaky with fear.

"You won't." I assure him, moving to undo his jeans and using my feet to push them down over his hips.

Lips find mine again and he kisses me until I'm breathless and moving against his fingers that are teasing at my entrance. When he pulls back and stands, I watch as he pushes his jeans down, revealing his hard dick, long and thick and intimidating.

Pulling a condom from his wallet he rips it with his teeth, then climbs onto the bed, reaching for my hands and helping me guide it into place. I expect him to move over me, but instead he drops his head between my legs again, licking me until I'm wet with desire and panting as a second orgasm threatens to explode within me.

His thumb finds my clit, circling and prolonging my climax as he hovers above me, his cock finding my entrance and pushing inside. He pinches my clit and I scream in pleasure as he thrusts inside of me, filling me completely as the burst of blissful sensation counteracts the sharp pain.

I lift my head, searching for his lips, kissing him hard, as he slowly pulls back his hips and slides part of the way out. I gasp, pain and pleasure mixing as he rubs my clit again, confusing my body and making me cling to him, never wanting to let go.

He's slow and gentle as he thrusts in and out of me, joining me in the rawest, most intimate way possible. "I love you," he whispers again and again as he claims me and I claim him until we're only one entity, so much in love that nothing else exists and all that's left in the world is me and him and the way we love each other.

For years I've lived in a world of books, wishing one day I could fall into the pages and exist within the stories that I love. But right now, right here with the boy I've loved my entire life, this is so much better than I've read about. All those love stories, all those happy endings and none of them could even compare to how perfect this, right here, right now and one hundred percent non-fiction.

GRIFFIN

"You owe me snuggle time," I shout at her retreating back as she walks away from me heading toward the stairs.

She shakes her head, twisting to look at me over her shoulder as she sashays away. She's always been beautiful, but the last six months she's come into herself, owning who she is and not being ashamed anymore. "You snuggle me all night every night," she says with a wink.

I can't help the smile that spreads across my lips. "I'm a lucky fucking bastard," I call.

Her laugh is the sweetest sound in the fucking world, and I drop down onto the couch instead of chasing after her.

She loves me.

Even six months later it still shocks the hell out of me. That day at her house changed everything for us, and nothing at all at the same time. She's still my best friend, still the most important person in my life, only now she's mine, and when I tell her I love her, she knows exactly what it means.

My beautiful girl still has every guy in a ten-mile radius hoping she'll notice them, but she only has eyes for me; and

Zeke, Valentine, and I make sure anyone who looks more than once knows that she's taken.

I spent seven years knowing that she was the only woman I'd ever love, a year thinking it was only a matter of time until I lost her, and now I have a lifetime to make sure she knows that she's my everything.

I have no idea what the future holds. Maybe we'll move home, maybe we'll travel, maybe not. All I know is that I don't care what my future looks like as long as she's part of it.

EMMY

I glance one last time at him before I dart up the stairs. It's been six months since I ran from my new life, straight back to the one I thought I was so desperate to get away from. Isn't it ironic that my past was exactly where my future lay?

It's taken me a while but I think I've figured out how to blend my past with my future, how to be normal and be me at the same time. Avery, Veronica and I spend a lot of time together, only now Nova comes too, she fits in with my new group just like I knew she would.

I love Griff more than I ever thought it was possible to love someone. He holds my hand, keeps me grounded, and encourages me to spread my wings and fly all at the same time.

Admitting my feelings for him didn't suddenly give me all the answers. I'm still figuring out who I am and what I want out of life, but I no longer think that my roots are holding me back.

Almost a year ago I was jealous of Nova and Valentine. I wanted what they had. I wanted someone to love me like they love each other. What I didn't realize at the time was that I already had that.

Archer's Creek no longer feels like a shackle holding me down, now it's just home and even though it's a small town, it's not so different to the big bad world I was so desperate to explore. We still have four years to decide what my happy ever after looks like. As long as I'm with him, maybe following my roots after I've spent some time flying wouldn't be so bad.

Roots and wings, my past and my future. I'm a Sinners Scion, I always will be, but that doesn't define me anymore, it's not an anchor holding me back. I have no idea what the future holds, but I'm not running towards it. For now, I'm happy to live in the here and now.

My name is Emmy Devereaux. I'm the daughter of the president of the Doomsday Sinners MC. I fell in love with my best friend. He's my past, my present, my future, and everything else in between.

The End

Acknowledgements

This book is full of my blood, sweat, and tears.

This wasn't the story I planned to tell, this wasn't the love I intended, but this is the one that refused to be ignored, and the one that in the end wore me down until I agreed and let the words come how they wanted.

I'm not sure if people will love or hate this book, but if you hate it, know that at times I have too. If you love it, then I get it, I've felt that as well.

Griffin and Emmy will forever be my nightmare couple. The only ones so far who refused to play nicely, but what else should I have expected from two biker kids?

This will be the last AC or Scions books I write for a while. It's not the end for these characters, but I have a thousand more characters who want to be heard and more stories to tell. If you think I'm wrong, then feel free to tell me, harass me with the stories you want to read, the characters whose voices spoke to you the loudest. Or you can just sit back and take this journey into new worlds with me.

As always, Sarah you get a mention. You've held my

hand and sometimes shoved me through the writing of this book. You know how much I've struggled, but you always believed I could finish it and as usual you were right. I got there in the end. I love you and I appreciate you more than you know. X

Andie M. Long, again I apologise for the commas, but know I couldn't do this without you. In fact, I refuse to do this without so NEVER leave me! X

This book looks so bloody pretty because of Kerry Heavens of Rebel Ink Co. Thank you so much for getting me and running with your instincts. The cover is utter perfection.

Lastly, but by no means least thank you to every single one of you who reads this book. I adore you all and I really hope you love Emmy and Griffin's story.

ABOUT THE AUTHOR

Gemma Weir is a half crazed stay at home mom to three kids, one man child and a hell hound. She has lived in the midlands, in the UK her whole life and has wanted to write a book since she was a child. Gemma has a ridiculously dirty mind and loves her book boyfriends to be big, tattooed alpha males. She's a reader first and foremost and she loves her romance to come with a happy ending and lots of sexy sex.

For updates on future releases check out my social media links.

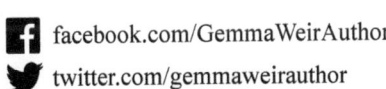

facebook.com/GemmaWeirAuthor

twitter.com/gemmaweirauthor

instagram.com/gemmaweirauthor

ALSO BY GEMMA WEIR

The Archers Creek Series

Echo (Archer's Creek #1)

Daisy (Archer's Creek #2)

Blade (Archer's Creek #3)

Echo & Liv (Archer's Creek #3.5)

Park (Archer's Creek #4)

Smoke (Archer's Creek #5)

The Scions Series

Hidden (The Scions #1)

Found (The Scions #2)

Wings & Roots (The Scions #3)

The Kings & Queens of St Augustus Series

The Spare - Part One

(The Kings & Queens of St Augustus #1)

The Spare - Part Two

(The Kings & Queens of St Augustus #2)

OTHER WORKS FROM HUDSON INDIE INK

<u>Paranormal Romance/Urban Fantasy</u>

Stephanie Hudson

Sloane Murphy

Xen Randell

<u>Sci-fi/Fantasy</u>

Brandon Ellis

Devin Hanson

<u>Crime/Action</u>

Blake Hudson

Mike Gomes

<u>Contemporary Romance</u>

Eve L. Mitchell

Elodie Colt

Lightning Source UK Ltd.
Milton Keynes UK
UKHW011858060121
376538UK00001B/149